Pure Murder

Other Cesar Franck mysteries by A. M. Pyle

MURDER MOVES IN
TROUBLE MAKING TOYS

A. M. Pyle

Pure Murder

A·THOMAS·DUNNE BOOK

St. Martin's Press † New York

Library of Congress Cataloging-in-Publication Data

Pyle, A. M. (Albert M.)
    Pure murder / A.M. Pyle.
        p.   cm.
    "A Thomas Dunne book."
    ISBN 0-312-03917-4
    I. Title.
PS3566.Y53P87   1990
813'.54—dc20   89-24126
                                          CIP

10 9 8 7 6 5 4 3 2

Pure
Murder

I

Dr. Don L. Poe was running. He was on what was for Dr. Poe the most sensuous and intensely pleasurable stretch of the run. As he checked them one by one, all of his systems were operating at their most efficient levels. His small strong feet, protected first by cotton and polypropylene socks and then by Nike Air shoes, were completely free of pain. He had never had a blister. Never. Nor a heel spur. Nor a plantar's wart. His Achilles tendons slid powerfully up and down in their casings, free of friction and free of inflammation. At 148 pounds, Don Poe weighed ten pounds over the ideal for his height of sixty-nine inches, but he had added those ten pounds slowly and carefully through upper body workouts, never putting any undue or sudden strain on his lower joints or on any of his connective tissue. From the center of his brain, where Dr. Poe's consciousness had taken itself, it almost seemed as though he could hear the tendons gliding in their casings, bathed in the cool stream of his lubricating fluids.

His flawless and powerful heart pumped in steady rhythm. He seemed to hear it at the same time that he felt his clean and filtered blood rushing to every fiber of muscle in his body.

There was no pain in his legs. Only pleasure. His knees operated flawlessly, with not the least hint of chondromalacia, the bane of so many less careful and less elegantly constructed runners. Running with classically perfect posture, his head and neck and torso precisely aligned and upright, Dr. Poe made scarcely a sound as his feet met the sidewalk in a heel-to-toe motion indistinguishable from that of Alberto Salazar, the marathon runner with whom he felt the greatest affinity.

And now it was time to increase the pleasure. His run was nearly over. He loved this part. Loved it. Gliding up Clinton Springs Avenue as the street rose from the dismal bottoms of Vine Street, he was as close as a human could come to feline perfection. For a few blissful, realistic, and startlingly erotic seconds, Dr. Poe was one of his own Burmese cats, swooping up the smooth sidewalk.

But what was this? Dr. Poe tore himself away from the pleasures of his gliding, clicking, pumping inner self as his brain registered the presence of another noncat ahead of him on the sidewalk. A white person, male, going in the same direction. And trying to run.

Odd. This was Don L. Poe territory. No one else ran here. Not at this time of the morning. Not on a weekend. That was part of the pleasure. His black neighbors always slept in on Saturdays, which allowed the doctor to pretend that there were no black people anywhere in the world, let alone in his own neighborhood. But this intruder wasn't a black person, so it had to be someone he knew. He knew every white person for blocks around. Of course it could be someone venturing far afield from the comfortable neighborhoods of Clifton or Walnut Hills, but that was highly unlikely. Avondale was not attractive to any but the most knowledgeable runners.

It was Maurice Eckmann, the fat shrink. More than half a block away Dr. Poe could make out the sound of Dr. Eckmann's big New Balances as they slapped the concrete under their 270-pound load. By the time he had reduced the distance between them to a little under half a block, Poe began to hear the frightening sound of the psychiatrist's breathing, which came in great heavy ragged gasps of pulmonary panic.

A faint smile played briefly across Dr. Poe's lips as he passed Maurice Eckmann, accelerating smoothly and swiftly. There was a moment when Dr. Poe was tempted to yell over his shoulder that, even though he was fresh and fast, this was his twelfth mile, but he thought it might be even more humiliating not to recognize his neighbor at all. The pleasure as he rounded the corner and began to ascend Washington Avenue was almost unbearable. The air was cool and clear. The sidewalks were empty. The trees were green. Dr. Poe was fast.

When he reached the corner of his own street Dr. Poe reluctantly slowed to a trot and then to a fast walk. His running systems began quickly and efficiently to step themselves down to the new lower demands of his body. For a couple of brief moments the doctor panted heavily and felt the terrific beats of a running heart, but by the time he had passed the shabby cottages of his nameless black neighbors and reached the open shade of his own end of the street his pulse was well down into the sixties.

Christa Poe's dark red Civic was out in the driveway. Her husband approvingly felt the warmth of the air around the Honda's engine as he passed. Christa had a bad habit of oversleeping on Saturdays, when their agreement called for her to get down to Findlay Market and back with fresh fruit and vegetables before Don got home from his run. But today she had obviously been out.

A flash of sunlight reflected from the polished glass of an open casement window caught Dr. Poe's eye and he looked up at his house as he approached it.

It was a very nice house. Very nice. Casa Poe sat with two others in fifteen acres of lawns and ravines at the private and isolated end of an otherwise depressed and unnoteworthy street. The doctor's house and its neighbors were as beautiful and glossy as anything in the much more popular neighborhoods for the well-off around Grandin Road or in Lafayette Avenue. And Don L. Poe, dermatologist to the carriage trade, could have bought in any neighborhood in town, but he was careful with his money, and it gave him great pleasure to own a small mansion that had cost one-fourth as much as those of his associates. Besides, what he truly liked to spend money on was rugs.

The alarm system was on, which meant that Christa was probably sunbathing. The idiot. He knew she left it off when he wasn't there. Don tapped out the code on the keypad to disarm the system and then tapped out another code to unlock the front door. There was a satisfying thunk as the bolt slid back. He turned the gleaming brass knob and let himself into the front hall, immediately sidestepping the antique oriental runner so that he would not drip sweat on it. Madame Nhu came screaming down the stairs to greet him while U Thant watched from the landing. Dr. Poe squatted to stroke Madame Nhu, who continued to screech in her own tongue. He straightened and caught sight of himself in the mirror.

Save for the long strands of pale red hair that had been lifted straight up from his scalp by the wind of his own running, Don Poe saw no flaws. He ran his slender hand over his hair, pasting it down in the sweat that gleamed on his pate. He was a very white man. White as milk glass. Skim milk glass, since he was a redhead and had just a hint of blue about him. Madame Nhu screamed at him again. She wanted to be picked up, but Dr. Poe was too sweaty to pick up a cat, even such a perfect cat as his own Burmese queen. He picked up his little tape recorder instead and started up the stairs, stooping to caress U Thant behind the ears. As he stroked the neutered tom, he noticed that the pathetic alcoholic his wife had hired to help with the house-painting had missed a spot on one of the banisters. Dr. Poe pressed the record button on the tape machine and began to speak.

"Christa, I told you that your painter was totally incompetent and now I'm looking at the . . . at the sixth banister from the east end of the landing and there is a spot that he missed. I hope to God you haven't paid him this week." He hit the stop button and climbed up to the second floor. Christa's tape recorder stood on his dresser in their bedroom, waiting to disgorge its messages, but he ignored it, passing through the bedchamber and into the bathroom.

It was still a thrill. In Buffalo where he had grown up, Don, his mother and father, his two sisters, and his grandmother had shared a bathroom that was no bigger than five feet by eight feet. It had contained a washbasin, a water closet, a bathtub, a clothes hamper, and a shallow linen cupboard. And at that, Don's grandmother had said it was too fancy for her.

Don and Christa's bathroom was different. Before moving into the house, the Poes had consulted an architect and a contractor who were more than happy to explain that it would be no trouble at all to knock the existing master bathroom and an adjoining bedroom together to form a state-of-the-art bath and exercise room. It was only a matter of money.

Now the bathroom was what their architect called "a free-flowing series of zones," and what Christa's sometime friend Greta called "the Poes' Y." There was a bathing zone, an elimination zone, a cosmetic zone, and a very large exercise zone. The room had a tub, a shower, a bidet, two water closets, two sinks, a rowing machine, a stationary bicycle, a treadmill, a weight bench, a weight rack, weights, and, above all else, mirrors. Mirrors covered nearly every available inch of wall space and most of the ceiling.

All of the equipment was used and used heavily by the two Poes, which made it necessary to have a cleaning woman come twice a week instead of once. There was so much sweat.

Don Poe sat on a commode and took off his shoes and socks, dropping them for Christa to pick up. He dropped his sweat-soaked nylon running shorts on the shoes and stepped into the exercise zone, which had the best mirrors.

Perfect.

He began his set of stretches, pleasantly hypnotized by the sight of so many fat-free images. When he was at last through with his stretches, he walked over to the window that overlooked the backyard to see if Christa was indeed stupidly exposing her skin to the carcinogenic sun. She was. He knew that she did it to annoy him, just as she always snickered when he applied total sunscreen before leaving the house on an early morning run. Let her laugh. She could find herself another dermatologist to handle the inevitable melanomas.

Christa's head was turned away from him, but something in the way that she lay betrayed a knowledge of being watched. She was naked, lying on her stomach on a quilt worth at least $400. The quilt was spread on the deck jutting out over the wooded ravine that crossed the property in back of the house. She couldn't be seen from the other two houses in the compound, but she wouldn't have cared if she could be. Her skin gleamed in the sun. Without meaning to, Don began to think about the details of Christa's strong and well-fed body, but when he felt himself beginning to react, he moved away from the window and into the shower. The time for that was later in the morning. That was the agreement.

It was a long shower. Don liked to use bathtime to visualize upcoming events. He had been quick to see the positive effect of visualization and imaging in all his professional and recreational efforts when articles on that technique first hit the magazines devoted to recreational perfection. And he was good at it. He had an astounding memory for details. As the water poured over him he took himself step by step through the upcoming Medical Association Crosstown Ten Kilometer race. With participation limited to physicians and surgeons and their families, the race was one of Don's favorite events. In his mind he went through every street and past every hospital and freestanding clinic on the race route, concentrating at the same time on the constant threat of his great rival, Randy Ziemann, the maxillofacial surgeon who was his only real competitor in their age group. Don gave himself a realistic sixteen-second lead at the end and then turned off the water.

Christa had moved the towels. Don went dripping wet into the bedroom, skirting the even more expensive upstairs antique runner until he reached the tape recorder. He switched it on with a savage snap.

"Christa, don't move the towels."

He went back into the bathroom, found the towels on their new shelf, and dried himself off.

Time for his treat. According to Don L. Poe's private sports theories, it was unwise to use cocaine within two weeks of a competitive event. This, then was the absolute last chance to dip into the latest little parcel. Moving languidly into the bedroom, he felt around in his leather bag until he found the small, brown, plastic pill jar to which he had transferred the coke on the day he got it. Christa had given him a bevel-edged hand mirror for his last birthday, and he got that out of the delicately inlaid drawer in his antique shaving stand. When the coke had been measured and lined to his satisfaction, he touched a wall switch that turned on the lights surrounding the deck where his wife lay. It was his signal to her to come inside for her next part of the agreement.

"The lights just went on."
"I know. I saw them."

"That means he's back, doesn't it?"

"No. I told you he's been back for ages."

"So this is the 'Get your ass upstairs' signal?"

"No, that's flashing lights. That's when he's pissed off."

"He's always pissed off."

"No, he's not. You just don't know him."

Christa Poe began to arch her back like a cat. She let the beautiful Amish quilt stick to her stomach and hands and feet so that it began to bunch up under her as she came to her hands and knees. As her head left the deck it became harder for her to see her companion through the cracks between the boards as he lay in the dark shade under the deck. He, too, was naked, sprawled on a brown blanket stolen from the United States Army. Christa put her head back down and left her backside up in the air where she knew it would interest Don. Now she could see her companion much better.

"You know, when he smiles he looks like he's trying to pass a hairball. Did you ever notice that?" asked the man under the deck.

"No, he doesn't."

"He does. Do you really have to go in?"

"That's the signal."

"I thought you said it wasn't."

"I said it wasn't the signal to get my ass inside. It just means he's ready for sex," said Christa. "So I have to go in. It's not the same. I'll take care of you Monday."

"But early. It's got to be early."

"Why?" Christa knew why; she wanted to make him say it.

"Because I can't wait to—*shit!*" Christa's friend had banged his head on the deck floor.

"Not so loud. And be careful getting out of there. And don't forget your blanket." Christa started walking toward the back of her house.

"Your house, right?"

"Unless yours somehow got clean."

"Your house."

Christa nodded agreement, not caring whether the man under the sundeck could see the movement of her head. Her mind was on the business ahead.

U Thant scrabbled off the counter by the food processor as he heard the door open. He stared from the floor up at Christa, who had a good idea where he had been. She passed him without speaking and walked through the kitchen, laying her shades on the counter under the wall phone. She stepped into the high heeled mules that were part of the agreement and walked deliberately through the swinging door into the hall holding the folded quilt in front of her. She climbed the stairs. Entering the master suite through the Y, Christa stopped to stow the quilt in a cupboard and then went into the bathroom. She picked up her husband's shorts and socks and dropped them down the clothes chute. She took the shoes back into the exercise area and put them on the wire rack with his other sport shoes. She walked back into the bathroom and spent five minutes washing her hands.

Christa brushed her long, dark brown hair into a pony tail and fastened it with the pornographic ivory clasp Don had bought for her in Thailand. She rubbed Opium into the nape of her neck and the skin behind her knees, checked herself one last time in the mirror, and opened the door into the bedroom.

"I'm here," she said, pitching her voice a little lower than usual. And then she said "Don?" The little shit wasn't spreadeagled on the bed. A first. "Don."

And then Christa Poe noticed something out of place on the floor by her husband's dresser. She had taken her contacts out in the bathroom, so she had to walk over to see that what appeared at first to be a crumpled bedspread was instead the crumpled body of her husband the dermatologist.

2

It required a trained observer to know that behind the mirrored sunglasses and impassive African features, detective Henry Chapman was quite impressed by Christa Poe. The brand new widow was talking on the telephone in the kitchen. Since the games with Don were off for good, she had switched from the spiky mules to a pair of red Reebok hi-tops and had pulled on short-legged white canvas overalls. But she was still naked underneath the stiffish overalls and Detective Chapman was politely keeping his head averted. Even so, he had had several breathtaking eyefuls without really trying.

It was the toothpick sticking through his beard and rolling from one end of his mouth to the other and back again that gave Henry Chapman's emotions away. It was really traveling.

Not just because Mrs. Poe's breasts were popping back

and forth behind the loose bib of the overalls. He could deal with that. It was the chill. This lady was cold. She was giving orders over the phone to her third friend in fifteen minutes to come up and take care of her. This lady did not need anyone taking care of her. She wasn't even shaking.

Before she started making the calls, Henry had been up in the big bedroom nosing around while the guys from the lab worked the room over. And then he heard this noise that he knew he had never heard from anything the lab crew ever did, so he stepped out of the bedroom following the sound until he got to the stairs, where Christa Poe was busy vacuuming the carpet on the landing. She was going like a pro, big strong strokes back and forth, breasts flying around like part of the machinery, and for a second Henry just stood in awe, but then he got a grip on himself and shouted, "Ma'am, you got to stop."

She didn't hear him. The big Electrolux was too loud. He went down to the landing and gently touched her elbow so that she looked up. He signed to her to turn off the sweeper. "You can't do that, ma'am."

"I have to do it. You all have tracked in a lot of dirt this morning. Look. Footprints all over the place."

"I'm sorry, but you can't run the vacuum. Not until they're through checking the house. You might pick up something we need to see."

Mrs. Poe glared at him. Henry had seen plenty of distraught widows. He knew that grief could make anybody a little crazy. But Mrs. Poe wasn't going crazy. She was just pissed off about the dirt on her rugs.

"When will that be?"

"I don't know, ma'am. It might be a while."

She shook her head in irritation. Then she asked, "Will it get me in trouble if I make a phone call?" Real testy.

"No, that will be all right."

So there they were in the kitchen while she made her

call. Which turned out to be three calls while Henry was waiting to use the phone himself. At last she hung up.

"Are you waiting for something or are you keeping an eye on me?" she asked Henry.

"I need to use the phone, ma'am."

"You shouldn't wear those sunglasses. It's rude."

Henry didn't take off the sunglasses. Who did she think she was? The toothpick picked up a little more speed.

"Can I leave?" asked Christa.

"The house?"

"The kitchen."

"Sure."

She banged out of the room, letting the door swing rudely close to Henry's face.

Cesar Franck felt a tug on his trouser leg. He peered down through the film of dust that coated his safety goggles and saw Stella Hineman standing at the bottom of the stepladder. It was a really good view, seeing her from above like that. She mouthed something at him that he couldn't make out, so he switched off the huge belt sander he was holding over his head, which was a big relief. His arms were starting to shake real bad from the strain of pushing the heavy machine against the ceiling. Cesar propped his elbows against his chest so Stella wouldn't see how close he was to giving out with so much of the ceiling left to go.

"Telephone," said Stella.

"For me?"

"It's Henry."

"Chapman?"

"Henry Chapman."

"He wants to talk to me?"

Stella shook her head a little and wondered if the paint and plaster dust was getting to Cesar's brain. "Yes, Cesar. It is Henry Chapman. The only Henry Chapman you know. He called here and he wants to talk to you. He is on the phone now. Get down off the ladder and go to the telephone and talk to him."

"I understand what you're talking about, Stel. I was just surprised." As he had often done, Cesar wondered what Stella really thought about him. Like right then when she seemed to think he was a little simpleminded when he was actually slightly stunned by the din of the belt sander. As he climbed down he realized that the same angle that gave such a terrific view of Stella's chest must give her a reciprocal and really bad view of his stomach. So he sucked in his gut. "What's he calling here for?"

"You'll have to talk to him. He's talking like a cop. You know how he does."

"Yeah, well, he's on duty."

Cesar wiggled through the sheet of heavy clear plastic he had taped over the kitchen doorway to keep the dust out. The phone was next to a frying pan with that morning's bacon grease still in it. He automatically moved the pan to the sink before picking up the telephone.

"Henry?"

"Good morning."

"What do you want? I'm working. I told you yesterday I was going to be busy."

"I know, man. I'm sorry."

"Well, what do you want?"

"I think you want to be out here."

"No, I don't."

"You don't know, Ceez."

"I'm working. I'm in the middle of a job."

"You don't have to stay long."

"I don't have to do anything. I'm not on duty. You're on duty. I'm working on this house." Cesar didn't think he should have had to tell Henry any of this, since he had told him the day before what he was going to be doing. Henry must have remembered or he wouldn't have called Stella's house. And anyway it was forbidden and impossible to reach Henry in a similar situation.

"It looks like this doctor blew his head off," said Henry.

"Did he leave a note?"

"With coke," said Henry.

"What are you talking about?"

"I'm out at this doctor's house. Called about an hour ago. The guy must have got some strange shit in his cocaine. It looks like he dropped in his tracks right after his noseful. The man wasn't even dressed."

"Another Len Bias, huh Henry?"

Chapman, touchy about black sports figures, didn't respond. Cesar pulled a chair away from the kitchen table and sat down under the wall phone, grateful to be goofing off. But he was also getting pissed off. He knew that Henry was preparing to hand him this case for some reason. Cesar was supposed to be off until Monday unless it was the end of the world.

"When'd he do it?" he asked Henry.

"This morning. His wife says he was out running and then he came back and dropped dead."

"I told you about running. That's what happens."

"From cocaine. Not from a heart attack."

"Why are you telling me this?"

Henry mumbled something.

"Henry, I can't hear you."

"You got to see this lady."

"Is that why I have to go out there? You've got some chick out there?"

"This one is something else. But what you got to come out here for is that I'm going on vacation Monday and you're going to get this anyway, so you better take a look while it's fresh. You know."

"You got vacation? Approved?" asked Cesar. It was news to him.

"Yesterday. Lieutenant signed it yesterday."

This was a typical Henry Chapman thing to do. Not a word to anybody and then he weasels in to see the lieutenant when Sergeant Evans is out sick because Evans always gives Henry, and anybody else who asks, a lot of shit about taking time off while Lieutenant Tieves, who thinks all blacks are treacherous time bombs, never gives Henry a bit of shit about it.

"You should have told me you were going on vacation."

"Yeah, well, I didn't know till Friday."

"How long are you out for?"

"A week."

"Where are you going."

"Alabama."

Which explained much. Henry Chapman hated going to Alabama worse than anything except maybe a country music concert. The only conceivable reason for him to go to Alabama was to drive his mother down to see her sister, Henry's Aunt Florence. Henry's mother didn't fly. She preferred the air-conditioning, leather seats, and flexible scheduling of her son's Lincoln Continental Mark IV. Besides, now that they were locking the door to the flight deck she couldn't get into the cockpit of a 727 to harass the pilots. Cesar started to feel a little better knowing that Mrs. Chapman wouldn't let Henry play his jazz tapes while he was out of town and off work. Henry's mother traveled with her own tapes. She liked sermons and church services. Henry was going to pay heavily for ducking out like this.

"If I come out there, I can't stay," said Cesar. "I got things to do here."

"I told you you didn't have to."

"And I'm not gonna change clothes either."

"Don't matter to me."

"And you have to explain this to Stella."

"I don't do explaining."

"Where is this place?"

Cesar had to write the address on a paper towel with a

crayon belonging to Stella's son Sidney. Stella never had a functioning pen anywhere in the house. Stella was at his elbow when he got off the phone.

"Are you leaving?" she asked.

"I'll be back. I got to see something."

"Before lunch?"

"I don't know. I doubt it."

"You want me to pack you something? I made this fruit salad. You could take that and a beer."

"Are you mad at me? I'm sorry to crap out on you like this."

Stella pulled the plastic aside and peered into the chaos that was the dining room. Cesar couldn't' bear to look.

"Hey," said Stella. "This is your project. It's your idea. You say you're coming back, I'll trust you."

"I'm really sorry," said Cesar. Stella planted a big kiss on his mouth and started dishing out some fruit salad for herself.

Cesar really was very sorry. It *was* his idea to pull the crappy-looking dropped ceiling out of her dining room and patch everything up so he could paint it. Stella would have lived with it as it was. But he hated to see her in such a slummy-looking room. So he had gotten up at five that morning to whip through the cleaning at his mother's house and was down at Stella's house by eight-thirty, and by nine-thirty he had pulled out the false ceiling. He has been using the big borrowed belt sander to grind off all the lumps and loose paint hidden by the ceiling tiles when the call from Henry came.

It took some doing to find the Poe's street in Avondale since the house was actually in North Avondale where Cesar seldom went. When the police had Avondale business it was normally farther south where everybody was black and the big old houses were chopped up into apartments. But there were still some white people in North Avondale, Jewish families and politicians mostly. And the black families who did live in the neighborhood were well behaved or rich for the most part. But even in North Avondale there were some crummy-looking streets, and the Poe's street seemed to be one of them. Cesar drove past the small crowded houses in the first part of the block. All black people and all out on the porch. They all knew he was a cop, too. He knew that they knew from their frank stares. They probably knew that he knew that they knew. He saluted and they nodded.

The end of the street was a surprise. There was no transition from the cruddy little houses on their tiny lots to the mansions sitting in the middle of what looked more like a good-sized park than a collection of yards. All of a sudden the street just opened out into a forest of huge old shade trees with three beautiful houses dropped in at odd angles to each other. The Poe house was easy to pick out since the driveway was full of police vehicles. A few civilian cars were blocking them at the end of the drive.

Cesar started to pull onto the grass so he wouldn't be in the way when he saw Henry coming down the driveway shaking his head. Henry was wearing a Hawaiian shirt, white pants, baby blue socks, beige Italian shoes with a fringe, and sunglasses. Cesar waited to see what he was doing wrong.

"Man, you can't park on the grass. I got the word," said Henry.

"Where else am I supposed to park? There isn't any place."

"Park on the street. You don't want to tangle with this woman, boy, and she's fussy about her grass."

"Shit," muttered Cesar. He backed out and halfway down the block to the first available space. Henry waited for him at the end of the drive.

"Are you going to tell me why I had to drop what I was doing? It had better be good. Sounds like no problem to me. Guy sticks cocaine up his nose gets what he deserves."

"OOOoo. You cold today."

"I got work to do," said Cesar.

"But you ain't anywhere near as cold as Mrs. Poe."

"She won't go out with you?"

Henry Chapman ignored his partner. "This Dr. Poe was a real little guy, too. Makes you wonder."

"Wonder what?" asked Cesar.

Henry turned his mirrors toward Cesar, checking to see if Cesar was kidding. "You know. Whips under the bed. That sort of stuff." Henry always suspected the worst of white people's sex habits.

"Is she big?"

"Cesar, they don't have to be big. She's just tough. You'll see. You'll be glad I kept you off the grass."

They were outside the front door, which was painted a dark shiny green. All the brasswork was highly polished. There were no shortcuts in the trim paint, no buildup or drips from past jobs. Everything about the place was clean and polished. Cesar looked at himself in Henry's glasses. There was dust in his hair and around his eyes where his filter mask hadn't covered. He looked down at his clothes and gave his shirt a smack. A puff of dust billowed out, forcing Henry to take a step backward. "I didn't know it was this bad," said Cesar.

"I wasn't going to say anything," said Henry. "I know you been busy." Cesar stepped out from under the little roof that protected the doorstep and started shaking his clothes.

"Forget it," said Henry as he pushed the door open.

"*Stop! Stop, stop, stop!!*" It was a woman's scream. "*No, kitty! No! Stop her!*"

There was a streak of brown fur. Henry just watched as it zipped past, but Cesar kicked out with his foot and connected with the cat. There was a howl of outrage as the cat sailed up on the end of the policeman's oldest black oxford and then flipped over on its back. The cat scrabbled to its feet and stalked stiff-legged back into the house as a woman in yellow shorts and a white T-shirt came out the door looking scared.

She peered down at the cat as it went back in the house and then turned to look at the cops.

"You can't let that cat out. It's declawed. It would die."

"I'm sorry, ma'am," said Cesar. His partner didn't seem to be sorry in the least, even though he had opened the door and presumably knew about the declawed kitty. Cesar looked to see if he was going to get an introduction to the woman, who could be the bereaved as far as he knew. But since Henry gave no sign, he had to assume that she was not the widow. Henry excused himself as he walked past the woman and on into the house. Cesar followed him, nodding at the woman as he passed her, watching to make sure no more cats got out.

"I told you not to go out there ever," he heard someone say. A woman talking firmly. "You could get killed. I've told you that." The voice came from the right of the entry hall and Cesar peered into the gloom of a huge living room. The Burmese cat was sitting on top of a woman who was lying on a long sofa. When the cat saw Cesar it screamed and flinched. The woman put the cat down on the floor by the sofa and stared at Cesar without getting up. Henry stepped past Cesar.

"This is Detective Franck, Mrs. Poe. He's going to be working with me."

Mrs. Poe held out a hand, still without getting up. Cesar went over and shook it. It was cool and dry. "I'm sorry about your husband, ma'am," he said.

"Thank you," said Mrs. Poe. She didn't say anything else. Cesar started backing away as she looked at him.

"We'll be upstairs, ma'am," said Henry, pulling Cesar away from the sofa. Christa Poe didn't answer. She turned and started talking to the three women who were sitting in armchairs they had pulled up to the sofa. Cesar listened to her as he climbed the stairs behind Henry. "Where was I? Oh. His mother. So when she said that it was my fault I told her I didn't want to hear that, and if she wanted me to hold the cremation until she got here, she was going to have to promise not to talk like that. It's no wonder Don was—"

Whatever Don was was out of earshot. "You got to see this first," said Henry when they reached the top of the stairs. He led Cesar to the door that went from the hall directly into the bath complex. "Do you believe it?" Cesar stepped through to see what it was he might not believe.

"Exercise room?" he asked.

"It's an exercise room *and* a bathroom. The whole thing," answered Henry. "It's awful." That was a compliment. "Must be five thousand dollars' worth of equipment in here. Look. That rower, that's an Avita. And that's an Airdyne. And that," he said, pointing to a gadget that looked like a mammoth can opener, the kind that screws to a wall, "that's the *new* kind of rowing machine. They've got both kinds. Can you believe it? And look at that treadmill." Henry went over and punched a button and the treadmill came to life. He shook his head in admiration.

Cesar didn't know anything about the exercise equipment and he was surprised that Henry did. Henry was strong, but he was also about a hundred pounds overweight and never seemed to be too interested in shaping up. Why should he, when he always had at least two very good-looking women calling him at the office every day of the world? Cesar figured that he himself was no more than twenty-five or thirty pounds over what he was supposed to be for his height but he had never gotten anywhere near the calls that Henry did. Cesar wasn't into exercise except for some push-ups and sit-ups he had been doing, which seemed to make him hungry. He slid a hand to his stomach and found that it was still there. Henry was looking at him, waiting for a reaction. Cesar raised his eyebrows. He was thinking that the Poes's bathroom looked like something from *Playboy*. Not real.

"This," said Henry, "is the way I want my bathroom to look."

"You want all this stuff?" Cesar couldn't keep the amazement out of his voice.

"This is the best you can get," said Henry.

"So what? What do you want it for?"

"To stay in shape."

"What are you talking about? You got to *be* in shape before you can stay in shape."

"Hey," said Henry. He reached over and took Cesar's hand and brought it to his belly. "Push." Cesar pushed. He didn't know what he was supposed to feel, but it felt to him like a big belly on someone holding his breath. Henry was grinning with his teeth showing, but that didn't mean he wasn't holding his breath. Cesar pulled his hand away. "See what I mean?" asked Henry. Cesar just shook his head a little and dropped it. He would never figure Henry out.

"Where's the doctor?" asked Cesar.

"Gone. They took him to University."

"Who did she call? Rescue?"

Henry nodded. "She was doing all the right stuff when they got here. Apparently she found him right after he took the cocaine because she said he was still warm. So, since she was still giving CPR when the medics got here they had to keep working on him until they got him to the hospital." Cesar nodded. "But get this," Henry continued. "When they got here, the rescue squad, she told them she knew this wasn't just a heart attack. She came right out and told them first thing that he used cocaine and that she was sure he had taken some just before he died and that that was what killed him. And she made them call us right in. Do you believe it? And—" Henry took off his sunglasses to show Cesar just how amazed he was—"she told the paramedics that she was, and I got to get this right, 'certain without a doubt' that he was murdered by his supplier. But you see how she was down there?" Henry stabbed a finger toward the floor. "All cool like that?" Cesar nodded. "That's not just the way she is now. That's the way she was when she talked to the paramedics and that's the way she talked to me as soon as I got here. With her husband in an ambulance on the way to the hospital."

"Real torn up, hunh?" said Cesar.

"Cold," said Henry. He backed out of the bath area and opened the door to the bedroom, where a couple of the lab techs were still taking samples. "Mrs. Poe wants to know if she can run the vacuum sweeper," Henry said to the techs.

"Up here? Not in here. Not yet."

"Not here. On the stairs."

"Jeez, I guess so."

"Is this where he was?" asked Cesar. Henry nodded. Cesar nosed around the room trying to get some kind of a handle on the Poes.

3

The Poes, or, now, Mrs. Poe kept a lot of their money lying around on the floor. Many trips into many houses had taught Cesar that rich people often liked to keep thin, almost threadbare, rugs with crummy-looking fringe like the ones that covered every floor outside the carpeted bathroom at the Poe house. Real orientals.

Several of Stella's friends had oriental rugs, some real, some fake, some confusing. The confusing ones, explained Stella, were authentically oriental but were new and less desirable.

There was no pile at the Poes's house. Every last rug from the largest one in the living room to the little scrap in the back vestibule was flat and limp. And every room in the house had more than one rug except for the health club where there was the constant threat of sweat.

Ten thousand dollars' worth of rugs? Forty thousand? A hundred thousand? Cesar had no idea, but the alarm system was top of the line and tied to a very expensive protection firm. It seemed to him that the security could only be for the rugs, since there was not much in the way of consumer electronics or even furniture. With the exception of the health club, every room Cesar had seen was almost sparsely furnished. The few pieces of furniture downstairs in the living room looked like pieces from hotel lobbies that were old-fashioned when Cesar was a little boy. The sofa that Christa Poe and her cat stretched out on, a dark wood and rose brocade number, had enough room at the end past her feet so a couple of her friends could have shared it with her and still had room for the other cat.

The large bedroom was also nearly empty, having only three pieces of furniture. Two of the pieces were chests of drawers; the other piece was the bed. And the bed was just a mattress and boxspring on a frame. There was no headboard. There wasn't even a bedspread, just plain white sheets and pillowcases. Cesar picked up a corner of the top sheet, which was nearly as heavy as canvas.

"Cold room," said Henry. He stood in the bathroom doorway, slowly shaking his head in disapproval. Cesar had never seen Henry's bedroom and didn't expect to, since Henry was intensely private.

"The whole house is sort of empty," said Cesar. "I guess all the money went into the rugs."

"Say what?" Henry pulled his sunglasses off to look at the floor. "These here?"

"Orientals," said Cesar. "They're all over the place. They're probably worth a fortune." He was surprised and a little pleased to know some consumer information that Henry, who knew every brand name in America, didn't. "Even the little ones are worth a couple of thousand."

"No shit?" said Henry.

"The older the better. They're all handmade."

Henry squatted, the better to examine the status goods. The strain his sturdy legs made on the fabric in his trousers was great, but the trousers held. "What else do you know?" asked Henry as he picked up the end of a medium-sized rug with no fringe at one end.

"It doesn't matter if they don't look symmetrical. That's just the way they do it. And I think the little ones are supposed to be prayer rugs."

"For Muslims?" asked Henry.

"Yeah."

"Are they African?" Henry had bought heavily into African history in the sixties and seventies. He was mostly over it, but he still had a soft spot for the continent, as he did for Islam. Cesar didn't think that Henry was ever going to do anything radical with Islam as long as his mother, a power-house Baptist, was still alive.

"I don't think so. I think they're from Turkey."

"So how come they're worth so much?" asked Henry, pushing himself back to an upright position.

"They're old. And rare, I guess."

"Yeah, well—" Henry had lost interest somewhere around Turkey. "They picked up some of his shit over there," he said, pointing to Dr. Poe's dresser. "And he still had some out. It was either real powerful stuff or else it was adulterated with something nasty."

"What kind of doctor was he?" asked Cesar. Henry shrugged. "You wouldn't think a doctor would be so stupid, would you?" Henry shrugged again. They had both run into enough doctors to know what a silly question that was. "Still, if I was a doctor, I think I'd check that sort of stuff out. It's easy enough."

"The dude probably just sticks his hand out and says coke," said Henry. "Just like in the operating room. He don't expect anybody to mess with him. They're just supposed to give him whatever he asks for."

"I believe that," said Cesar. "But still—"

"Can you believe that bitch?" asked Henry out of the blue.

"Real torn up," said Cesar, understanding the conversation had swung back to Christa Poe.

"It wouldn't surprise me if the man was just trying to get away from her. I have to say I'd shoot her after a day. I can't take that type."

Something made the two policemen turn simultaneously to the door. Perhaps it was a noise. Perhaps it was joint guilt over the shared desire to see the absolute last of Christa Poe. And both men jumped ever so slightly.

The woman in the doorway was tall, attractive, and vaguely familiar, although Cesar could not place her. "I'm Kay Gallery," she said. Her strong voice was vaguely familiar, too. "Are you the gentlemen from Homicide?"

"Yes, ma'am," said Cesar. He wanted very much to know who she was before she told him. She was in a suit, so he thought she might be a lawyer, except that it was Saturday and he had never seen a lawyer dressed for business on a weekend. Also the woman's suit was bright red, which didn't seem to go with the bar.

A reporter, he guessed. Television. But what channel?

"I guess your job gets to you every now and then, doesn't it?" she asked. And then she laughed.

"Ma'am?" asked Cesar.

"Didn't I hear you say you'd kill that poor woman downstairs if you were married to her?"

Was she kidding around or were they going to hear themselves on the five-thirty news? Cesar sensed that Henry, whose fear and loathing of reporters was exceptional even for the police, was closing up. In another minute he would drop to the floor and roll up into a ball of quills, leaving Cesar to deal with the TV woman.

"Are you two all right?" asked Kay Gallery. "Can you talk?"

"We didn't—" began Cesar. But he did. And he knew

that the reporter knew because she was about to laugh at him. Channel Three. That's who she was. But not an anchorman.

"She's really a case. I've met her," said Gallery. "And you aren't the first men to want to murder her. There's a big line ahead of you."

Cesar felt Henry relax a little. Cesar thought that it might be too early to drop his guard. Kay Gallery seemed to have a lot of confidence. He'd been sucker-punched before by reporters and he bet she could do it.

"Can you confirm that this is a cocaine overdose?" she asked all of a sudden, confirming Cesar's fears.

"No, ma'am. There'll have to be tests."

"But the tests will be for cocaine?"

"There'll be an autopsy." *How did she get in here?*

"But he was a user?"

"We automatically look for drugs. It's required in these circumstances."

Kay Gallery looked good. Wherever she had bought her suit, and it looked expensive, it wasn't from a career shop. Not that she wasn't dressed for success. But she also looked beautiful.

Big teeth. White.

"Did Christa mention her insurance?"

"Life insurance?" asked Cesar.

"Two million dollars."

"No, ma'am." Cesar choked a little.

"Two million?" asked Henry, speaking for the first time to Kay Gallery.

"You're Henry Chapman, aren't you?" she asked, and she turned the full smile on the unwitting policeman.

Henry was stunned. "Yeah," he said after a moment of confusion. He was mystified, but he wouldn't ask how she knew him.

Kay Gallery saved him the trouble. "We have a friend in common. I know Calquetta."

"Oh," said Henry.

"She showed me your picture. You're much more attractive in real life."

"Oh," said Henry. Cesar was happy to see Henry at a loss for words.

"Was Dr. Poe a big user?" asked Gallery.

"Say what?" Henry, stunned again and confused by the sudden switch in topics, stared at her for a moment, looking dopey. It was all Cesar could do not to laugh.

"Oh!" said Kay, turning her big dark blue eyes and white teeth on Cesar. He stopped wanting to laugh, feeling a little wave go through his knees. "Are you Officer Franck?"

"Mess, ma'am. I'm am." *Shit!* screamed Cesar to himself. *I can't talk!* He knew that Henry was staring at him. Kay Gallery hadn't batted an eye.

"Is this the first physician to die of a cocaine overdose in Hamilton County?" asked the reporter. Cesar nodded at the same time that he felt Henry try to nudge him back into the right time zone. He shouldn't have nodded. He shouldn't have nodded. "What about Ohio?" asked the reporter quickly. "Is it a first for Ohio?" But Cesar's head was finally starting to clear and he didn't move a muscle. "What about . . . shit." The lights went off in Ms. Gallery's eyes as she snapped at a beeper somewhere under her jacket. "Don't go away," she ordered and then she went to the phone by the bed and stabbed in a number.

Cesar wished he had disobeyed her and left the room. Instead he had to watch as she talked to her television station and got the bad news that she was getting pulled from the assignment. Kay Gallery tried to argue but the station wasn't having any. The woman who hung up the phone barely resembled the fast-talking charmer who had blown into the room earlier. She sat on the edge of the bed, her shoulders sagging, thinking private thoughts. At last she looked up at Cesar. "Larry Wilmot's coming over. He wants to talk to you himself."

The hell with that idea. Cesar was not going to be around

for Larry Wilmot. The pop-eyed gee-whiz news anchor might be the ratings leader and the middle-aged ladies' heart throb, but as far as Cesar was concerned, Wilmot was nothing but trouble. Because he was stupid. Cesar knew this for a fact, having dealt with him before. And feeling more sympathy for Kay Gallery than was good for him he said, "He's stupid."

Ms. Gallery looked up at him from the bed and nodded slightly.

"Doesn't he usually take the weekend off?" asked Henry.

"Usually," said Gallery. "But this is a big story with the cocaine. And then the dead man's a doctor. And he's got friends. *Had* friends."

"Like Wilmot?" asked Cesar.

"Like Wilmot. *And* like Rick Albers. Probably more like him."

"Who's Albers?" asked Cesar.

"He's the vice-president for news. He redid Wilmot."

Cesar chewed over that one for a second until he remembered that Larry Wilmot had been a band director on one of the old live variety shows before he became a news authority.

"How did they get the idea there was cocaine?" asked Henry. "As far as I know nobody's said anything one way or another."

Kay Gallery took a moment before she answered. "I really shouldn't tell you. She's a source."

"Her?" Henry pointed downstairs where, presumably, Christa Poe still reclined in her grief.

"She called the station. Actually she called Larry and Rick at their homes first, but they were both out. *Then* she called the station. I took the call, so I took the story. She blamed me personally for Rick and Larry not being home."

"And she told you something about cocaine."

"I'm not supposed to tell you anything. You know that."

"Well, you said she called," said Henry.

"I'm just so mad," said Kay. "This just really stinks!"

"Pulling you off the story?" asked Cesar.

"Yes. For no reason at all except that Rick and Larry and this Dr. Poe all knew each other."

"But she told you about the cocaine?" asked Henry. "Or what she thinks is cocaine?" Kay Gallery looked uncomfortable and didn't answer but the men understood that Christa Poe hadn't hidden anything.

"See what I mean about her?" Henry turned to Cesar. "She is *crazy!* Calls the rescue squad and tells them. Calls me and tells me. Calls her friends and she's probably telling them. And she calls the TV and tells *them!* You figure that out. This is her dead husband she's talking about. If my wife did that to me, I'd kill her."

"But you're not married," said Kay.

Henry stared at her. He had forgotten she was there. Then he said, "That's right. Now, are you through with us?" Kay nodded slightly, taken aback.

"I'm through," she said, and she got up from the edge of the bed. "I'm sorry to have bothered you."

"No problem," said Cesar.

"Are we shooting in here?" asked someone.

Henry, Cesar, and Kay turned to the doorway to see a man in a polo shirt holding a minicam with a big 3 on it. "Not till Larry gets here, Tony," said Kay.

"Larry's coming in for this? What for?"

"Never mind what for," said Kay. "Just go back to the van and wait for Larry. These gentlemen are still working."

"You guys Homicide?" asked Tony, turning his camera on them.

"I said outside," said Kay. She strode over and pushed Tony out the door. "Thanks anyway," she said to the policemen. Cesar waved a hand as she backed out into the hall, reluctant to leave her story, shoulders still drooping from the humiliation.

"She is *beautiful!*" Henry said softly when he thought she was out of earshot. "I got to ask Calquetta about her."

Cesar walked over to the window and looked out back. "Nice deck," he said. "Must have cost a mint."

"That's where she said she was when Poe was snorting his shit. She was out there sunbathing while he was out running. What do you want to bet she sunbathes in the nude?"

"Do we know for sure he was out running?"

"I haven't checked. You think he wasn't?" Henry began to sound a little defensive.

"I'll check it," said Cesar. "There's no reason to make it up, I guess."

"You won't get much help out of the street though. He was up pretty early."

"You know who lives in the other big houses?"

"It's not those ladies downstairs. They all drove."

"You want me to check out the neighbors?" asked Cesar.

"If you feel like it."

"What do you mean, 'If I feel like it'? Do you want me to?"

"I told you, man, I got to go somewhere. You know this is gonna be yours. You decide."

Henry could really be a pisser sometimes.

Cesar slipped past the widow and her attendants and out the front door, heading toward the big white frame house to the south of the Poes. By the time he got there, the door was open and a woman was standing in the door waiting.

"I hope you're the police," said the woman as Cesar followed the square paving stones that curved from the driveway to the front door.

"Yes, ma'am. I'm Officer Franck."

"Well, Officer Franck, it's taken you a very long time to get here, I can tell you that. I'm Mrs. Harris. My husband is Dr. Harris. You probably know him."

Cesar shook the hand that was held out to him and found that he was not required to confirm that he knew Dr. Harris, which he didn't, as Mrs. Harris pulled him into the house and continued talking.

"I must have called about an hour and a half ago. What if it had been an emergency? Would you like to explain finding me on the floor with a knife through my throat? Would he like to explain that, Joey?"

The last was to a little stiff-legged terrier making its way down the curving staircase from the second floor. The dog, who really did look pretty intelligent, stopped to stare at Cesar.

"Did you call about—?"

"I called about what's going on over at Dr. Poe's. I suppose you want something to drink. God knows it makes me thirsty to talk so it probably makes you thirsty to listen.

"Deloris! Deloris, stop what you're doing and come in here a minute." Mrs. Harris called to the back of the house before Cesar could say that he wasn't thirsty. "You go in and sit down there. Joey, you go with him."

Cesar and Joey went where Mrs. Harris pointed, which was a living room as big as Christa Poe's but with the usual amount of furniture and with eggshell plush wall-to-wall carpet instead of fifteen oriental rugs. Deloris turned out to be a black woman holding a dust cloth.

"Deloris, would you get us two Cokes? Diet for me." Mrs. Harris dropped her voice to talk to the maid, but not low enough that Cesar couldn't hear everything. "Is Classic Coke all right, officer?"

"That's fine. Whatever."

"Because there's New Coke, which we keep for Dr. Harris who seems to like it. I don't care for it. But you're welcome to have that if you want it."

"Classic's OK with me."

"Good. Deloris, did you get that?"

Deloris, who would have to have been deaf as a post not to get that, nodded and disappeared. Mrs. Harris took the two steps down into the living room very carefully.

"I have to be so careful since I broke my hip. I'm as old as Mount Ararat, you know. Sit down."

Cesar sank into a down-filled fauteuil and watched Mrs. Harris settle into the end of an eight-foot sofa. Her feet just barely reached the ground even with the high heels. "So what is all this business going on over at the Poes's?" she asked. "And don't try to take it easy on me. I'm old. I've seen it all. She shot him, didn't she." The last remark wasn't delivered as a question. Mrs. Harris sounded as if bullets at the Poes were as inevitable as the next ice age.

"No," said Cesar.

"No? That's it? Just no? I don't believe that. You know I saw the ambulance. I'm old but I'm not blind. And I saw her out watching the ambulance so I know it was him. So I'm shockproof."

Deloris came in then carrying the tray with the drinks. Cesar took his glass and napkin and thanked Deloris. When Mrs. Harris had her drink they both started sipping, holding out for each other to start talking. Finally Mrs. Harris couldn't resist.

"You know, you hate to see young people destroying themselves when you're my age. It's a terrible thing. So much talent. Good looks. And what do they do? They throw it away." She set her drink into the coaster Deloris had set on the table. "How's your drink?"

"It's fine."

"There's plenty more out there."

"It's fine."

"So if she didn't shoot him, what is it? You're not going to tell me he just dropped dead from a heart attack at thirty-six. Not Dr. Run-Six-Miles-Every-Day-of-the-World-No-Matter-What-Kind-of-Terrible-Weather-We-Might-Be-Having."

"Nobody got shot, Mrs. Harris."

"But this was not a 'natural death.'"

"I don't think anybody—"

"You don't call in a mobile forensic laboratory for a simple heart attack, young man."

Mrs. Harris pursed her lips at Cesar and waited for him to try to shovel more bullshit. Not in her living room. Not on a carpet like this.

"Mrs. Harris, right now I'm just trying to find—"

"So. Since you don't contradict me I can see we're not talking heart attack. So now we're talking drugs. Now, I can tell you want to know how I know the Poes are involved with drugs. And I'll tell you that it's cocaine, by the way. The reason I know is my husband.

"You know, people like that," and she jerked her head in the direction of the Poes's house, "think they're so smart. They never had any Cubans or Negroes in the house. No drug deliveries that you could notice. I am right, you know. You're sitting there as if there's some chance that this old broad doesn't know what she's talking about, but you know you have to believe me. I can see it in your face. I'm glad to see we have policemen like you. Anyway I can tell you absolutely that Dr. Poe didn't take his deliveries over there, but he was taking deliveries somewhere because my husband said to me, 'Lenore, that little punk—'ordinarily he's very polite, but he didn't have a lot of respect for Dr. Poe—'that little punk is doing coke like a colored pimp.' Now, believe me, my husband doesn't make charges like that without a reason. He's a doctor. He has to be careful. So how did he know?" She waited a moment for Cesar to come up with the answer. "He talked to him for five seconds. Five seconds." She recrossed her legs and folded her arms and waited for Cesar to be dumbfounded.

Cesar sipped his Coke and waited. He wasn't quite dumbfounded yet, but it was very convenient dealing with Mrs. Harris. He hadn't had to ask her much of anything and he was getting a respectable load of information.

"You know my husband is a physician." She said that as though you would have to be from Indiana not to know it. "He talked to Dr. Poe for five seconds the day they moved into that place and he knew that we had a cokehead for a neighbor. He's a trained observer. He doesn't miss something like that.

"*But—*" Lenore Harris took a portentous sip of cola. "If he *had* happened to miss that, if he hadn't had a chance to see the man eye to eye, he would have known anyway. It was common knowledge among certain people."

Cesar shook his head, waiting to find out which certain people.

"The entire staff of Baptist. The entire staff."

"Dr. Poe was on the staff at Baptist?"

"You don't think he would be on at Jewish, do you? An anti-Semite if I ever saw one, and I've seen plenty in my lifetime, you'd better believe it."

"Is Dr. Harris on the staff at Baptist?"

"Dr. Harris is welcome at any hospital in this city, Officer Franck. He's that kind of physician. A fabulous man and a terrific doctor. But Jewish is his home."

"So . . . so what did they say about Dr. Poe at Baptist?"

"You want to know that? I'll tell you. I happen to know that you can't slander the dead. What they told him—"

"*Who* told him, Mrs. Harris?"

"A dear sweet colored woman whose life my husband saved fifteen years ago and who has of course been devoted to him ever since, who works in their dietary department and who makes, I must tell you, the best chocolate layer cake since my mother—she has one for him every birthday—this colored woman, whose name is Rosetta, pointed to Dr. Poe once when my husband stopped in to say hello to her and said he was going to be the death of somebody some day and my husband asked why and she said he used more cocaine than a movie star."

"How did she know that?" asked Cesar.

"Gossip, I imagine. My husband told her she shouldn't say things like that and she said she supposed not but it was the truth and she believed it because she said he acted just like her nephew who's in Lucasville." Mrs. Harris took a sip of her Diet Coke. "That's the penitentiary," she added unnecessarily. "She raised that nephew from the time he was a baby. My husband said he was a born criminal if ever he saw one."

"Did anyone else say that Dr. Poe had a drug habit?"

"Do I know? Isn't that enough? If you knew this Rosetta you'd know that she's the soul of discretion, who wouldn't say an unkind thing unless it was absolutely true. She's that kind of a gal."

Cesar wrote down, "Rosetta, Baptist, dietary," and started thinking about getting out of the Harris house and possibly even getting back to work on Stella's ceiling. But Mrs. Harris seemed to sense his restlessness.

"Just like my son. I can tell you want to get away."

"No. You've been a help, ma'am."

"I understand. You've got things you need to do. My sons always have things they need to do. That's the way it is. So I'll just bite my tongue and not bother you with anything about Mrs. Poe and what she's been up to with that French horn player in Esther Green's house while her husband is out running the streets in his little nylon pants."

4

Mrs. Harris and Cesar eyed each other across the expanse of eggshell carpet as they waited for the word or words that would dislodge the rich nugget of information about Mrs. Poe's adulterous private life and its possible bearing on Dr. Poe's private death. Mrs. Harris obviously thought it was Cesar's obligation to ask her just what she meant about the French horn player. That way he would be tearing the scandalous information from her reluctant lips. Cesar, on the other hand, not being sure that allusions to Christa Poe's real or imagined love life had anything to do with anything, was reluctant to take responsibility for airing the subject. As the pregnant silence lengthened, Joey the terrier who, exhausted from his trip downstairs and across the living room, had sunk senseless to the floor, sensed the electricity in the air, awakened from his senile nap, and straightened his stiff front pins, the better to stare back and forth from Cesar to Mrs. Harris.

"Is this someone—?"

"I hate to have to—"

Mrs. Harris and Cesar both began to speak at the same time. Joey let his front legs buckle and passed out once again.

Honor having been satisfied, Mrs. Harris continued. "Since you ask, I'll tell you this Mrs. Poe, whose name, by the way, is Christa, which always sounds to me like a name for a hooker, has been at it hot and heavy with the fellow who bought the other house here." Mrs. Harris twirled a hand toward the front door and Cesar understood that she meant the other big house in the little subdivision rather than one of the cramped bungalows on the street. "He got it for a song, you know. Esther left it to her niece who still thought we were having race riots every night so the niece sold it to this Gupta for maybe a tenth of what it was worth. May God forgive her ignorance."

"Gupta?" That was one of the things about Jewish people. They had all these Yiddish names for everything.

"George Gupta." Mrs. Harris rescued Cesar from his confusion. "He's half Indian. His father's a surgeon, only I can't imagine who would be so desperate that he would go under that particular knife, and his mother used to be Peggy Schwegman whose family owned the Hub downtown when it was still a nice place to eat, and you can believe they cut her off without a dime when she got married in a Hindu cere-mony. She went to Oberlin."

Mrs. Harris gave Cesar a you-know-Oberlin look over the top of her Diet Coke as she took a deep draft. "I don't know how Dr. Gupta found out about Esther's house, but one day I was out working in the yard when this Mercedes comes down the street and pulls into Esther's driveway and Dr. Gupta gets out with Bea Heiple from West Shell and three days later there's a construction crew in there remodeling the place for George, who turns out to be very handsome if you like a man who's too good-looking, and of course I recognized him right off from the symphony. But I had never seen him close up before.

"So you can imagine there's a string of girls in and out of Esther's bedroom. Or at least there was until the Poes moved in. Now, of course, it's a completely different story."

Cesar jiggled his ice and then drained the glass, waiting to hear the completely different story.

"It wasn't a month after the Schwartzmans moved out and the Poes moved in that those two started carrying on. And let me tell you you would have to be blind and deaf not to know what was happening, and with these glasses I can see like I did when I was sixteen and I've never had a bit of trouble with my hearing. Thank God. So many of my friends have gone deaf. It's getting harder and harder to find anyone who can carry on an intelligent conversation. Believe me, if I do lose my hearing you can count on me getting a hearing aid that afternoon. Anyway, I would be up in my son's bedroom, which is in the front of the house where it gets a lot of sun, and I go in there very often to take a little nap—when you get old you like to feel the sun on your bones; you're just like a lizard—and I would hear Dr. Poe going out the driveway and then five minutes later I would hear George Gupta's car—he's got a sports car so you can always tell it's him—coming into his driveway, and I would look out just to make sure. We have to do that. These houses are so tempting for certain people. It's sad, but that's the way it is. And he'd get out and the first thing he would do is look up at the Poes's window and there she would be waving to him and he would go into his house through the front door, but thirty seconds later you could see him crossing over from his backyard to hers. I guess they think nobody can see that because of the way the hill goes down in back. And you can't see from downstairs. You really can't see from upstairs except that he's so tall and I could see the top of his head when he went over and occasionally when he came back.

"So what do you think of an old lady who spends her time spying on the neighbors? You don't have to answer that. And I can tell you're not going to tell me anything I don't already know about what's going on at the Poes's, and don't deny it. I know it's your job. But even so, I'll be glad to do anything you need to carry out an investigation. I told you I've got excellent vision with these glasses." Mrs. Harris laughed at herself and Cesar figured it was time to go. He stood up.

"You've been a help already, ma'am. Believe me."

"You're a nice polite boy. Now, are you going to ask if I saw Dr. Poe out running this morning?"

"That would help."

"You see, I was waiting. I figured I had to leave something for you to ask." She laughed again and poked Cesar's elbow, steering him to the front door. "I did see him. I saw him leave the house at eight-thirty sharp and I saw him come back at ten."

"Are you sure of those times?" asked Cesar as he wrote them down.

"Even if I hadn't checked the clock I would have been sure. Every Saturday it's exactly the same thing. That's the kind of man he was. Dr. Harris said he was anal retentive and who am I to argue?"

Cesar and Mrs. Harris stood in the open doorway. Joey had escorted them to the two steps that led up to the hall and decided not to make the effort. He stood looking sleepily at the detective.

"That's Gupta's, of course," Mrs. Harris said, pointing at the third house in the complex. "He's in. I think you should go talk to him right now while he's upset, which I know he has to be. He's a real nervous boy. It'll take you maybe five minutes to break him."

Cesar started to laugh but stopped when Mrs. Harris smacked the back of his shirt. They both watched the cloud of plaster dust as it drifted away.

"You know," said Mrs. Harris, "you should get out of

those dirty clothes. What kind of an impression do you think you're going to make?" And then she patted the back of his arm to let him know he had made an OK impression on her regardless of the filth.

Henry Chapman stood waiting by his car as Cesar made his way across the lawn. "What you been doing?" he asked.

"I've been doing your work for you," answered Cesar. "Looking for witnesses. Now I'm going to go back and finish the job I was doing when you called."

Henry waggled his toothpick lewdly.

"Very funny," said Cesar. "You know what I was doing." He leaned over the hood of Henry's Lincoln and began to thump his chest, letting plaster dust fall on the heavy wax job. Henry whipped out a big linen handkerchief and wiped off the dust.

"Anybody else but you, man." Henry was only half kidding. "But I know you got a long day ahead of you."

"That's right. I got a long day working on Stella's house. Which is where I'm going, in case you think you're going to slide a little work my way while you take off for Alabama." Brave words. Cesar knew by Henry's expression that he was too late and that a call to the homicide squad office would confirm orders putting him on the Poe case. Henry spoke in confirmation.

"I am really sorry, Cesar."

"Shit," said Cesar.

"I'll be back as quick as I can." Henry Chapman put on his best sympathetic expression while Cesar wondered what he could do to ruin Henry's trip.

Cesar stood on George Gupta's doorstep with his back to the house, waiting for someone to answer his ring. A puff of warm air slithered around his neck and moved on, reminding him that a hot and muggy day lay in wait for him whenever he left this little pocket of oak-shaded air. As he stared at the

Poes's house, a cloud shifted somewhere and a ray of sunlight pierced the leafy ceiling and hit the Poes's front door so that the house looked like an ad for a house. Cesar wondered if the Poes were ever going to have any children, since it looked like a perfect setup for kids. Then he remembered that Dr. Poe was unlikely to have any children now.

There was a rustle of leaves. He turned his head in time to see a man's head pull back around the corner of Gupta's house. Cesar leaned forward to peer in the direction of the disappearing head. "Sir?" he said. "Sir?"

The head reappeared and stayed out. Whoever it was wore a vomity-looking little grin of embarrassment on his mouth. He finally stepped out and started walking in storklike strides toward the policeman, keeping his hands in his pockets. Cesar had seen that particular walk several times before, although it was the first time he had seen this man. That walk meant the person suffered under the goofy illusion that he would get shot or arrested if he walked normally.

"Are you Mr. Gupta?" asked Cesar.

"Yehes." Mr. Gupta was too nervous to talk right. This strongly suggested that he was going to prove to be a stupid interview. "I was going," he said. Cesar didn't know if he was going *to* or what, but when Gupta raised his arm in a jerky wave toward the street. Just going. Cesar waited. "My car's in the garage," said Gupta. Cesar waited. "This one." Gupta poked an arm in the direction of his own garage. "Not the service station." Cesar waited. "Did you want . . . Did you want to see me? I can stay."

"I rang your bell," said Cesar.

"I heard it," said Gupta. "No! I *thought* I heard it! I wasn't sure. But you . . . should we come in? The house?"

"If you've got a few minutes," said Cesar.

"Minutes? SURE!" Gupta turned red. He hadn't meant to shout. It was nerves. Rather than take the easy way around, Gupta squeezed between Cesar and an evergreen, keeping his back to the policeman as if he didn't want his breath smelled. He got to his front door and tried to turn the knob. "Locked," he said, fumbling in his pocket for a key. "I locked it." Cesar imagined that was what happened. At last Gupta came up with his keys and, after a little fumbling, got a key into the door, but it wouldn't open. "I don't know what's wrong!" he said to Cesar.

"Have you got it bolted inside?"

"No. Yes. Yes. I bolted it from inside. I don't use this door. I always come in from the garage." Gupta squeezed past Cesar who followed him to the garage door. Gupta looked at the door and then yanked it, but it didn't move. "It's automatic," he said. "Electric." He fumbled in his pocket again and then stopped. "I don't know what to do. The remote's in the car."

"Is there a back door?" asked Cesar.

"Sure. Sure! That's how I came out! I tell you—!" Cesar followed Gupta around the house in the back door, which stood wide open behind a screen door. "It's open," said Gupta. He pulled the screen door open and stepped inside, letting it slam before Cesar could catch it. "Oh, Christ! I'm sorry!" He pushed the door out and held it for Cesar, but since he was leaning through the opening with one arm stuck out to hold the door, it was a tight squeeze. Cesar wished he could turn around and go home, but he led Gupta into the kitchen.

"It's dirty," said Gupta.

"That's OK," said Cesar.

The man was still about as nervous as you could get without your nose starting to bleed. People were often that way around murders, Cesar had noticed. If Cesar had seen him on the street when there wasn't a major crime to set the mood, he was sure that Gupta would have been a pretty arrogant son of a bitch.

He was big and good-looking. Six three or four. Two hundred pounds. Black, wavy hair. Sun tan, although on second thought it was probably not a tan but Indian coloring.

And a muscular build. But he didn't look like he felt powerful. He still looked like he was afraid Cesar was going to shoot him.

Gupta was right. The kitchen was very dirty. It was very modern and full of new appliances and gadgets, but since the gadget to straighten up hadn't been invented, Stouffer boxes and Lean Cuisine trays lay everywhere beckoning roaches.

"Here," said Gupta. "Why don't you just sit down here." He pointed at a built-in breakfast nook that had somehow escaped a tidal wave of high tech. They slid onto maroon vinyl cushions and sat knee to knee, arms resting on a maroon linoleum table surface. It was sticky and, in spots, a little lumpy, with a huge pile of newspapers and magazines at the end of the table where it met the wall. A lot of the newspapers were still in their plastic wrappers. "You want some coffee?" asked Gupta.

"No, thanks," said Cesar.

"Make it in the microwave. Just take a second."

"No thanks."

"But it's OK if I have some?"

"Go ahead."

Gupta wriggled back out of the nook, banging Cesar's knees and feet as he went. Cesar, tired of waiting for the man to calm down, asked, "Did you know Dr. Poe?"

"Yeah. I do. But he's dead?"

"Right."

"Not real well, though. He's a busy guy. So am I."

"Have you been here all morning?"

Gupta locked the door on a cup of water and poked the control panel on the microwave. "Yes."

"Since last night?"

"Right."

"Would you be aware of anybody visiting the Poes?"

"Would I?"

"Would you?" asked Cesar, wondering how a guy so dense could have such a big house.

"If I saw them," said Gupta.

Jesus.

"But I don't usually see. I don't keep track of them, you know. I'm usually in here or watching TV. You can't hear cars coming in when you're sitting here. You can hear them when they come into *my* driveway. But I don't think you can hear theirs. But somebody could have come. I wasn't here."

"You said you were here." Cesar scratched at something that might have been a raisin at one time.

"I know. I did. I was. But I meant after I got back from the opera." He looked at Cesar, perhaps waiting for the policeman to ask him what he was doing at the opera. But Cesar just waited, knowing that Gupta was still in no state to tolerate too much silence. "I'm in the orchestra."

"What time did you get back?"

"Gee. I don't know. I usually get back by eleven-thirty. I didn't stop anywhere on the way back." He stared bug-eyed at Cesar for a moment. And then he asked, his voice cracking, "Is Christa—? Do you—? Is Christa—Mrs. Poe—is she a suspect?"

"I don't have any suspects right now, Mr. Gupta. I'm just trying to get some information so we can find out what happened."

"But what happened?"

"We don't know what happened, Mr. Gupta. That's what we're trying to find out."

"But this is a murder!"

"It might be."

"What do you mean 'might'? Christa told me—!" Gupta stopped in shock and turned as pale as his tan would let him. Cesar wanted to laugh. Mrs. Harris was right. No doubt about that. Mrs. Poe and Mr. Gupta were better-than-usual neighbors. Right now Gupta was remembering that Mrs. Poe had told him not to tell the cops they had discussed Dr. Poe's problem. It was written all over Gupta's face. He stared, stricken, at Cesar. After a few seconds he got a grip on himself and said, "She called me on the phone." Then, recognizing the inanity of that explanation he added, "She has my number."

For sure.

"We all sort of look out for each other here. We have to because of the neighborhood."

"Seems like a nice place," said Cesar.

"Oh, it's great. Where we are it's great. But we're surrounded by blacks." He looked quickly at Cesar to see if he had screwed up, but Cesar wasn't about to tell him. "Break-ins," Gupta explained.

"You been broken into here?" asked Cesar.

"Not yet."

"The Poes?"

"Somebody tried. We think. The alarm went off."

"They'll do that," said Cesar.

"You're right. I know. They want to charge you now for checking on it when it goes off. I guess you know all about that. But they have a really good system. The Poes."

"Did you see Mrs. Poe this morning?"

"Yes. No. Not close. I saw her through the window. Twice."

"When was that?"

"This morning. She was doing something with the car. And then I saw her when the ambulance came."

"What was she doing with the car?"

"She had to turn it off, I think."

"It was running?"

"It must have been. She went out and got in it and turned it off."

"You didn't talk to her."

"I talked to her on the phone."

"Did you see Dr. Poe?"

"Sure. Yes."

"When?"

"When he went out to run."

"When was that?"

"Around eight-thirty."

"You can't see from here."

"I was upstairs."

"Did you see Dr. Poe after that? When he came back?"

"No. I couldn't."

"How come?"

"I was—I wasn't upstairs any more."

"Where were you?"

"I don't know. How could I know if I didn't see him?"

Gupta started to look a little cocky. Cesar couldn't figure out why unless he thought he sounded tough. Then it dawned on Cesar that Gupta was finally remembering to tell him what Christa Poe had told him to tell him. Cesar let it ride. Gupta was bound to start forgetting his lines again soon.

"I understand Dr. Poe exercised a lot," said Cesar, hoping to get Gupta started again.

"God, did he ever. He was a maniac. I never knew anybody in my life exercised so much. He probably had a heart like a seventeen-year-old. I know he thought he was going to live forever. Didn't make it, did he? Just goes to show you." Gupta let a little laugh slip out and then looked panicky. Cesar stared and waited. "I mean he was always making remarks about body fat and what percentage he probably had, all the time looking at me like I was lard city." As he talked, Cesar straightened his spine and tried to be subtle about sucking in his stomach. But Cesar didn't see that Gupta had anything to worry about. He should see some of the porkers in the division if he wanted to see some body fat. Cesar began to tighten those of his own stomach muscles that still remembered how to go about it. Then Gupta let his stomach out. "But women like a little weight on a guy. You know? They don't go for the sticks. They never did."

Cesar hoped that was so.

"Have you been over there?" asked Gupta. "Have you

seen the exercise equipment in that place? They've got a fortune in it. That and the rugs. Christ."

"You go over there often?" asked Cesar.

"I—" Gupta interrupted himself. Cesar heard the wheels going in Gupta's head. There was going to be black smoke in another second. "I . . . I think I want to talk to my attorney, OK?"

"Sure. Go ahead." For a moment Cesar was tempted to tell the man he knew all about him and Mrs. Poe and to just give him a break for Christ's sake and stop pretending like he wouldn't recognize the lady if he tripped over her, but he didn't. Instead he made a show of closing his notebook and packing his pencil and started to wiggle out of the breakfast nook. He paused with his legs swung over the end of the bench and looked at Gupta, who seemed ready to cry in gratitude over Cesar's imminent departure. "Do you know if Dr. Poe used cocaine?" asked Cesar.

Gupta closed his eyes for a full second and tried to sneak in a steadying lungful. "No," he said. And then he said, "Yes." He turned in confusion and started toward the back door. "I'll have to check on that," he said.

"Okay," said Cesar. He wondered who Gupta's lawyer was going to be.

Cesar left Gupta at the end of his flagstone walk where it met the driveway. For some reason Gupta was staring at his own house, his back to Cesar.

There were new cars on the scene. One was a Bronco with a big Channel 3 on the side, the other a Channel 3 Sable sedan parked behind Kay Gallery's older and dirtier Channel 3 Chevy. Kay Gallery was standing in the middle of the space between two of the cars talking to a man whose back was turned to Cesar. Cesar started toward them, and Gallery, spotting him, waved a jerky greeting, which made the man she was talking to turn around.

It was one of those awkward moments. Cesar had

interrupted a heavy discussion. Kay Gallery was as tense as a bowstring, her arms folded against her chest as if to keep them from flying out and doing damage. The man she was with, while not ready to explode, stood balanced on the balls of his feet, ready for anything. They were both smiling at Cesar now. Gallery's smile was brittle, the man's was coolly polite, an "Is-there-something-I-can-do-for-you-if-not-please-shut-the-door" smile. But not rude. Somewhere back of Kay Gallery's eyes was a plea. Did she want him to come to her? Kill her friend? Go away?

Since what he wanted to do was see her up close again, Cesar interpreted her look as a plea to join them.

"This is Detective Franck, Rick."

"Rick Albers," said the man as he stuck out his hand.

"Rick is our news director," said Gallery. "My boss."

The one who pulled her off the job, remembered Cesar as he shook hands.

"Nice to meet you," said Albers. "I've heard good things about you."

Cesar couldn't help it. His eyes went to Kay Gallery's in embarrassed pleasure, but she shook her head ever so slightly.

"Grace Golden seems to think you're going to be chief someday."

Now Cesar was even more embarrassed, and it must have shown, because Kay Gallery stopped looking distressed for a minute and looked a little amused. Grace Golden was a beautiful woman who was also president of a multimillion-dollar business. Cesar knew her, but she was way over his head. Still.

"She's hard to impress," said Albers. Cesar stood grinning, he was sure, like an idiot. Albers took him off the hook by changing the subject. "I was just trying to make things up with Kay about bringing in my anchor," he said. Cesar looked blank. "Wilmot," said Albers. "The anchor." Oh. "I gather you were here when I called."

That's right, you jerk.

"I was a jerk," said Albers. Cesar began to think that Rick Albers might have a different management style from Lieutenant Tieves, Cesar's boss. "But I get paid an indecent amount of money to be a jerk, so I just had to close my eyes and do it." Cesar wondered who Albers was talking to. Kay Gallery's expression suggested that she had heard this line before. "Anyway, just think, Kay. Someday you might be a little too far over forty with no other markets calling you for audition tapes. I admit it's not likely given your brains, but it could happen. You'd appreciate a break. You know you would."

Albers stood there, looking intently at Kay Gallery. For a long moment she would not meet his eyes. At last she drew in a deep breath and looked back at her boss. She was not going to sulk.

"Do you ever manage *him*, Rick?" she asked at last. "Larry?"

"Give me some credit, Kay. If you think about it, you know I do. All the time."

They seemed to have forgotten that Cesar was there.

"Should I be learning from you?" Kay Gallery asked her boss. It was just short of an impertinent question the way she asked it.

"Yes, you should. You have right along, and there's no reason to stop now. You'll pass me in a little while anyway."

Interesting. The two newspeople were about as intense as you could get, but something about them, the way they talked, the way they stood, stated that this was not in any way a lovers' quarrel. Albers turned to Cesar, surprising the detective, who had begun to feel invisible.

"You'll be seeing her on network news before two years are out," said Albers.

Before Cesar could respond, there was a commotion at the Poes's. The front door opened to let the Channel Three film crew crash and bumble its way out of the house and set up for action in the front yard. Wilmot, the anchorman, and Christa Poe followed the crew outside. They were deep in conversation; Christa Poe kept a hand on Wilmot's elbow, and from time to time he patted it. She reached up and smoothed the hair on his temples. An enraged little moan escaped from somewhere deep inside Kay Gallery and a shadow of a smile flickered over Rick Albers. Cesar, who had seen plenty of anchormen, turned to leave, but as he stepped quietly away he felt a firm grasp on his elbow.

"Please stay, Officer Franck," said Albers. He held Cesar's arm but his eyes were on Wilmot, the news leader. "I'm sure we're going to need you."

Cesar pulled his arm free from Rick Albers's grasp, wondering who the hell Albers thought he was to grab a cop like that. Or anybody. He was going to tell Albers where to get off, but then Kay Gallery put a much gentler grip on his other elbow and Albers grinned at him in a peacemaking way so Cesar let it slide.

"Please talk to him," pleaded Albers, still smiling. "It would be a favor to me."

"I know you'd do it for me," said Gallery.

It was confusing. A couple of minutes ago Gallery and Albers had been in the middle of a major engagement, but now they were working together like a couple of luxury-car salesmen teaming up on a sale. Cesar looked at Gallery, his onetime damsel in distress. She smiled into his eyes, sending what he took to be an unspoken promise of delights to come. It was either that or she was about to start laughing at the plaster dust in his mustache.

"He's got to keep it short," he said.

Wilmot kept them waiting. Gallery, Albers, and Cesar Franck stood on Christa Poe's walkway and watched Wilmot as he went over and over and over a little speech about his late friend whose loss was going to be such a blow to Cincinnati's medical community. Cesar had the little speech memorized long before Wilmot did. But at last the lights went off and Wilmot came bouncing over.

"I don't know," he said, laughing, "sometimes the easiest things give you the most trouble. I guess," his face became suddenly solemn, "it might have something to do with losing a friend. Have we met?"

The question was directed to Cesar and it startled him, because as soon as Larry Wilmot started talking Cesar started to feel as if he were watching television and the television had suddenly started talking back.

"You interv—" Cesar began.

"There's something familiar about you. Have I interviewed you?"

"This is Detective Franck, Larry. He's from the homicide squad," Albers said briskly.

"Right!" said Wilmot. The questioning face went off and the serious face came back. "Terrible accident. Great doctor. And a personal friend. If only the drugs—" Wilmot broke off his speech and allowed an expression of bitter grief to take over his face. He stared at the ground for a moment while everybody waited for him to collect himself. Then he stared seriously up at Cesar, man-to-man, his eyes just slightly damp.

Cesar waited for the news to continue. He had seen Wilmot go through this on television before when Stan Pancoast, a trusted and popular bank executive, had gone for a ride in his garage after it came out that he had been fiddling with a couple of trust funds for many, many years. As Cesar recalled, Wilmot and Pancoast had been on the same businessmen's basketball team.

At last Wilmot set aside his private grief and resumed his professional expression. "Detective Franck, I've been talking with Mrs. Poe. She's badly shaken, of course."

Of course.

". . . but she did have some important information about Dr. Poe. She said that he had been using cocaine—"

Wilmot could not prevent a censorious shudder—"for years. Although never in excess."

Of course not.

"She also said that he always got it from the same place and that it was always reliable. She said he insisted on that. He's a doctor, you know."

What was *that* supposed to mean?

"But she says she doesn't know where he got it. She, by the way, does *not* use drugs." Wilmot shook his head, saying no to cocaine. "But she says the drugs killed him."

"How's that?" asked Cesar. He still felt as if he were talking to a TV set. It had something to do with the voice. Did Wilmot talk like that in his own house?

"A real tragedy," said Wilmot. "A real tragedy."

"How are you going to handle it, Larry?" asked Kay Gallery. If she felt the real tragedy, it didn't show in her voice, which sounded pretty matter-of-fact.

"Handle what, Kay?"

"About your friend overdosing. Are you going to put that in your report?"

"Overdosing? What are you talking about? Who said he overdosed?"

"Or whatever. How are you going to handle it?"

"You mean report about the cocaine? I'm not going to report about that! Christa told that to me in confidence!"

"You have to report it, Larry."

"I certainly do not. Rick! I don't have to report that. It's not confirmed."

"Then what," asked Kay, "are we doing out here with three cars, a mobile unit, a reporter, an anchorman, and a news director? And if what we're doing is getting ready to sit on a story, how are we going to explain it to the people who get the whole story on every other channel and in every newspaper since this confidential information is the same information that your late friend's wife has been telling everybody in earshot including her bridge ladies in there and every policeman and fireman that's been in the house, which is a lot. And how come your late friend's wife is running around in overalls with no brassiere when she's supposed to be prostrate with grief?"

"Hey!" said Wilmot, deciding she needed calming. "Hey! Take it easy!" He chuckled. Cesar didn't know why.

"Rick, he doesn't believe me." Kay sounded calm. She seemed to be ignoring Wilmot.

"Larry, she's right," said Albers.

"She is?"

"I have to tell about that?" asked Wilmot. He was shocked. Rick Albers nodded. He looked so solemn that Cesar wondered if he was trying not to laugh. "But," said Wilmot, "I thought we were here to make things better. I thought we were going to give Christa a little privacy. I mean, if we can't do that for a friend—" He broke off, leaving his mouth open in amazement. Then he began to stare angrily at Kay Gallery. Albers headed off Wilmot before he could say anything stupider.

"Don't look at Kay, Larry. Look at me. She covers stories the way I want them covered. And she's right about this. It's out. It's public. You can't put it back in the jar. I know how you feel. Don was a friend of mine, too. We all go way back. But he knew how I run a news operation. He'd understand. Christa understands. We're not here to put a lid on things. That's not how we operate." Here Albers took a quick look at Cesar to see if he was listening. He was. "The only thing we can do for Don and Christa is make sure that what goes out is true. That nothing gets reported out of context. That nothing gets said that doesn't need to be said. All right?"

"All right," said Wilmot. He understood. Cesar knew that Wilmot understood because while Rick Albers was talking Wilmot's face was registering greater and greater comprehension. If there had been a live camera, Wilmot would have turned to it and said, "There you have it, ladies and gentlemen." Since there was no camera, Wilmot turned to Cesar and said, "That's how we'll handle it. Nice of you to stay around."

"No problem," said Cesar, and he started to back away from the group before Wilmot or anybody else remembered that the purpose of his staying was so that Wilmot could interview him. Seldom had escape seemed so necessary. Wilmot made Cesar's brains feel scrambled and he needed to get back on the job so he could regain his bearings. He started to slip away without saying good-bye, hoping to catch Henry. But as he walked toward the Poe house he heard Kay Gallery's quick footsteps behind him, so he stopped and waited.

"You can see why we're number one in the ratings," she said as they stood side by side, looking at the Poes's house.

"Any idea," asked Cesar, "where Dr. Poe got his cocaine?"

"No. I wish I did." That made Cesar look at her. She continued to stare at the house. "Not for me. I don't use it." Cesar grunted softly in relief. "It just seems like that's where the story is. You *are* about to go in there and get to know Mrs. Poe, aren't you?"

"'Fraid so," said Cesar. And meant it.

"Will you call me?" she asked. Cesar turned to her, wondering what she meant. "Of course not!" she answered for him. "I can call you?"

"Sure," answered Cesar. "Anytime."

The front door of the Poe house was unlocked. Cesar let himself in carefully, not wanting a repeat of the cat incident. When he stepped into the cool, dark, front hall, he heard two voices going at once. From one side came the sound of Christa Poe, who seemed to have kept her audience of friends captive in the living room all the time she was dealing with Larry Wilmot. She sounded exactly the same as she had when Cesar first got to the house. From the other side of the house came the more familiar sound of Henry Chapman muttering into a telephone, trying not to be heard. But he was muttering so loud that Cesar knew Henry was talking to his mother, who was going a little deaf. Cesar ambled over to tune in. Henry stared an opaque stare at Cesar to make him go away, but Cesar was pretty good friends with Henry's mother and didn't feel as if he had to leave.

"I know you do," said Henry to the telephone. "I know you do. . . . you told me. . . . I know you do. . . . That's right. That's right." Little squawks escaped the earpiece from time to time as Henry shifted the phone, continuing to glare at Cesar. "No. It's all ready. . . . Everything's ready. . . . It ain't ever dirty, mama. No, ma'am. . . . No, ma'am. That's all set. Cesar. . . . That's right. That's the only Cesar I know. . . . Yes. Right here. He can't. . . . Because we're not at the office. . . . No. We're at this house. . . . No. Look, I got to get off the phone. . . . No, ma'am. I am all ready. . . . No. I've got to go back to the office and stay there until my shift is over and then I will stop by and we will leave right away. Just as soon as I get there. I got . . . I got to go. . . . I will. Now?" Henry looked at Cesar in impotent fury. "Okay. Cesar, my mother says hello and she wants you to come to supper as soon as she gets back."

"Tell her thanks," said Cesar. "Tell her I hope she has a good trip and I'll be there whenever she says."

Henry relayed Cesar's message through his teeth, but he was careful not to sound sassy, which would be big trouble. When he got off the phone at last, he started for the door without speaking to Cesar.

"Hey! Wait a second! I got to talk to you!" said Cesar. Henry stopped and turned just enough to let Cesar know it had better be good and important. He really hated for Cesar to hear him talking to his mother.

"If I have to talk to Mrs. Poe, I want to know everything I'm supposed to know."

"You know it," said Henry, starting again for the door.

"I don't know shit," said Cesar. "You haven't gotten any lab reports? Nothing? You haven't talked to her anymore?"

"Only lab report I got is unofficial."

From one of his girlfriends.

"But you'll get it pretty soon. Lab says that's the purest cocaine they've ever seen. They want to know where he got it, too. They said he must have brought it in himself for it to be that good."

"Could he have done that?"

"Seems to me doctors can do just about anything they want to."

"Did you ask his wife about that?"

"Naw. I left that for you, man. I got to get out of here. You know everything I know. That's it."

Henry pulled his sunglasses out of his pocket, slipped them on, and strolled to the door. He was big on exits, and this one would have been just great except he had to do some tricky and unscheduled maneuvers at the door to keep the cats from streaking out. If he hadn't been in a house of bereavement he would have kicked Madame Nhu across the hall. Things being what they were, he opened the door as little as possible and squeezed his massive bulk through the crack, executing little dance movements to counter the cat's thrusts. At last the door closed and Cesar was left alone with Christa Poe and her handmaidens. He tuned into the conversation.

". . . said maybe two months ago, and this is what I mean by pretentious, that when he went, he wanted to be wrapped in his first prayer rug, the little one over there by the fireplace. He wasn't kidding, either. He said he was going to see his attorney about it to make sure and I said that was criminal since it's eighteenth-century silk. There's no way on earth I'm going to cremate something like that. I don't care if he did bring it with him, I just won't stand for it. But I think what I will do, if this is OK with his attorney, who can be just as shitty as Don about details, what I'll do is make a grouping with that rug and the Persian enamel I got him last year and that tulipwood box he bought for himself without telling me and see if that doesn't take care of any legal obligations."

"How?" asked one of the women. Cesar wanted to know too, although he had begun to guess.

"Well, it would certainly meet the spirit of his silly plan for the rug."

"To be buried with it?"

"Madeline, are you paying attention? Don's going to be cremated. They always give you the ashes back. I'll put them in the tulipwood box. It's exactly the right size."

"I thought you were going to go on a cruise and scatter them."

"This is better. It takes care of the rug."

Cesar had heard enough. He stepped quietly into view, and Christa Poe looked up to see him. "I thought you had all left," she said. "What do you want?"

"I'd like to talk to you, Mrs. Poe. Ask some questions if you don't mind." Cesar let his eyes wander to the women friends to let Mrs. Poe know that he knew that she wasn't exactly so wracked with grief that she couldn't give him a little of her time. She followed his glance and then looked back at him with her own message. "Don't get smart with me, cheapo public servant," came through loud and clear. But then she stood up and turned her back on her friends and Cesar and headed for one of the doors that flanked the fireplace at the end of the long living room. Cesar followed.

The room had been Dr. Don Poe's den. There was a huge desk. Antique, Cesar assumed, given the Poes's taste. Yet another patterned and threadbare rug lay on the floor between the desk and a vast, leather club chair complete with a matching, five-hundred-pound ottoman. Christa Poe twitched her red Reebok hi-tops around the desk and sat firmly in the glove-leather swivel chair that had belonged to her husband before the marriage. It was hers now. In fact, the room was hers now. She established that clearly with a gesture, taking a framed photograph, the only ornament on the desk, and dropping it in the leather waste basket.

"What do you want to know?" she asked the policeman. Cesar had not been invited to sit, but his legs had begun to ache in the last half-hour or so, probably because of the way he had had to lean backward on the stepladder at Stella's this morning. He decided to sit on the ottoman.

"Did Detective Chapman inform you about the lab analysis of the substance found near your husband?"

"He didn't need to. I told *him*. It was cocaine."

"The preliminary report—" Cesar stopped to stare. Christa Poe, ignoring the detective, had suddenly dived into the wastebasket and pulled out the picture she had just thrown away. She slid the back out and took the frame apart, examining each layer of paper, cardboard, and fabric until she got to the picture, which she threw away without a glance. With quick movements she reassembled the frame, and then, without excusing herself, strode out of the room. She was back in a few seconds without the frame. "The preliminary report," repeated Cesar, having decided not to ask her what the hell she was doing, "indicates that the substance was cocaine—"

"I told you that. You were supposed to find out what *else* was in it," snapped Mrs. Poe.

"—in its unadulterated form."

"What do you mean, 'unadulterated'? I specifically told the forensic specialists that something in that cocaine killed my husband and that they should find out what it was." Christa's eyes were wide open in amazed outrage over the stupidity of public lab persons.

"Did you have reason to think there was something in the substance beside cocaine?" asked Cesar.

"He was dead. Isn't that reason enough?" Christa Poe rolled her eyes in appeal to the heavens. Then she had another thought. "Wait a minute. Is that an accusation?"

It hadn't been. But if it would help . . . "You just

seemed very sure that there was some sort of extraneous agent in the substance."

"Do you mean poison? If that's what you mean by extraneous agent, of course I'm sure. I found my husband dead on the floor with his cocaine kit out and cocaine on the floor around him. It was obvious to anyone that he had died suddenly from something in the cocaine. Certainly obvious to *me*. I don't see any reason to make any bones about his use of it. He *was* a physician. He knew exactly what it was doing and how it affected his body chemistry. I can tell you that he was in complete control of himself at all times and that he never used cocaine when he had any medical business to conduct. The only time he ever used it was when he knew he would be off duty for forty-eight hours, and then only when he intended to have sex."

Cesar coughed.

"Do you have a problem with that?" asked Christa.

"No, ma'am."

"*I* don't use it for that, but that's one of the attractions, in case you didn't know."

"Mrs. Poe, do you know where your husband bought his cocaine?"

"He didn't buy it. He never bought it. It was given to him. All the time."

"How—?"

"Just a minute. I want to make it absolutely clear that my husband was not addicted to cocaine. He only used it when he wanted to, and that was no more than once a week, and a lot of times he went without. Now. What do you mean unadulterated?"

"That means that there wasn't anything else in the substance."

Christa Poe let out a little sigh of exasperation and twisted her chair to the opposite corner of the room so that Cesar could see what a pain it was for her to have to deal with such an idiot.

"I *know* what unadulterated means! What I don't know is what that has to do with my husband's death. I've just explained to you that he was an experienced user. This was not the first time he ever took it."

"Ma'am, what I mean is the cocaine was pure. There wasn't anything but cocaine in it."

"So? He always said it was the finest available."

"Normally, ma'am, even what you call the finest cocaine is diluted with something. It's usually diluted two or three times between the time it leaves the lab where it's made and the time it gets to the user. It's usually diluted with quinine or milk sugar, but sometimes it's something dangerous."

"Not the cocaine Don got. He was very careful."

"Ma'am, all I know is that what was sent to the lab didn't have anything in it to dilute it at all. It was pure cocaine."

Someone had knocked on the door to the study while Cesar was talking. "Who is it?" snapped Christa.

"It's me, Christa," answered a woman.

"Open the door."

The woman who stepped into the room smiled nervously at Cesar before turning to Christa. She was wearing a halter top, a long khaki skirt, and yellow espadrilles. Cesar wondered whether that was fashionable.

"Christa, I hate to have to do this, but I've got to leave. I told the children I'd pick them up by now, and I've just got to go."

"Will you be back?" Christa Poe expected to dismiss her friends. She did not like for them to decide to leave. They all knew that.

"I'll be back later for sure. Also, I think—" The woman bit her lip nervously—"I think Alice needs to leave too."

Mrs. Poe stood up. "I'll be right back," she told Cesar firmly, and she strode out of the den, sucking the woman in her wake. Cesar stood up quietly and reached into the wastebasket to retrieve the photograph Mrs. Poe had tossed out. He slipped it into his pocket without looking at it and listened to locate Mrs. Poe. It sounded as if she were in the hall and as if she were not real pleased that her friends were leaving. There were sounds of wounded feelings followed by sounds of soothing. He couldn't hear specific words.

He walked over to take a look at the small painting that hung on the wall opposite the desk. It turned out to be some sort of sketch rather than a painting. Cesar couldn't read the signature, but he guessed the little drawing was something original and valuable, since the frame looked expensive and since Dr. Poe had rigged a light to shine on it. The picture and the rug were the only decorative items in the room. The other three walls were taken up with windows and book-shelves. Cesar went to the door to see if there was time to snoop through the books. Mrs. Poe was still in the hall, standing with her back to him, her arms crossed, listening to the miserable excuses of her so-called friends, all of whom had gathered to leave. The big living room that lay between Cesar and Christa was empty of humans. Two cats sat on warm spots left by the visitors. Cesar stepped around the door and squatted to see what kind of books Dr. Poe was into.

Medicine, of course. Lots of those. He pulled one out and noted approvingly that no dust had been allowed to settle on the edges. Books were real dust collectors. He ootched a few steps to the right and noted that medicine gave way to running. As he started to pull out a volume on brain disease he heard the thunk of the big front door closing, so he straightened up, nearly blacking out as he did so, and made his way back to the ottoman, his head still swimming. Christa Poe whipped back into the room as Cesar's backside hit the leather.

"You were telling me about this unadulterated cocaine." She was into the chair and swiveled around to face Cesar in one crisp motion.

"Ma'am, I have to remind you that it's a preliminary report. We'll have more information on it later. So it might turn out different. But if it *is* unadulterated it's just as dangerous as if it had contained some kind of poison. It's a matter of what your body's used to. See, most people don't ever get pure cocaine. It's usually been what you call stepped on or diluted, like I said. Now your pure drug is very, very powerful, and what it does is it attacks the heart muscle. When it does that, it can be fatal." Cesar watched Christa Poe carefully to see how she would take a little bit of frank talk. She took it like a pro. Didn't bat an eyelash except that she looked a little impatient.

"When *will* you know?" she asked.

"Later today. It really won't be too long."

"Is this widely known? What you say about pure cocaine?"

"I think so. There's been a couple of prominent athaletes who died from it."

"Athletes," corrected Mrs. Poe, removing Cesar's extra syllable.

"And they were in pretty good shape. I hear your husband was, too." Not sure about the correction, Cesar decided to ignore it.

"Excellent shape."

"Now, you said a while back that your husband didn't buy his cocaine? He got it free? Is that right?"

"Always. He made a point of never paying for it."

"How was that?"

"He was very careful with his money. Not stingy. But careful."

"So did he just ask people for it? It's kind of expensive, you know."

"Not as expensive as it used to be. There's a lot of it available now. But, no, he didn't ask for it. He got it regularly from the same source. Person. I assume it was a person. Always. He called it his source. And he told me a couple of times that it was a reliable source."

"Did he tell you who it was?"

"Please. Give me some credit. If I knew who it was, I

would have told the police. I'll be going through his papers, of course, and it's perfectly possible that I'll find the answer myself, in which case I will act promptly. I want results. Which I don't seem to be getting from the experts."

The expert thought she ought to give it a few more hours before she started complaining.

"Do you have any *idea* who it was?"

"I think I've already answered that. Now, when you say that it's generally known about the fatal effect of pure cocaine, what exactly do you mean?"

"A lot of people know about it. That's all. It's been in the papers."

"I don't read the papers."

"And television. It was big news about the basketball players."

"I never watch television. All I want for you to tell me is that this is not a bit of knowledge that would be limited to the medical professions."

"I guess not. No."

"Of course that would have been convenient in some ways, since it would limit the field," said Christa Poe.

"Ma'am?"

"Are you on the homicide squad?"

"Yes, ma'am. That's why I'm here."

"You don't seem very quick."

"Ma'am?"

"I would think by now that we would be narrowing down the people who could have killed my husband and talking about serious suspects. I can't *believe* how slowly you policemen operate. That fat man who was here before you barely moved. He just seemed to stand around staring. I don't suppose he cared what kind of image he gave."

Cesar looked down at the small notebook in his hands. If he looked at Christa Poe he might start telling her off. She didn't have any business talking about how homicide detectives were supposed to work.

"Ma'am, you seem pretty sure that your husband's death was not accidental."

"I'm not pretty sure. I'm absolutely—"

"Okay. Why are you absolutely sure?"

"He's dead! He's dead from what you say is pure cocaine!"

"I know. But, you have to understand, that sort of thing can still be an accident. There may have been some sort of slip up in the process."

"No. No, officer, you're wrong. I don't think you've been paying attention. This cocaine came from my husband's usual supplier. He had often commented on how stupid it was for people to go to someone they didn't know and buy something to put in their bloodstream. He explained to me that he would *never* have anything to do with an unknown and untrusted source."

"Had you warned him? Is that why he was telling you?"

"No. He was commenting after he had told me about some of the hospital cases he had seen. People who mishandled their drugs. He thought they were extremely foolish and he was bragging about how he was in no such danger.

"I realize you didn't know my husband, but whatever else he was he was very intelligent and he was vitally interested in his body and its health. He would never . . . I repeat, never do anything to endanger his health."

Cesar was still pissed off at Christa Poe for her crack about Henry. Even if she hadn't said what she did he would still have disliked her. Mrs. Poe was very good at getting across without actually saying it how dumb she thought Cesar was and how he was wasting her time. Still, he had to listen to her. And for all she didn't really have proof to back any of her contentions about her husband's cocaine rules and regulations, Cesar believed her. He had seen the bathroom with its fortune in health equipment, all of which looked used. He had also heard Mrs. Harris say how Dr. Poe was regular as clockwork about his running. Even his office supported the picture of the doctor as a thoroughly methodical person. It was stripped and clean far beyond the usual standard, even for doctors. He wondered who the cleaning lady was.

"If what you say is true, Mrs. Poe, I mean about somebody intentionally giving your husband cocaine in a form that would cause his fatality—" Cesar couldn't shake the habit of talking around death even with such a cool customer; maybe she'd appreciate it some day—"we normally have to wonder why anyone would want to. Would you know anything about that?"

5

Cesar waited calmly for Christa Poe to answer his question. She sat behind the desk, her lips pursed, and he was quite aware that she was appraising him. Her eyes traveled over his clothes rudely. At last she settled on his eyes, which stared patiently back into her own. There was the tiniest moment of embarrassment on her part and then she looked away. Cesar waited.

"Will I have to go all over this again for someone else?"

"I can't promise you won't, ma'am." Mrs. Poe pursed her lips again and looked annoyed, but Cesar wasn't about to apologize. He waited again.

"Well, of course, he's never had any death threats. He's a doctor!" she snapped at last. Cesar wrote down "No death threats" in his little notebook, leaving out the "of course" since he didn't understand what she meant. "And, of course, you can forget about his patients. His patients are all very grateful for his help. He's the finest dermatologist in the city." Mrs. Poe looked to see if there was going to be any impertinence about that. But there would not be. Cesar had no reason to doubt that Dr. Poe had been the finest dermatologist in town. But then Cesar had never had cause to see a dermatologist. No sooner had that thought registered than he remembered the bad spot on his ankle where one of his pairs of service oxfords had rubbed, a spot that had never quite gone away. Anytime he remembered it, he had to consider that it might be cancer. His hand slid down toward his sock, but then he stopped. She would know what he was doing. And indeed, when he looked up at Mrs. Poe she narrowed her eyes slightly.

"But that's not to say there weren't people who would do anything they could to drag him down. Are you writing?"

Of course he was writing. He looked up again from his notebook and twitched his pen slightly, just enough to call her attention to it.

"The other man, the detective who was in here before, didn't write down anything that I could see." That was probably true. While Henry did write things down, it was seldom where anybody could see him doing it. Henry seemed to like to have people believe he was either forgetting everything or nothing depending on the situation, so he kept his notebook pretty much out of sight. "All right. Don used to be partners with a man named Lyle Ullner." She spelled the name for Cesar. "Lyle graduated a couple of years before Don, and he had taken over his father's practice. He asked Don to come in with him, which he did. This was before I knew him or it wouldn't have happened. Lyle's father had a good reputation, which he didn't deserve, but Lyle turned out to be utterly incompetent and Don wound up with all the patients. All the good ones. Lyle couldn't stand it, and he made a big scene until Don agreed to dissolve. Of course everybody followed Don. Everybody. And Lyle, who was barely functional with Don around to hold his hand, just collapsed without him. He wound up working at the VA. So of course he hates Don's guts.

"There's also a nurse at Baptist you'll need to talk to. Her name is Elaine Robison, and she's a tramp and a congenital liar. She tried to get Don in a paternity suit. Again this was before we were going together, although I met him while he was still clearing it up. She's very cheap-looking. He never was able to explain adequately what he had seen in her. At any rate, she dragged the administration at Baptist into the business. So she's someone you have to see.

"I also want you to check out a lab technician named Chester Patel. He's an Indian. Don caught him selling supplies to one of those pathetic Indian surgeons and blew the whistle on him and got him canned."

"Did your husband—" Cesar interrupted himself, surprised at the angry look he got from Christa Poe. She must not have liked being interrupted. But this was business, so he plowed on. "Did your husband see that this Ms. Robison lost her job, too?"

Mrs. Poe's nostrils flared a little and she tossed her head slightly before answering, "No. He should have, but he didn't. I don't know why." She was not going to try to guess, either.

"Another person you'll have to see is a man named Victor Imwalle and you'll have to go to Price Hill. That's where he lives, even though he has some very nice rugs." Cesar looked up to see what she meant by that. "My husband bought a rug that this man thought should have belonged to him, which was just so much bullshit. You probably wouldn't know about the Warren collection." She waited.

"No, ma'am."

"I didn't think so. Ethel and Stanley Warren had one of the better collections of rugs in the city. They lived on Annwood. You know where that is?" She didn't think he would, but Cesar had had business on that short, elegant street, so he was able to nod. "After Stanley Warren died, my husband got to know Ethel. She had some moles that were getting caught in one of her necklaces and my husband removed them. He had heard about her rugs, so of course they talked about them. She wanted to come over and see his, but she never got around to it. But he did go over and see hers, and because she liked him and appreciated his expertise, she sold him that Ushak that's in the living room shortly before she died. Then it turned out that Victor Imwalle believed he had been promised first refusal on the rug, and he took Don to court when he found out that he had bought it. He's a disgusting man. You'll find that out. I'm not sure how he could involve himself in cocaine dealings, but he's very passionate about this. I think he's a serious danger."

"Now, I also want you to check out his friends."

Not unheard of.

"I'm talking about his close friends."

Heard of that, too.

"He's had some friends since he was in high school. But just because he's known them for a very long time doesn't mean they might not be jealous of him. Many people are jealous of my husband. Were jealous of him." She corrected herself, but there was no sign that the reminder of her husband's past tense was a great strain. "And I think some of them may have resented Don at times."

Cesar tilted his head enough to let her know that she would have to explain friendly resentment.

"I don't know how well you know physicians. Do you know any?"

"A few."

"Well, then, you should know that they tend to know a great deal about a number of things. They're achievers. They have to be to be successful. They're used to the best in a number of important areas. And they tend to be impatient with people and things that represent less than the best. I think that's understandable. But certain people, people who just get by with a minimum of effort, resent it being pointed out that they have failed or aren't trying hard enough."

"You're talking about his friends still?" asked Cesar.

"Yes. What did you think?" Christa's answer was quick and impatient.

"Well, when you say friends, ma'am, are these people he spent a lot of time with?"

"I don't know what you call 'a lot of time.' Since my husband was a physician, he didn't have a lot of free time. His first concern was always with his patients. And then he took up running, and that was very time-consuming. And we did a lot of things together, things that wouldn't interest or involve his friends. So, no. He didn't spend a lot of time with them."

Cesar sat, waiting to see why he should concern himself with Dr. Poe's friends. So far Christa Poe hadn't given him much to think about. Not that he didn't see the need to look into friends. In Cesar's experience friends were just as likely to go goofy and kill someone as strangers were. But there was more here that Christa Poe was not telling. She was squirming a little in her seat, and she glared at her hands, which were toying with her husband's letter opener.

"I think," she said at last. And then she stopped, looking even more irritated. Cesar didn't see how he could be the irritation. It looked as if there was something she knew she had to tell him that she didn't want to.

He was right. Christa Poe finally stiffened her back and turned with a glare to face Cesar. "It is possible," she said, "that my husband was a . . . that my husband was in a position to pressure someone." She waited to see if that was all she was going to have to say, but Cesar didn't have the slightest idea what she was getting at. So she sucked in another breath and said, spitting her words out with little gaps between them, "I think he may have used some of his knowledge about someone to cause that person to do something he or she may not have wanted to do."

Oh. You mean blackmail.

"Professional knowledge?" asked Cesar.

"Oh, I don't know!" Christa Poe came close to yelling as she stood up impatiently from the swivel chair. She managed to give the impression that Cesar had been badgering her. She was a handful.

"Could you tell me what makes you think that?" asked Cesar, sure that he wasn't badgering.

"How would I—?" She started to snap at him again, but something, his expression, maybe, reminded her that she was the one who had brought up the subject and she was the one who was going to have to support the nasty contention. She plopped back into the chair, her expression sullen. "Don liked to control things," she said. "That's one of the reasons he was such a successful doctor. He liked to control disease. Problems. He also liked to control people. Not me of course. We had a mature relationship. But—"

It was a constant source of amazement to Cesar the way people put themselves through contortions when they had something to tell you that they didn't want to tell you and didn't have to tell you. Why did they tell?

"Ma'am," asked Cesar, "could you maybe give me an example of what you're talking about?"

"Why?"

"Well, it would help me to understand a little better. You say that your husband liked to control people and maybe that might have something to do with his death. That's what you said, I believe."

"That *is* what I said. Only that's not the way I said it. And you should remember that I gave you other reasons and people. Those are important. I wouldn't even mention this other problem except that I want to be thorough."

"OK. That's fine. I've got those names and I'll check them out. Do you have some names of people you think he might have controlled? These friends of his?"

"*God*, I knew I shouldn't have brought this up. You *don't* understand what I'm saying. Not at all. You just sit there and write and it's all apparently just meaningless to you."

"Ma'am, I think you're mistaken. I imagine you're a little upset, and I don't blame you. I'll be perfectly glad to finish this after you've had some time to yourself."

It was time to get out of there and down to the office to explain the phone calls that were certain to beat him to Ezzard Charles Drive, calls that were just about guaranteed to complain about how he was harassing a poor widow. He closed his book and started to get up.

"Where are you going?" asked Christa Poe, surprised.

"Downtown, ma'am."

"Why?"

"That's where our office is. I'm sure you'd like some time by yourself. I can come back later."

Mrs. Poe's reply was cut off by the buzz of a telephone. Dr. Poe must have had an office line in addition to the household number. The telephone on the desk was a pre-breakup set with a row of buttons at the bottom. Christa Poe mashed the flasher and then held the same finger up, ordering Cesar to sit tight.

"Yes? . . . Yes. . . . As I'm sure you know . . . all you have to do is look. . . . No. In a little while." She whapped the phone smartly back into the cradle, giving the caller not a second's extra thought.

"You've already met two of his friends and you may have met another. I want you to pay particular attention to them."

"Who would they be, ma'am?"

"Larry Wilmot and Rick Albers, those two men from Channel Three who were outside a while ago. Just because they're on television doesn't mean a damned thing."

"No, ma'am."

"And I want you to pay special attention to Rick Albers. He's very, very smart. And he's also very ambitious. You'll see that he's quite ruthless."

"He's a friend of your husband?"

"Yes. They were academic rivals, but they were friends all the time growing up. But don't let that overshadow Larry Wilmot. He is extremely stupid. You'll find that out right away if you can't tell from his asinine news show. But he's got just enough brains to be dangerous from time to time. Don used to tease him about that once in a while."

"All right, ma'am. I've got their names. Is there something I should know that would help me to check them out?"

"Do we have to discuss it now?"

"No. Like I said, I can always come back."

"Good. Do that. I'm starting to feel very tired."

"Fine. Now, I've got those two names. You said there was someone else I would want to know about."

"Yes. I want you to check on a Bob Tieves. He's the one you should have met. He's on the police force. Only I think he's an officer."

He knew what she meant. She meant he wasn't just your basic police officer. But that wasn't what sent two or three ounces of brutal digestive acids into his empty stomach, nor was it what made his vision cloud up like a close-up shot of Doris Day for a full fifteen seconds. It wasn't the rank. It was the rank and the name. Bob Tieves, the officer in question, the "friend" of the late Dr. Don L. Poe, was without a doubt Police Lieutenant Robert Francis Xavier Tieves, the handsome, spotless, and incredibly ambitious chief of Cesar Franck's homicide squad.

Cesar let his mature Camaro find its own way out of the driveway and down the ratty little street that led to Washington Avenue. There were ruts in the driveway and potholes in the concrete, and the Camaro found them all, but at ten miles per hour the shocks were not unbearable. Cesar didn't even notice them. He was lost in his own misery and confusion. How was it, he wanted to know, that if there was something happening, anything happening that had to do with homicide, or for that matter, any police business, that would somehow turn out to be sticky business, business involving the kind of people who could and would make any investigation extra-complicated by virtue of their being connected to, or, as in this case, not just connected to but one and the same with people who controlled his, Cesar A. Franck's, life, and we're talking real power and real control, it was guaranteed just as sure as anything that that sort of not-straightforward, slip through your hands, got-you-from-behind case would land up in his, Cesar A. Franck's, hands. It seemed to Cesar that somewhere, somehow, along the way, when he didn't even know he was doing it, he had managed to get his name on the master shit list. It had to be. How else would he wind up sitting across from a new widow hearing that he had better look into the involvement of his own lieutenant in the drug-related death of a blackmailing physician. Tieves. Of all people. He should have guessed, though. There was a lot of the same feeling to Dr. Don. L. Poe's den as there was to Lt. Tieves's office. No dust. No dust, and no comfort. No mental comfort. No emotional comfort. The ottoman wasn't bad. The leather club chair would probably have been really comfort-able if it weren't the kind of chair you felt like you were in for the night. But, see, it wasn't that kind of comfort that wasn't there. They were cold places. Really cold.

Another thing he should have thought of was that Lt. Tieves had turned into a big runner, too, a couple of years back. It was bad enough that he was in better shape than any of his detectives when all he seemed to do was get in the occasional softball game, but then he had to get serious about running. Really serious. Nothing stopped him. Cesar didn't know how many times he had been driving out in a smacking cold rain on his way to the Kroger or the bakery for some pastries or other arteriosclerotic agent only to find himself overtaking a lone runner on Harrison Avenue, Westwood's aorta, and knowing a block away that it was going to turn out to be Lt. Tieves. And it always was. By himself. In the cold. Hard-charging. It wasn't too long after he started running that he started racing. Everybody heard all about Lt. Tieves's racing career from the one person in the squad who actually gave a rat's ass, which was the one other person in the squad who was into running, Carole Griesel.

Carole didn't seem to be real fast, but Lt. Tieves was cleaning up in the races the way Carole told it. She was always congratulating him on Monday morning or asking the lieutenant if he had seen his name in the sports section where they printed the results of the weekend races. Lieutenant Tieves always said he hadn't seen it. Didn't know it was there. Sure.

The Camaro overtook a runner, a sight that did nothing to improve Cesar's mood. He seized control of the car, made an awkward right, and promptly got hung up at a red light. Two dudes in Air Jordans sitting on a bench seemed to find the white man in the tired Chevrolet in the heart of black South Avondale hilarious. Cesar felt like giving them the finger, but he could just about count on the Camaro stalling at such a time, so he just stared ahead through the windshield.

How bad was it? Were Lt. Tieves and Dr. Don L. Poe really big friends or were they just running buddies? Did they go back to the beginning of time the way a lot of friendships in Cincinnati went, or had they just gotten to know each other in the Chamber of Commerce training and networking program for future municipal and corporate ball-busters? Was it possible that this was a mistake? That Christa Poe was confused and had screwed up the names? That there was another Bob Tieves in the police division? Naah.

Cesar was behind the zoo now. The warm wind brought the scent of the thousands of zoo animals and their droppings along with the smell of thousands of decaying bag lunches through the cyclone fence and into the open window of the Camaro. The air conditioner hadn't worked in three years. Cesar heard the whoop of one of the whooping baboons on its monkey bars on the monkey island. Whoop! Whoop! Whoop! It had been maybe years since Cesar had been to the zoo, but he knew what the baboon looked like and knew that it was laughing at him.

One thing was for sure. Lt. Tieves had nothing to do with cocaine. That was absolutely impossible. Lt. Tieves had his eye firmly on the top spot. Colonel-to-be Tieves. Future Chief of Police Robert Tieves. Chief Robert F. X. Tieves, youngest man to head the respected Cincinnati police division. Fastest man to head the respected Cincinnati police division.

Cesar Auguste Franck. Homicide detective with the worst luck in the respected Cincinnati police division. First cop ever to be asked to check into Lt. R. F. X. Tieves and his connection with a dead, cocaine-using physician.

Having returned control of the journey to the Camaro, Cesar found himself well into the crosswalk at a stoplight in Clifton. A powerwalker wearing not much more than a Walkman approached, swinging handweights up to his shoulders and glaring at Cesar. What was his beef? Oh. The crosswalk. The all but naked goof stood glaring directly into Cesar's eyes, waiting for the detective to get the hideous blue coupe out of his way. But Cesar had to wait for the light. The powerwalker clucked his tongue and ostentatiously walked out into the street in front of the car while Cesar pretended interest in the clock tower on the school across the street. What a pain in the ass.

As he drifted down the hill and slid onto the lazy curves of Central Parkway, Cesar entertained the idea of never mentioning anything about Christa Poe and her suspect list to anybody and just forgetting the bit about Lt. Tieves altogether. Yeah. That was it. Just forget it.

That plan held up for about half a mile. Then Cesar had to admit that it was wishful thinking. Mrs. Don L. Poe was the type of person to make sure that every last one of her ideas and suggestions got thoroughly investigated. Failure to do so would be certain to result in calls from above releasing a load of shit on the detective below, the detective whose failure to check out the widow Poe's theories had resulted in calls to the mayor.

It was actually surprising that she didn't mention the mayor. At the very least a councilman. Of course, since she knew Lt. Tieves, she didn't have to mess around with councilmen. Not where Cesar was concerned. Lt. Tieves was plenty to have to deal with. Plenty.

Another wave of panic washed over Cesar for thirty seconds. Then he started to come out of it, realizing that he had no memory of driving during that time. He sincerely hoped he hadn't hit anyone.

And why should he get so upset? All Christa Poe had done was say that Cesar needed to look into the possibility that one of Dr. Poe's friends, having had a little too much of Dr. Poe's "control," controlled Dr. Poe back. And then she had said that one of Dr. Poe's friends was Bob Tieves, a policeman.

That was all. That was it. Nothing to worry about. Not only was Tieves the least likely man in Cincinnati to have anything to do with cocaine, he was also the least likely man ever to let himself be in the control of someone who was not a member of the police division, except maybe for Mrs. Tieves.

Cesar made the turnoff for District One, the headquarters of the police and the building in which the homicide squad was housed, but instead of heading for the parking lot he let the Camaro amble around the corner leading to Stella's house, which was just a couple of blocks away. It was time to face the music in the dining room, where he had a very big mess to clean up. He didn't think Stella was going to be mad. That wasn't the kind of thing she got mad at even though she would have been well within her rights. The Camaro pulled up by the curb near Stella's. Cesar got out and locked the car, nodding to the neighbor ladies drinking Colt 45 on the stoop next to Stella's. They waved. As Cesar entered the gate and started up the short walk, one of them said, "She gone. They went off with her daddy." "Yeah?" asked Cesar. He didn't want to be impolite, but for crying out loud they didn't have to tell the whole neighborhood. "They been gone about a hour," said one of the ladies. The best-looking of the women smiled enigmatically at Cesar. As he got to the front door, Cesar spotted the note taped to the glass. Right where anybody could find it. Frankly, he didn't know how it was Stella hadn't been burgled down to her last sewing machine needle the way she kept the world informed of her movements.

"We went home with dad to supper. Probably stay the night so we can do washes. Don't worry about the D.R." was what the note said. Cesar tried the door and found, to his surprise, that it was locked. He crumpled the note and slipped it into his pocket, and as he did, his fingers ran into an unfamiliar item. It was the photograph that Christa Poe had tossed into the wastebasket and Cesar had salvaged. It had become creased, jammed as it was, and then forgotten. He stood on the covered stoop, his back to the house, smoothing the photograph and staring at the picture. The group stood on risers around a handsome young priest. They seemed at first glance to be college boys, but on closer examination Cesar decided they were high school seniors. He had to take the photograph out on to the walkway to get enough light to read the inscription at the bottom: "The Senate. St. Julian 1965." Even without the sign Cesar would have guessed the date within a year. Everyone was in a suit or sportcoat. A few crew cuts showed, but the boys closest to the priest, the boys with the confident looks of top dogs, had begun to let their hair grow out just a bit. They would have been a little shaggier or a little hoodier at one of the public high schools, but they were Saint Jay boys. The best and the brightest from the parochial elementaries, the boys from the families with ambition, boys with money, boys with smarts. Never the best athletes, but always respectable. Always wiping Elder and Purcell off the map when the College Board scores came out.

They were still wearing white socks, and about half of

them wore the laced-up shoes still favored by building and loan officials. They would have looked totally ordinary except that the majority of them smiled a message of confidence, security, and, perhaps, superiority that marked them as the best of the best. And not just in their opinion. For the priest in the center smiled an adult version of that very smile, one that seemed to speak for the group to all who should be fortunate enough to see the photograph. "Here," said his smile, "are the best. I defy you to match them."

Cesar scanned the faces, wondering if he would recognize anyone but doubting it. These boys were ahead of his class, and although some of them were undoubtedly from Westwood, they had certainly gone to parochial schools. Still, he might recognize someone from the neighborhood. He imagined that one of them must be Dr. Don L. Poe, but he hadn't the faintest idea what Dr. Poe looked like now, much less then. And then he came back to a face. And another face. Two boys standing next to each other. One boy grinned openly into the camera. Something about the grin and his posture suggested that he was a senator because he was well liked rather than the smartest kid in the school. The smartest kid in the school stood next to him. Maybe not the smartest. That was probably the guy in the shortest crew cut with the face like a fox terrier. Maybe the boy next to Mr. Popularity was the most mature, the wisest. His expression was that of someone much older and his smile was fainter.

Why did they look familiar? They conjured up no one from Westwood. He might have stared all night except that he was helped by neighbors. A television set was blaring from the front room in the second floor apartment next door. And it was the familiar sound of the Channel Three Newsfocus team theme that tipped him off. Even before the serious baritone of the city's most popular newscaster reached him, Cesar matched the adolescent face on the popular kid with that of the well-known adult face of Newsfocus anchor Larry

Wilmot. The kid next to him, the one with the brains, had to be Channel Three news director Rick Albers.

What do you know. Cesar looked closer and decided that Larry Wilmot looked a whole lot like Dave Radtke, the biggest jerk in Cesar's own class at Western Hills, a popular pain in the ass who had gone on to State and become a bald dentist with the largest practice in Green Township and a close friend of Cesar's own disgusting brother-in-law, Fred the weasel. What do you know.

Another face in the picture caught his eye. It belonged to a tall, thin boy in the back row next to the crease in the photograph. For a moment Cesar forgot about the face and wondered where he stood with the rules of evidence, since he had filched the photograph. Well, he had filched it from a wastebasket. But it was a privately owned wastebasket. And he hadn't had a search warrant. But it was from the scene of a murder. Well, it was from the same house. The other end of the same house. Finally he decided that the photograph had been sitting out in the open. It wasn't something you had to search for.

He looked again at the skinny guy in the back row. Now, why did *he* look familiar? And not good familiar, either. He was probably a basketball star at St. Julian, but their basketball stars never made it to the pros. They didn't make it to the big sports schools either. Too small and too smart, usually. So if he wasn't a sports figure, who was he? Not someone from the past. Not a neighborhood kid.

Oh, shit. Cesar sighed a little. There was no mistaking it. Put fifteen pounds on the guy, part the crew cut and flatten it, leave the superior smirk in place, and put the guy behind a steel desk, and there you had, without a doubt, Cesar's own supervisor, Lieutenant Robert Francis Xavier Tieves.

He looked like a jerk even then.

"Go take a shower," said Sgt. Evans before Cesar could even sit down at his desk.

"What are you doing here?" Cesar asked the sergeant. Saturdays were Sgt. Evans's drinking days.

"I'm working. Go take a shower. And make it fast. And get clean. Do you have any clean clothes?"

"What is this? An inspection? I don't have to take a shower. I'm not even supposed to be on duty."

"Yes, you are, Franck. It's already set up. You know it. I know it. You know that I know. I know that you know that I know. Use soap. What about the clean clothes?"

"I might. How come I have to take a shower?" Cesar's question came halfway to the locker room. The short but still powerful Sgt. Evans held Cesar's arm firmly at the elbow as he steered him toward the soap and water. Cesar tried to pull away, but Sgt. Evans had a grip like a pit bull.

"Because you look like a vagrant. Have you been in the homes of taxpaying citizens looking like this or did you become filthy sitting in your filthy car?"

"I was working this morning."

"Police work? Jesus Christ! Stand back!"

They were in the locker room and Cesar had pulled his shirt over his head, sending a cloud of plaster dust out into the atmosphere. It immediately mixed with the warm locker room fog to create a light glue that began to settle on the cool lockers as well as the shiny toes of Sgt. Evans's service oxfords.

"I've got a life of my own too, you know," said Cesar, pulling off his trousers. Heavy, sandy dust fell from the waistband to the terrazzo floor where it crunched under the soles of his shoes.

"Does this life of your own force you to live under a viaduct somewhere? I can't believe you went out looking like that. I can't believe I didn't get a telephone call from a taxpayer about what a dirtball we've got on the force."

"I was working on Stella's ceiling. I told you I was going to do that." Cesar knew that Sgt. Evans had a soft spot for Stella Hineman and hoped the mention of his girlfriend would get Sgt. Evans off his case. He stepped into the shower and turned it on full blast. They had really good water pressure at the station. Better than at home. Plaster dust washed out of his hair and onto the floor of the shower. Jeez, what a mess. He still didn't understand what he had to get cleaned up for.

"You're going out to see the lieutenant," said Sgt. Evans, reading Cesar's mind. He had taken a seat on a bench near the shower. Cesar wondered if the man was going to check his ears when he got out.

"What?"

"You heard me," said the sergeant. "You're going out to his house as soon as you get cleaned up."

"What the hell am I doing that for?" Cesar stood in the door of the shower, outraged and dripping liquid soap. "I don't want to go there. What is this? I'm not going! No sir!"

"So make sure you get really good and clean. Use some of that soap on your hair."

"What the hell for?" asked Cesar as he rattled the bejeezus out of the helpless soap dispenser. "What's so important I have to see him at home? Wait, don't tell me." He slapped soap on the top of his head and began to punish his scalp. "I can guess. It's about his friend the dead doctor, isn't it? Am I right?"

"He didn't tell me, Cesar. And I didn't ask him. But since the request came immediately after I told him that you were over there investigating the death of Dr. Don L. Poe, I would have to guess that you're probably right. Get your ears good and clean."

Cesar sloshed soap everywhere he could reach and then sluiced off. He wanted nothing more than to stay under the pounding hot stream until it was time to go to bed, but he hadn't the slightest doubt that Sgt. Evans would reach in and pull him out if he stayed in thirty seconds longer. He stepped out of the shower and into the sergeant's critical glare.

"I'm not kidding, Franck," said Sgt. Evans. "You're

gonna have to do something about that pot. You're getting big as a house."

Cesar tried to stay out of Lt. Tieves's neighborhood as much as possible. That was not hard to do; there was no crime there. Dawn Vista Drive, where the Tieveses lived, was one of a handful of long, dead-end streets in the quietest and most expensive section of Westwood.

Cesar Franck, although he too lived in Westwood, didn't think of the Tieveses as neighbors. Cesar lived a mile away with his mother Lillian Franck in the house where he had grown up with his sister Kathy and, before he died, their father. But he knew who most of Tieves's neighbors were. Like right there. That sprawling four-bedroom number at the corner was where Allen Grote lived. Grote, in addition to being the sharpest young political strategist around, was far and away the best political fund-raiser in the city, regardless of age. He was a low-profile guy, though. The only reason Cesar knew about him at all was because his brother-in-law Fred the weasel filled him in, although now that he knew about him, Cesar had learned how to tell when Grote was influencing the councilmen who influenced the police. As a matter of fact it was thanks to Fred that he knew who lived in any of these houses. Fred and Kathy had a huge Buick sedan, and they liked to come over and take Lillian for a Sunday drive, since the rest of the time she had to get around on the bus or in Cesar's disgusting Camaro, a car she loathed and feared. She always made Cesar come along so he would see what a nice car the Buick was.

About every other trip Fred would swing through the Tieves's subdivision. Fred would invariably point out his cousin Ron's house, and then point out the house that he thought was the greatest, which looked like every other house on the street except for the street number, which was written out in wrought iron over the garage.

Something that drove Cesar crazy about the Buick was

the way it was sprung so soft. He actually got carsick once, although that might have been due to Fred's spastic driving and the fact that Cesar had to sit in the back.

Even after all these years Cesar was still amazed by the relationship between his sister and her husband. Did Kathy really like him? Or was this just some stupendously long joke she was playing on Cesar to see if he would actually believe she would marry such a jerk?

Another person who had the power to make Cesar miserable lived on Sybaris Court, one street over from Lt. Tieves. That was Charles Vollrath. Vollrath was a deputy city manager who was so slick that he had stayed on the job through three city managers even though it was an appointed position. Some of the guys had taken to calling him the J. Edgar Hoover of Cincinnati.

And of course there was the chief. Not just in the neighborhood. On Dawn Vista Drive. Lt. Tieves's very own street. Three doors down from Bob and Diane. Most of the police division who knew about that situation assumed that Lt. Tieves, the consummate brown nose, had moved his family onto Dawn Vista to be near the chief and his wife Marge. But the truth was that Lt. Tieves got there first, thanks to his father-in-law Herman Vielhauer and his unbeatable connections at the building and loan where he was able to find out just what the Stagges were going to do about their house after they moved into the condo by the golf course. It was the same Herman Vielhauer who tipped his son-in-law off about the bigger and more luxurious ranch down the street that was about to go on the market just as the chief landed his position and needed surroundings to match his title. Tieves passed that bit of information to the grateful chief real fast.

You almost never saw a for sale sign on Dawn Vista Drive.

Cesar didn't pull into the Tieves's driveway. The Camaro had a benign oil drip and Cesar didn't want to be the first person to put a mark on the Tieves's concrete.

Mrs. Tieves answered the door. Cesar, who accepted relationships pretty easily, was always a little surprised to see Diane Vielhauer Tieves, since she didn't look right for her part. She looked older than her husband in some ways. Her nearly colorless hair was cut and curled very much like the practical mop Cesar's mother had ordered up at Cathleen's Cut'n'Curl for the past twenty years, and her clothes were always very plain. This night she had on a light green shirtwaist she might have bought when she was a senior in high school. She wasn't ugly. But she didn't seem to have any of the vanity her husband did. She was also a little hefty, which Lt. Tieves was never going to be, no matter what.

"Hi," she said to Cesar. "You're Detective Franck, aren't you?"

"Yes, ma'am." This was really kind of funny, since they grew up so close and were the same age.

"He's down in the rec room. He told me you were coming, so he's expecting you." She coughed out a little giggle. Cesar followed her, sneaking a peek at the gigantic living room to the right of the entry hall. It looked like a new TV under the picture window. Mrs. Tieves led him to the basement door in the hall across from the kitchen. The sounds of two different television programs floated through the hall from two different bedrooms. "You've been here before, haven't you?" she asked, holding the door open.

"A couple of times," Cesar answered.

"Then you know how to get down there all right?"

He nodded. It was pretty basic. You went down the stairs and there you were in the rec room. He figured Mrs. Tieves was being polite. He hoped neither he nor she was as dumb as the question.

The rec room belonged to Lt. Tieves. There was a big family room with a huge fireplace off the kitchen. That was Mrs. Tieves's room. She had a TV and a telephone in there and the utility room was just around the corner, so she never had to leave if she didn't want to. She only went into the rec room to dust. She never had to straighten.

Lt. Tieves, looking much better dressed than Cesar in a bright yellow and teal sweat suit, was sitting on a bar stool, one of five along the bar, working on paperwork. "I'll be right with you," he said. "Sit down and get comfortable. Won't be a minute."

Cesar threaded his way between a sofa and a coffee table and sat down. The big Mitsubishi projection TV was on and tuned to ESPN with the sound turned off. Golfers somewhere out west were in the second day of a tournament. Cesar didn't follow professional golf much, so he didn't recognize the fat man with a moustache who threw his sand wedge at an oak tree as his ball dribbled off the tiny green, but he had played enough to feel for the guy.

He looked to see if his boss had seen the shot, but he was concentrating on the paperwork. The only light turned on in the rec room was a track light aimed at the bar top. The rest of the room gave back the dim colors of the projection TV. Cesar leaned back in the sofa and, with no warning, fell asleep.

He had no idea how long he slept. One minute he was watching the fat guy miss his putt, the next he was getting his knee rapped by Lt. Tieves. He was afraid it was pretty bad. The inside of his mouth was dry, so he'd probably been far enough out to let his jaw drop. Stella had let him know he snored when he did that. Jesus Christ.

"Burning the candle at both ends, Franck?"

Cesar smiled sheepishly and shook his head. Of all the stupid things to do.

"You want something to drink?"

"Sure, sir. That's be great."

Lt. Tieves didn't ask him what he wanted. The last time he was here a drink meant a draft beer from the restaurant-quality tap, and Cesar's mouth watered. But Lt. Tieves had a new gadget, a mineral water cooler. He pulled down a couple of the tapered beer glasses from the overhead rack and drew off a round of Talawanda water, pausing to drain his glass and refill it before bringing Cesar's over to the sofa.

"I'm addicted to this stuff," he said. "It's great. No fluorocarbons."

"No, sir."

Cesar sipped from his beer glass and waited. Lt. Tieves took a seat in the sofa around the corner of the table and put his feet up. They were unusually long and thin, even for such a tall man. Cesar didn't recognize the logo on the running shoe. It could have been a dollar sign.

"I don't know if you know this," said the lieutenant, dropping his voice to its official pitch, "but I knew Dr. Poe."

Cesar waited to see what he was supposed to do.

"The homicide."

"Right, sir."

"Did you know that?"

Cesar couldn't help himself. He let his fingers run along the bump in his pocket where rested the picture of the youthful doctor and his high school buddies, including Lt. Tieves. "Yes, sir. That came up."

"Mrs. Poe?" Tieves's eyes got steely, which was what happened when there was badness in the air. That must mean that Mrs. Poe was bad.

"Yes, sir."

"Excellent doctor. Physician. Excellent." Tieves didn't want to say something. Probably had to do with his friend the excellent doctor's cocaine habits. "I really hated to hear that there is some indication that a controlled substance contributed to his death."

"It seems to have been the sole cause, sir."

"Does it? Well, until the autopsy is complete, we're going to have to give him the benefit of the doubt. What . . . What could make him—? Why would a guy like that need—?" Cesar was interested. He had never before seen Lt. Tieves so rattled. "Franck, this guy, Don Poe, had everything. Everything. He was a track star. He was brilliant. The best science student I ever saw. Left high school a year early and then finished college in three years. State! Premed! I was always a little shocked that he turned out to be a dermatologist. I sort of expected him to specialize in something more . . . special. You know? I also kind of expected him to live someplace else. Chicago, maybe. Maybe even New York. That's what *he* said he was going to do."

"Did you talk much to Mrs. Poe?" The change of subject was abrupt. Cesar put down his water.

"I talked to her some, sir. I didn't want to, you know, upset her too much since it was so soon after the homicide."

"Of course."

"And Henry had talked to her before I did."

"Chapman?"

How many Henrys are there in the squad? And how many of those Henrys did you talk to today? Of course it was Henry Chapman.

"Yes, sir."

"I meant to tell you I appreciated your having to fill in for him. I'm sure you understand that he had a serious personal emergency."

"Yes, sir."

"You know, until the autopsy is in, we don't really *know* the cause of death. I don't want you to forget that. I'd be disappointed if I picked up the papers and read a lot of irresponsible bullshit about what did or didn't kill him. You know that, don't you?"

"That pretty much goes without saying, sir."

"Hell, Franck. I didn't mean you were going to call up the television stations." Tieves was irritated. So maybe he had meant it.

"Right, sir. But maybe you ought to know that there was

at least one station out at the house. Channel Three was there."

"It was? Do you—? Did they talk to you? Who was it?"

Cesar told him about the Channel Three coverage. Lt. Tieves's irritation slacked off as Cesar went through the story, particularly once he learned that Rick Albers had been on the scene to see that things went the right way. But he got irritated again when Cesar started talking about Mrs. Poe. Cesar had to tell the lieutenant that he didn't think Mrs. Poe was going to keep her lip buttoned about anything, since she had already told her pals, the rescue squad, the police, and Channel Three that her husband was a drug fiend.

"*Damn* it!" said Lt. Tieves, leaning back on the sofa with his arms crossed. "Damn it!" He glared at Cesar, but Cesar didn't feel responsible for Christa Poe's loose talk. Escaping the glare, he picked up his beer glass and, forgetting what he was drinking, sipped. He choked and spit the water back into the glass. Some of the water escaped and dripped onto his trousers and a little bit splashed onto the table. His peripheral vision told him that his boss was glaring even harder.

"You're checking her out, aren't you?" asked the lieutenant as Cesar brushed the water off his pants leg. Should he get a napkin? There were little napkins up on the bar. "What?" The question sank in.

"She's a suspect, of course."

"Of course." Cesar was very glad the lieutenant could not read his mind the way the assistant city manager around the corner could, since he had actually not given two seconds' thought to the idea of Christa Poe as her husband's murderer. For Christ's sake, why should he? She was the one who called the police and everybody else in sight and pointed out all the cocaine on the floor.

"Your leading suspect, I assume."

"Well, the wife—" Cesar hoped Tieves would fill in the blanks.

"And this one wasn't your usual loving wife. Never was. I don't know what got into Don. I really don't."

About a teaspoonful of pure cocaine.

"Nobody even knew her. I never met anybody who knew anything about her. She's from some place in West Virginia, for pete's sake. I think he met her at Nahighian's."

"Where's that, sir?" Cesar thought he knew most of the local singles bars, but this was a new one.

"Fourth Street." Lt. Tieves looked at Cesar as if he were asshole of the year. "It's the rug store. She was working there. She found out he was a doctor and got her hooks into him and never let go. Till now."

Cesar looked at the lieutenant. Tieves glared across the top of his water glass, not at Cesar but at a framed poster of Pete Rose hitting his big one. He sure seemed to have it in for Mrs. Poe.

"She didn't seem too upset, sir. I noticed that. In fact she's a pretty cool customer. Still, I don't know."

Lt. Tieves shifted his glare from Pete Rose to Cesar Franck. "Don't know what?" he asked.

"It just didn't seem to me that she would have called in the reporters and the police the way she did if she had something to hide. She seems just as interested as anybody in finding out who did what. Anyway, that's my impression."

"It is," said Tieves, stating an irritating fact. "Well, I didn't call you here to question your judgment or tell you who to investigate. You know that."

"Right, sir."

"And I know you were going to check out the wife as a matter of course."

"That's right." Eventually.

"So that's not what I called you here for."

"No, sir."

"No, I really just called to tell you that I'm counting on you to use your discretion in this matter. As a personal favor to me. Do you understand?"

"I think so, sir."

"Franck, for God's sake, you don't have to look like I'm asking you to cover anything up. You're sitting there like doomsday. Knock it off."

Cesar tried to make his face blank. He was a little surprised as he thought he had made his face blank five or so minutes ago and left it that way. He really didn't have any desire whatsoever to get the lieutenant riled up. It was unusual for him to be so testy and show it. Maybe it was because he was at home. Some people were that way.

"Do you have any family friends?"

"Sure, sir."

"Of course you do. Now if there were some kind of tragedy in the family of one of your family friends and it was in your power to see to it that the family might suffer a little less, would you do something about it?"

"Yes, sir."

"Of course you would. That's the way you were raised. That's all I'm asking."

"Sir?"

"I'm just asking," Tieves was beginning to sound really exasperated. Cesar wished he knew what he was doing wrong. He never knew how to do things right where the lieutenant was involved. Frankly he wondered how he managed to stay on the homicide squad. "I'm just asking," repeated Lt. Tieves, "for the sake of Dr. Poe's family, that you do everything to keep the hysterical drug-related bullshit out of the news. Now don't let me down."

"I won't, sir."

Tieves stood up, signaling Cesar's imminent departure. Cesar drained the Talawanda water and stood up himself. Was that all he had been brought out for? Just for a little warning about tact and discretion? He looked at Tieves to see if there were any other message forthcoming. But the lieutenant was headed for the bottom of the stairs. He wasn't even looking at Cesar.

"Lieutenant?"

Lt. Tieves turned impatiently to see what Cesar wanted.

"Are you aware of what it was actually about the cocaine that killed Dr. Poe?"

"It was pure. Straight stuff is what I heard. Why?"

"That's right. Or that's what they think. Mrs. Poe thinks that was intentional."

"That's possible. It's also possible that she doesn't just think. She may actually know."

"Right, sir. But she thinks the only reason this could happen was that his regular supplier, somebody he trusted, gave him the stuff that way. On purpose."

"That's possible, too. So if she didn't provide it, all you have to do is find out who hated him enough to want to kill him. That's going to be the hard part. Aside from his wife, everybody thought he was a great guy."

"But, you know," Cesar's voice stopped the lieutenant once again, "She seemed to think that the guy he was getting the cocaine from was one of his friends. One of his old friends."

Lieutenant Tieves lost control of his handsome face for a second, and a wave of anger passed before Cesar's eyes. It was not something to take lightly. Tieves opened his mouth in what was all too close to a snarl and then snapped it shut before getting control of himself and saying, "That sounds like something she would say. I'm not surprised. Still, you'd better check it out."

The interview was now over. Cesar followed Lt. Tieves up the basement stairs and into the hall. The TVs were still going in the bedrooms. If the kids were in the house, they were nowhere to be seen. The sound of Diane Tieves talking to her mother on the telephone came from the kitchen, blended with the softer sound of the family room television. Cesar followed Lt. Tieves to the front door. He tried to walk out, but the lieutenant stood in his way, facing him and staring at his belt. What was the matter? Cesar looked down to see if he was unzipped. Nope.

"You getting any exercise, Franck?" Oh, Christ.

"Oh. Here and there sir."

"Tried running?"

"Not recently. No, sir."

"Give it a try," said Tieves, patting Cesar's belly with the back of his hand. "Blast that gut right off. Two months. That's all it takes."

"Sounds like a good idea, sir."

Cesar was in his own driveway in five minutes. He thought about putting the car away so he wouldn't be tempted to go out again, but that would mean moving a few things including the automatic garage door opener, still in its box, that Lillian had given him for Christmas.

He let himself into the house by the front door and knew right off from the silence that his mother was out some place. Cesar headed straight for the refrigerator and pulled out a cold Hudepohl. He couldn't get over Lt. Tieves giving him a glass of Talawanda water on a Saturday evening. The first hit of cold beer rushed to salve the deprived lining of his mouth.

He pulled four burritos out of the freezer and stuck them in the microwave. By the time it beeped he was ready for another beer. He put the burritos and the beer on a tray and took them out onto the tiny screened porch that opened off the living room, setting up shop at the little outside table that his mother would never eat at even though she bought it. She didn't think it was possible to get it clean enough, given all the dust from the street.

He peeled the cellophane off one of the green chili burritos, took a bite, took a swallow of beer, and leaned back to think about his day and the death of Dr. Don L. Poe.

The first thing he thought about was the last thing he had done, which was to visit his boss in his own den. He had gone there with warnings from the widow that Lt. Tieves was one of a close group of Dr. Poe's friends who were on Christa's list of possible murderers. He still didn't think that was a possibility. No. But was that because he didn't want to? Without paying much attention, Cesar opened the second green chili burrito. The first had vanished in seconds, and he hadn't really noticed how it tasted. Did Lt. Tieves intimidate him? Yes. Well, that was his job. But did that mean that Cesar was incapable of treating him like just another citizen when it came time to investigating a murder? Yes. But he hadn't completely chickened out. He had at least mentioned Christa Poe's suspicions and gotten a reaction. That was at least sort of brave. And the lieutenant had definitely reacted. Definitely. Only Cesar didn't have the faintest idea what the reaction meant. Guilt? Anger? Contempt?

The second burrito was gone. Cesar weighed the beer and decided there was enough to go with the last two burritos. He opened one of the red bean numbers and began to chomp, moving a littler slower than he had with the first two. The summer evening sky was still a bright blue, the world still visible outside. But on the porch in the gloom of the screens it was getting dark.

Should he even be listening to Christa Poe's theories? Was she someone to take seriously? Did she have axes to grind? What were they? If the doctor really did have a regular cocaine habit, no matter how controlled, was it believable that she wasn't a part of it? And was it possible that she truly would not know where he got his stuff? If he did keep his source a secret from her, why did he? What kind of marriage was this? Why didn't they have any kids? Why did they have rugs and exercise equipment? Why did they live in the middle of nowhere in Avondale instead of one of the medical suburbs? Why did Cesar's muscles twitch when Kay Gallery laid a hand on him?

As soon as he thought of Kay Gallery he was reminded of

how his day had started and with whom, and he felt very bad. After all, it was his idea to get in there and tear Stella's dining room apart, not hers. And then, to disappear like that. Of course that was duty. But what about Kay Gallery? Well, that wasn't anything to worry about. She was actually sort of like a movie star. Not a real person to feel guilty about. It was just a little bit funny to have a movie star turn up in real life like that and turn her smile on you and break down in front of you and lay her hand on you and leave it there. Nothing to think about.

Cesar unwrapped the last burrito, only to discover that he had inadvertently finished his beer. He looked at the burrito, knowing he should skip it. That he should have stopped at two. He went and got another beer anyway. And by the time he was back in his chair, burrito in one hand, beer in the other, he had set aside thoughts of Stella and her ceiling and Kay Gallery and her touch and put his mind back on the much less pleasing subject of Christa Poe.

Christa Poe. She didn't talk like people from West Virginia that he knew. And she wasn't a hillbilly. Or if she was, she had done a pretty good job of disguising the fact. That boob that kept peeking out from her overalls, it was all the same shade of brown. She really must sunbathe in the nude. Cesar blushed in the dark of the porch.

Did she do her nude sunbathing out on that back deck? And if she did, did she do it where Gupta could see? Did Gupta come out and take a ringside seat? Was Mrs. Harris right about those two? Given Gupta's spastic and guilty reaction to Cesar's references to Christa Poe, Cesar would bet the farm on Mrs. Harris's accuracy.

Christa Poe hadn't mentioned Gupta once. Not surprising. But he would have to be checked out. Was Christa Poe someone you'd murder for? She wasn't Cesar's type. Not the way she looked and not the way she carried herself. She had all the earmarks of a real pain in the ass. Maybe she had a

Ph.D. in sexual recreation. That was a real possibility. Cesar had once had a short but very draining relationship with a paralegal from Covington, across the river, who had the same sort of bossy, businesslike, cold-blooded attitude.

A car slowed on Epworth and pulled to a halt in front of the house. It was a clean, undented Skylark in a taupe shade favored by a lot of his mother's friends, and sure enough, the passenger door opened and Lillian Franck worked her way out in her deliberate fashion. As usual, she leaned back into the car to keep talking to the driver. Then she closed the door and talked some more through the window. She had a paper bag with her, not a grocery bag, but not from one of the department stores. At last she straightened up and said good-bye to whoever was driving. The car pulled away, with Lillian at the curb watching and waving. Someone in the back seat waved to her.

As Lillian turned toward the house she looked up at the living room window. "I'm up here," called Cesar. A little startled, she shifted her gaze to the porch and didn't respond. Cesar realized she couldn't see him because of the screen and the fading light. He watched her take the stairs a little slower than usual. She must have been on some sort of outing to get that tired. He waited, and in a few minutes she came out on the porch.

"Sit down," said Cesar. His mother took a couple of her short steps over to the chair that matched Cesar's and peered down.

"I don't think so," she said, although she was pooped.

Cesar knew what the trouble was. He went into the kitchen, got a rag, came back out to the porch and wiped the chair down. His mother plopped into the chair without thanking him, which was a reminder that he was supposed to have cleaned the porch off the week before. He was spending too much time with Stella.

"Where'd you go?" he asked.

"Metamora," she answered. "It's in Indiana."

"Is it nice? Did you have a good time?"

"It's cute. My legs are killing me. Betty wanted to see everything. You'd think I'd know by now."

"What'd you get?"

"Something stupid. I knew it as soon as I bought it but I didn't want to go take it back."

"What is it?"

"A cookie jar. It's a cookie jar that's made like a panda."

"Like the one we used to have? The one I broke?"

"It's a little bigger, but it looks just like it. I won't tell you how much I paid for it. Those antique places are real ripoffs. Every time. I swear it."

"How much did you pay for it?"

"I told you I wouldn't tell you."

"Fifteen dollars?"

"Are you crazy? Did you get her ceiling fixed?" "Her" being Stella in Lillian talk.

"No, I got called out. This doctor over in Avondale died."

"He just died? Why'd you have to go?"

"He didn't just die. He might have died from a drug overdose."

"Suicide? They've got the highest suicide rate in the world, you know. Except for Sweden. Is there any more beer?" Cesar went to the kitchen and got his mother a beer. He debated getting one for himself since he only had about a third of a can left, and then figured Lillian wouldn't finish hers. He got a little mug she liked to use, filled it, and took it to her.

"Wasn't suicide," he said. "There was something funny about his cocaine."

"He took cocaine?" Cesar nodded. "A doctor? Who was he?"

"You don't know him. He's a young guy. A dermatologist."

"Was it Dr. Poe?"

"Yeah! How'd you know? Is it on the radio?"

"Betty never plays the radio. No. I know because he took that mole I was worried about off my shoulder. He's the only dermatologist I ever went to in my life. I'm not surprised."

"You're not? I think that's pretty surprising. You go to one dermatologist and it's him."

"No, Gus." Lillian Franck alone in the world called Cesar Auguste Franck Gus. "It's not surprising that somebody killed him. He was a real jerk."

6

hat doesn't make it right, of course. You know what I mean." Mrs. Franck glared at her son, warning him not to get fresh with her. "I'm just saying it's not surprising."

"How come?" asked Cesar.

"I don't know. I didn't see him that often. Actually I only saw him twice. But that was enough to get the impression that he was a very cold fish. And also I got the impression that he thought he was doing me a big favor treating me for this mole."

"What did he say?"

"Now, Gus, you're getting all bothered over nothing. I'm just trying to tell you that he wasn't going to win any popularity contests. Although, if you think about it, you don't want your doctor to be like a salesman, you know? Now that I'm thinking about it, I can't even remember what he looked like except that he was kind of small. Kind of bony, I guess. Not much hair."

"He was a big runner," said Cesar, involuntarily running a hand along his hairline.

"Well, that figures." Mrs. Franck was convinced that the runners and joggers who littered the streets and sidewalks of her city were all potential heart-attack victims waiting to collapse in front of her bus or her son's car. "I remember," she said. And then she stared earnestly out the screen at the fading sky. "I remember what he did say to me. I got real mad at him at the time. And it's no wonder. Of course I didn't say anything back to him. But he said to me 'You'd have very nice skin if it weren't for all these moles.' Can you believe that? How do you suppose I was supposed to feel about that? Was that supposed to be some sort of helpful remark? You'd think the moles were my fault. And I'll tell you, I actually sat there while he was working on the mole I wanted off wondering if I had really done something to get moles like they were some sort of disease. Now if Dr. Rieckhoff had said something like that I would have known what to do. But I didn't know this guy, so I took it seriously." Dr. Rieckhoff was their family physician. Lillian pretty much told him how to do his job and since she was basically very healthy, he usually went along with whatever she said. He still charged only fifteen dollars a visit. "Of course you wouldn't catch Dr. Rieckhoff snorting cocaine, either. I didn't know doctors were doing that, Gus. It makes you wonder."

"I don't think too many of them are, Ma. Maybe a couple of the young ones. Some of the residents. Guys just out of med school."

"Did he have any kids?"

"Just a wife."

"That's too bad." Cesar knew from the sound of her voice that his mother's attention was wandering. "Gus, do you think you're gonna have time to scrub this porch down tomorrow? I didn't know it was getting so dirty." She ran her fingers along a piece of molding under one of the screens. It was too dark to see dust, but she could feel it. Cesar knew she could because he had felt it earlier. He should have stayed inside in the air-conditioning. "I'll tell you something else I remember," said Mrs. Franck.

"What's that?"

"I remember sitting in his waiting room up on Highland Avenue watching his receptionist and his nurse and thinking they looked like two of the unhappiest people I'd ever seen."

"Not like Mrs. Rendigs?" Mrs. Rendigs was Dr. Rieck-hoff's nurse and receptionist, a position she had held as long as anybody could remember. She was always real cheerful. Too cheerful, sometimes.

"No way. Both of them looked like they were exhausted and ready to cry all the time I was there. They say he's the best dermatologist in the city, but I don't know how they ever get anybody to go back there. Give me your plate."

"Where are you going?" asked Cesar. His mother had stood up and was heading for the door.

"To the bathroom. I haven't been in a clean bathroom all day. One of the places had an outhouse." Lillian Franck was Holiday Inn all the way.

Cesar handed her the plate with the burrito wrappings and stuck his empty beer can on top. She didn't ask him if he wanted another. He wouldn't have said no.

He sat on the darkening porch and listened to his stomach as it processed the beef, beans, and beer. The traffic on Epworth Avenue was light. The evening was quiet. Most of the cars that did pass had just been washed and waxed and had high school kids at the wheel. A husband and wife in their fifties walked past the house talking hot and heavy about the man's sister. Cesar couldn't think of their names but he knew they lived a couple of blocks south. After them came a woman in her seventies wearing running shoes and following a fat pug on a leash. The woman was carrying a plastic SuperX bag with dogpoop in it. Cesar knew the woman and the dog. The woman was Mrs. Flaherty, who Lillian Franck said was pretty dumb, and the dog was Pep who was about forty-four years old. Mrs. Flaherty let Pep pee on the little pear tree the city had just put in by the sidewalk. She snuck a look up at the house to see if anybody was watching Pep pee, but since Cesar was sitting in the dark she thought she was getting away with something. A man in his forties ran north on the sidewalk across the street. Cesar knew who he was too. His name was Steve Wille and he managed the Glenway Avenue branch of the Fifth Third Bank. Cesar didn't go to that branch unless he absolutely had to because Wille was such a big talker. Seeing Wille reminded Cesar of Lt. Tieve's parting shot and his hand went to his stomach. It got there in a shorter time than he had counted on. He had forgotten to factor in the burrito supper. What did Stella think? She hadn't said anything about it. Did she have to pretend she didn't see it?

The telephone rang inside the house. Cesar waited a couple of rings, but Mrs. Franck didn't get it. He hustled into the house and banged his stomach on the corner of the counter in the kitchen as he reached for the phone. It was Kay Gallery.

As soon as the name and voice registered in his brain, Cesar straightened up and sucked in his gut. Was he busy? No, he wasn't busy. Did he mind that she had gotten his number from District One? No, he didn't mind. To hell with the rules. Had he watched the six o'clock news? No, he hadn't, but if he could have, he would have. He was really sorry.

She laughed and told him he hadn't missed much. She just thought he would have enjoyed seeing how Larry Wilmot managed to make the death of his friend Don Poe sound as if the angels had come and carried away Albert Schweitzer. Instead of a close-up of the bedroom carpet with its dusting of cocaine, Wilmot had selected a tasteful shot of the front of the house. Was it true that Dr. Poe had snorted up some of the purest cocaine ever to be abused in the county of Hamilton? Cesar didn't know if it was the purest exactly. Would he like to meet her someplace for coffee after she was finished putting together her weekend piece of fluff about two sisters in Monfort Heights merging their Hummel collections. Sure. What the hell? What about waiting for her at a coffeehouse near the television station?

A coffeehouse? OK.

Lillian came in while he was on the phone, bringing her unfinished beer, which she poured down the drain. Cesar watched her little ears twitch under the tight gray perm as she tried to figure out who was calling to make a date with her son if it wasn't Stella Hineman.

"Are you going out?" Lillian asked as soon as Cesar had hung up the phone.

"Yeah. Why? Do you want the car?" That was a big joke since Lillian didn't drive. She never thought it was real funny.

"Did you finish working on her house?"

"No."

"Are you gonna work on it tomorrow?"

"Maybe. Probably."

"So what do you think about cleaning the porch?"

"If I can do it, I'll do it."

"Was that her just now?" At last.

"No."

Lillian Franck gave her son a modified fish eye. He would have gotten the full fish eye, but Mrs. Franck had mixed feelings about her son's relationship with Stella Hineman. What she liked was that Stella Hineman was extremely pretty, that her mother and father were very nice people who didn't live too far away and there are a lot of nice people in Price Hill no matter what you hear, and that Stella and her son were always polite to her, which was not something she could say about most young people today. What she did not like about Stella Hineman was that she persisted in living in a house in the slums, that she would not take a regular job with fringe benefits, that she dressed unlike anybody Lillian knew, and that she did not seem to be interested in getting married. There had to be a basic problem with a single mother who didn't know how to make better use of a nice single policeman who didn't mind the way she dressed and volunteered to try to bring her house up to date.

Lillian waited for her son to volunteer the name of the party he was meeting at this hour on a Saturday night. She certainly wasn't going to ask him. Cesar didn't cooperate. The fact was, he was a little bit uncomfortable about the whole thing. For one thing, he didn't know whether he was considering this meeting with Kay Gallery as a date or as business. He didn't know whether Kay Gallery was coming on to him or just wanted to pump all the facts out of him. And then he didn't know whether he was hoping for anything more than a cup of coffee out of the whole deal, and if he was hoping for more, what did that have to do with the mess he had made of Stella Hineman's dining room?

Cesar and Lillian Franck stood in the spotless little kitchen, each waiting for the other to give in. The awkward silence was broken by a long groan from Cesar's midsection. "I can't believe," said Lillian conceding defeat for the moment, "that all you had for supper was four burritos. You think that's good for you?"

"I didn't feel like fixing anything," said Cesar, looking at his watch.

"Well, it's no wonder you're starting to put on a little weight, Gus. You can't eat like that and expect to stay normal."

"I'll see you later," said Cesar, and he beat it out of the kitchen before she could get in any more licks.

The burrito racket got louder and steadier as he drove across town from Westwood to the coffeehouse in Mount Auburn. At one point it got so bad that he had to undo his seat belt. He wondered what the hell he thought he was doing going anywhere in public in such a state, but it hadn't been so bad when Kay called. Or if it had, he had forgotten about it while he was talking to her. Now he was sitting at a tiny table next to a big fern at the Sign of the Crab, which was the stupid name of the stupid coffeehouse, waiting for Kay and praying to God that each heave and groan was the last. He was almost tearfully grateful for the recorded reggae that covered his sea lion noises. Almost covered. A little dude with an orange crew cut and an earring shaped like the space shuttle had brought him a menu, and right while Cesar was explaining that he was going to wait until the party he was meeting got there before he ordered, the long sound of a trumpet wailing in a buried coffin came floating up around the edge of the table. The music hadn't been loud enough for that, and the goofball in the orange hair was so awed that he stopped chewing his gum and stared at Cesar for a second with his jaw hanging. Cesar tried out a "Noise? What noise?" look, but that was asking too much of the waiter and he finally just turned away, his face burning. What did they do about this in Mexico?

Cesar almost failed to recognize Kay Gallery when she came in. She had changed out of her television reporter clothes into a sweatsuit and white leather gym shoes. She had also pulled her hair back and tied it behind her neck and scrubbed off most of her makeup. As soon as Cesar realized who she was, he stood up. The flimsy little table started to go over on its side, but he caught it in time and put it right in one quick motion that she might not have seen.

"Yeah, well—"

"Have you ordered?"

"No, I was waiting for you."

Cesar picked up his menu and started reading. He was a unhappily surprised by the huge selection of coffee drinks and ice cream dishes, all costing a lot more than he would have thought possible. He really hadn't expected to choose more than regular or Sanka. There wasn't any Sanka at all, just virgin coffee beans that had been given cold baths. He had sort of been thinking in terms of decaf, not wanting to stay up all night, but the price put him off. He looked for regular cup of coffee.

"I just want an espresso," Kay told the waiter. The boy turned to Cesar, stepping back a little and looking at Cesar's stomach as if it might blow up in his face.

"Same for me," he said.

"You know Larry Wilmot and Rick Albers and Don Poe were all three big friends," said Kay to a somewhat startled Cesar as soon as the waiter left. Cesar nodded. "But did you know that they went way back? I mean way, way back?"

"I did. I mean I found that out."

"I don't know if it means anything," said Kay. "I thought it was interesting, though. Okay, if you know that, did you know that Christa Poe's brother is doing time in Lewisburg, West Virginia, for running a drug supermarket?"

Cesar had to admit that he hadn't. How on earth had she found out?

"He was dealing right there on the West Virginia turnpike. He used CB radio and truck stops."

"How long ago was that?" asked Cesar.

"Up until this year. They only caught him last February. Apparently he'd been doing business there for years."

"Did you get this from Mrs. Poe?"

Kay shook her head. "That's not the kind of thing she likes to tell about herself or her family."

"So how did you get onto it?"

"You want me to reveal my sources?"

Cesar hadn't been thinking about her being a reporter. That was partly because of the sweat suit, but mostly because of the way she had been talking to him, as if they were a couple of friends with the same interest. Cesar got sucked right in.

"No. I understand you can't do that," he said, wishing she could.

"Actually, I don't know. I got an anonymous call at the station, a woman, which makes me think it must have been one of those poor women who had to come over and console the grieving widow today. Who else would know that I had been involved with covering the story? Anyway, whoever it was called this afternoon and said, and I quote, "I think you ought to know that Mrs. Poe's brother is a drug dealer in Beckley, West Virginia."

"That's all?" asked Cesar.

"That's it. I tried to get more out of her, but she was obviously scared to death and wanted to get off. I even told her we couldn't trace her call, but she didn't believe me."

"Can you?" asked Cesar.

"Of course not. Can you?"

"Once in a while. Not for something like that. You have to be expecting it and get set up."

"Good. I won't be scared to call you." She said it seriously, but Cesar thought she might be laughing at him. "The funny part is that I actually have a connection to Beckley, West Virginia. But I'm sure she didn't know that. My uncle lives there. He works for a coal company. So I called him to find out if he knew anything about it and he did. It was a very big story down there when the state troopers finally caught this man. And it was especially interesting since he and Christa are from this very prominent Beckley family. Their father's a big banker."

"Rich?" asked Cesar.

"For those parts, yes."

"Was Mrs. Poe involved?"

"My uncle didn't think so. She doesn't go there very much."

The waiter brought their coffees. Cesar picked up the tiny cup and wondered what he was in for. The coffee slid around and stuck to the sides the way his own did after it had been on the stove for a couple of hours, before his mother got the microwave. He pecked at the coffee, letting a little bit dribble down his throat. Disgusting.

"How can you drink it without sugar?" asked Kay.

"I can't, I guess. I never had it before."

"Try some sugar. It really makes a difference."

He stirred in a spoonful, tried it, and was relieved to find that he didn't throw up.

"Are your usual widows so cold-blooded?" asked Kay.

"She wasn't real torn up about her husband," said Cesar. He was beginning to think about maybe ordering some of the ice cream. A lot of the people at the tables around him were putting it away and they looked pretty happy. "I just wonder about how she would get pure cocaine from her brother if he's in prison."

"She wouldn't have to. My guess from talking to her and seeing her house and the way she lives is that she's a meticulous planner."

Cesar didn't quite understand.

"I guess what I mean is that she's so well organized and so unemotional that she wouldn't have any problem shopping ahead for pure cocaine to kill her husband maybe even months in advance."

Cesar quickly looked around the table to see if anyone was tuning into this hot stuff, but the only couple in hearing distance were hot and heavy into a discussion and their dishes of ice cream.

"Do you want some ice cream?" he asked.

"No, thank you." Kay Gallery unconsciously patted her flat stomach. "But don't let me stop you."

"Oh, no. I don't want any," lied the policeman. "I see what you mean about being organized and that. But I kind of wonder about the other part. About her being unemotional."

"A cold fish," said Kay.

"Whatever. What I mean is, if she's such a cold fish, if she doesn't care too much one way or another about things, why would she bother to kill her husband? That's a pretty emotional act usually. That's our experience."

"Oh, I don't think she's *totally* unemotional. I think you have to be psychotic to be totally unemotional, and I don't think she's psychotic. I just wish I knew more about her." She leaned back in her chair with a bit of a pout. "Rick won't tell me anything about their private life."

"Your boss?" Cesar started looking for the waiter.

Kay nodded. "I *know* he knows more than he's telling. He's very smart. Very perceptive. He really is. Ordinarily he'd have all kinds of things to say about a woman like that. He can be very funny."

"But this isn't a straight situation, is it? You said they were big friends."

"He and Don Poe were big friends is what I said. I don't think anybody is close friends with her. No one I know."

"What about Larry Wilmot?"

"What about him?"

"Well, he looked pretty friendly with her this afternoon. Maybe he knows something about her." He finally located the waiter. He was sitting at a table with two other boys and a girl who all looked a lot like the waiter. They were laughing real loud.

"Oh, God. Do you really not know about Larry?" Kay laughed a short and bitter fake laugh. Cesar shook his head. "I didn't know there was anybody left in the city who didn't know that Larry Wilmot is about as stupid as it is possible to get and still be able to tie your shoes."

For all his interest in her and for all his thoughts about how she was really smart and about as good-looking as anybody he'd ever met, Cesar hadn't completely lost his head, and it seemed quite possible to him that there might be a little professional jealousy in play here.

"Of course I'm jealous," said Kay, reading his mind. "How can I not be jealous of someone who gets two hundred and fifty thousand dollars a year for such a little bit of not very hard work."

"Jeez!" said Cesar. "Is that how much he makes?"

"That is absolutely the *least* he makes. That was what he made four years ago when one of the secretaries blabbed in the ladies' room. But he's had raises since then. We know that for sure."

"Boy, that's hard to believe." Cesar tried waving his little coffee spoon at the waiter. Then he realized he probably looked like a complete nerd and put it down.

"Hard to believe and hard to take. I'm telling you this is a stupid man we're talking about. He has to let Rick Albers do all of his thinking for him. All of it. And from what I gather, Rick Albers has been doing Larry's thinking since they were in high school."

"With Dr. Poe."

"With Dr. Don L. Poe. So let me assure you that even if Larry might want to tell the world about what a bitch his buddy the dermatologist married, if Rick Albers told him to sit on it, he wouldn't think twice about it. I use the term think for lack of a better word."

She really didn't have much use for the city's favorite anchorman.

"I heard that Dr. Poe was kind of hard to get along with," said Cesar.

"Well, that's not what Rick and Larry and the widow Poe would have you think, but I think you're probably right. I have a friend who's doing a residency at Baptist where Dr. Poe sent most of his patients, and she said that everybody there hated him. She said he was arrogant even for a male doctor. She also said that when the word got out this afternoon that he had died, everybody jumped right away on two theories."

"What were those," asked Cesar politely. At the same time he finally caught the waiter's eye.

"A lot of people assumed that he had been hit by someone when he was out running, since he was famous for insisting on his right of way, but most people just assumed he had OD'd."

"Really? They all knew about it?"

"They didn't *know*. But Wendy, my doctor friend, says that a lot of people were awfully sure."

"How come?" asked Cesar as the waiter finally reached the table. "Can I get a dish of plain vanilla?" He thought that might sound like a diet food.

"It's special french vanilla."

"OK."

"You don't want anything on it? No liqueur?" asked the waiter with a nasty little smirk.

"No. You sure you won't have anything?" He would be a lot more comfortable if Kay joined him. She smiled and shook her head. "What about more coffee?"

"No thanks." So she was going to just let him eat ice cream by himself while she sat there and got thinner watching him.

"Well, for one thing, the only orderly he ever treated with anything less than total contempt was the one orderly that everybody really did know for sure was able to come up with cocaine on a moment's notice. And then another thing, he was always making references to it. Little jokes."

"They do that on the 'Tonight' show."

"I know what you mean. That's what I said to Wendy, but she said that it was about the only kind of joke he would make. She said they weren't actually jokes, just sort of cracks. Very hip stuff. Which fits in pretty well with his being such an arrogant person."

"Does she know who this orderly is?"

"The one with the coke?" asked Kay. Cesar nodded. "She does. So do I. I asked her, of course. Would you like his name?"

"Sure."

"You realize I'm just giving away the whole candy store telling you everything I know like this."

"Yes," said Cesar, hoping this didn't mean she was about to stop.

"You won't tell on me, will you? I don't know what Rick would say about it, and I don't want to put him to the test."

"You're safe with me," said Cesar with no further meaning, so that when the reporter gave him an archly questioning look he didn't know what the hell she was doing. "What's the guy's name?"

"Who? Oh, the orderly. It's Marcus something." She reached into the pocket of her sweatsuit for a little notebook. "Marcus Brooks."

The ice cream arrived while Cesar was writing down the orderly's name. He dug into the dessert without looking at Kay Gallery, wishing first that he hadn't ordered it and then, after a couple of bites, wishing that he hadn't ordered it without some kind of topping, since it wasn't all that great a vanilla. "My supper got sort of screwed up," he said, taking a little break.

"I know how that is. Mine gets messed up all the time. If it weren't for breakfast I'd never have a regular meal."

"It doesn't seem to affect you the same way," said Cesar. "You don't need to lose weight."

"Well," said Kay, "I guess that's because I run."

Shit. Cesar stopped with a spoon full of french vanilla in mid-air. He lowered it sadly and pushed the bowl to the center of the table.

"Finish it," said Kay. "Don't you want it?"

"It's real filling."

"Do you think Christa Poe has a lover?" asked Kay, graciously turning the conversation away from health matters.

"Do you?"

"Well, it would tie up my theory about her spiking Dr. Poe's cocaine if she did. So I suppose I do. It seems like something she would do. She didn't work, you know."

"I didn't know that."

"She just kept that house. Can you believe that?"

"It's a big house." Cesar had not yet got around to assuming that all women had careers unless otherwise engaged. Lillian Franck went to work when Mr. Franck died, not before.

"She's a doctor's wife. They get issued cleaning women with the marriage certificate."

"Maybe. She was doing the vacuuming today, though."

"I'm just saying that she didn't have to do the cleaning. They could pay somebody. She could go to work."

"Maybe she didn't want to."

"Well *obviously* she didn't want to. People like her don't do *anything* they don't want to. But it's really sort of insupportable to be just hanging around like that, living off her husband. Don't you think that's disgusting?" Kay Gallery was beginning to sound a little testy.

"Oh. Well. I don't know. I guess I don't think it's disgusting. Maybe it is getting a little unusual."

"Just a little. You aren't married, are you?"

"No."

"Well, if you were, wouldn't you have a problem with a wife who just stayed at home while you were out putting your life on the line as a policeman?"

Cesar didn't feel very comfortable with the way the conversation was going. The uneaten ice cream had not melted, and he began to think about going back to it. "I talked to one of the neighbors out there by the Poes today," he said, reaching for the bowl. "She seemed to think Mrs. Poe might be a little bit unfaithful."

"Well? See? What did I tell you? And with her brother in the drug business—"

"I'll definitely be checking *that* out," said Cesar, spooning in the last of the ice cream. "You really sure you don't want anything to eat?" Kay shook her head no. "I'll also be checking out some names she gave me."

"Who?"

"People she thought might have some sort of reason to want to do something to her husband. They don't all make a lot of sense, but it's got to be done."

"You don't think she's just trying to call attention away from herself?"

"Maybe. If she is, it's not doing much good. First thing my boss starts talking about is how she's the likely choice. Now you're doing it."

"Well? Isn't she?"

"Sure."

"But not your choice."

"I don't have a choice yet."

"You know . . . and I know this sounds awful. I don't mean it to. But sometimes you really answer things like a politician. A good one."

Cesar put his spoon back in the bowl and shoved it away, his appetite finally dead. He had been called a lot of things in his time, but nothing ever alarmed him the way being called a politician did. And probably because of that remark and maybe because of the ice cream, it started again.

NnnRRRRgggggnnnFFFnnn!

Kay Gallery's eyes bounced wide open in alarm. "What? Are you—?"

Gagagagannnnnnooooorrrrffff!

Jeez. Jesus. The damned burritos had started to howl again.

"Are you—? Are you all right?" she asked.

"I'm fine. No kidding." What could he say? The couple at the next table was staring at them. "Something . . . Something I ate. No problem."

OOOOOOOnnuhnuhnunuhnnnnrr!

It wasn't getting any better. It didn't hurt. Maybe it would have been better if it did. He could maybe clutch at his chest and fall on the floor. But all he got was noise.

"The ice cream?" asked Kay.

He shook his head. "Mexican. I ate some Mexican food for supper." Kay was sitting with her mouth agape.

"Oh." She shut her mouth for a moment and then asked again, "Are you sure you're all right?"

The real loud stuff seemed to be over. "I'm fine," he said.

The reporter didn't believe him. She stood up and grabbed the check. "I think you ought to get home," she said. "That really sounds like a problem."

Cesar had to agree. He knew he wasn't going to die, but he was never going to be able to convince anybody. Besides, there might be worse to come. So far everything had remained localized, but you never could tell.

He squeezed his way through the tables and sensed the fear of the patrons. Jerks. Kay Gallery had the check paid before he even knew what was happening. He reached for his billfold, but she shook her head. "No. I got you out here. You should be in bed. I feel terrible."

"I'm really okay," said Cesar, following Kay to the door.

Her own car, a Pulsar, was just outside the door, parked at an angle that would have gotten her a ticket in Cesar's uniform days. There was a another moment of embarrassment before she got in the car. Cesar tried to thank her at the same time that she started to thank him for his concern about her getting pulled off the story. And then she just broke off and got in her car. She started away from the curb with a lurch and vanished down the street, turning east at the first stoplight.

Cesar, wide awake from the espresso, went to North Avondale.

7

The frantic and hideous howl of his digestive system had stopped as soon Kay Gallery disappeared into the night. That was the way things seemed to go in the world. Now, as Cesar rolled through the dark streets of the city on his way to North Avondale the only noises to be heard for which the detective was directly responsible were the rumble of the cancerous exhaust system and the creaks and groans of the rusting bodywork against the tortured frame of the car. The shocks were really bad.

It wasn't that he had business in North Avondale. It was too late to call on anyone unless it was an emergency. What he wanted to do mostly was feel like a functioning detective, and visiting the scene of the crime was the only thing he could think of to do at that hour. He had taken a beating at the hands of Lt. Tieves. He had abused his own body with microwavable burritos and too many beers. He had eaten ice cream when he had had warnings all day about his weight. He had drunk coffee made from all the caffeine washed off of all the Venezuelan coffee beans for the decaf customers, and now he would never sleep again. And then he had driven Kay Gallery away with his uncontrollable abdominal imitation of moose mating calls. What a jerk. Now it was time to be a man.

Cesar was so deeply involved with his self-recriminations that he missed the turnoff to Kerley Avenue, the crummy little street leading to Denmark Place. He had to turn around in a driveway and endure the stares of a passing police cruiser. Maybe Lillian was right. Maybe it was stupid to continue to drive a model of car that seemed to be the vehicle of choice for every last petty criminal in the city. He pulled to the side of the street and killed his lights and engine. The dark and the quiet were deep. There were no streetlights on Denmark Place, just one gaslight emitting its useless glow where three driveways branched out. The sound of Saturday night drums barely reached this hidden glade.

There was a slight flicker in the corner of his vision. Someone had come to stand at a second floor window at Mrs. Harris's house, a silhouette in the light of a bedside lamp. Since the figure barely reached the middle of the sash, Cesar assumed it to be Mrs. Harris checking on the intruder in her street. He flicked the car lights a couple of times, hoping she would recognize him as a friend. Doubting it. He now had anywhere from five to sixty minutes before the police arrived in response to her call. Depended on how busy things were.

There was no lights on at all at Gupta's place, not even a light over the door. Someone had parked a big Saab in front of the garage door. The outline was unmistakable even in the feeble gaslight.

The Poes's house, however, was lit up like a Christmas tree upstairs and down. Someone was either at home or had walked out without switching off a single lamp, something he didn't see Christa Poe doing. Odd, though. After seeing all those cars there this afternoon, there's wasn't a single one left in her driveway.

What was it with these people? In Cesar's experience it didn't matter whether you were black or white, Christian or Jewish, rich or poor, when there was a death in the family, people came to sit with the survivors and sympathize from the first minute the word of death went out until the last of the cold roast beef had been eaten after the funeral. Somebody was always around to make sure the bereaved didn't get morbid, or to vacuum, or to call everybody else. But there was no one at the Poes's. Henry had told him that Christa Poe had ordered those ladies to come over that afternoon. Would they not have come otherwise? Was there no family? Maybe Mrs. Poe had given orders for the world to stay away. If anyone could give an order like that it was Christa Poe. If ever there was anyone that people might imagine not to need or want family it was Christa Poe. If ever there was anyone you might not want to visit without being ordered, it was Christa Poe.

Cesar sat there in the sordid automobile thinking about Christa Poe and Dr. Don L. Poe and their world of rugs and exercise machines. Somewhere near the car, insects had begun to chirp, and the rhythmic sound worked its way through his brain and began to massage his hippocampus. One by one his extremities began to relax. One by one his limbs began to get go. Cesar didn't pay any attention. The long day, a day that had begun with the destruction of Stella Hineman's ceiling, moved to the destruction of Dr. Don L. Poe, and thence to the destruction of Cesar's stomach, ending at last with the destruction of an unborn relationship with beautiful reporter Kay Gallery, that long day had caught up with Detective Franck. He caved in. His head tilted back against the seat and his eyes glazed over. His brain went into free fall.

Cesar came to with a start, his brain trying to tell him something. Something bad. He shook his head and stared around and listened and then he heard it again. A woman's cry. A shriek. Cesar straightened up and began to tense for action, still unsure where the shriek came from or what kind of shriek it was. He opened the car door, wincing as it creaked on its hinges and thunked over the detent. He swung out of the car and stood, closing the door enough that the light went out but not latching it.

Mrs. Harris had heard it too. She was back at the window. A taller, male silhouette, presumably Dr. Harris, joined her. Cesar took a step away from the car, listening intently. There it was again. But this time there was in the shriek a quality that told the detective the shriek was not quite for real. Or at least that there was no immediate danger. He relaxed just slightly and continued to walk slowly and quietly in the direction of the noise, moving closer and closer to the Poes's house. There was another sound, a short loud yip. Cesar went off the path and into the grass toward the end of the house that faced the Gupta place. More and more light began to reach him, reflected from some source behind the Poe house. Again there was the shriek, but now he began to pick up a deeply pitched huffing underneath. And as he got closer to the end of the house, the huffing picked up in volume and became a more vocalized grunt. And then there came one more shriek, but this time the shriek changed into a whoop and then a laugh and the accompanying grunt became a cry of triumph followed by a sharp shush from the shrieker. Cesar turned around and headed back to the car. He saw no reason, or at any rate no defensible reason, to break them up. The shrieker was Christa Poe. The grunter was unmistakably Gupta. There was no present danger.

The first thing Cesar did the next morning was call Stella to see if he could come down to her house and get back to work on the ceiling anytime soon, but there was no answer. He figured she was still at her parents' house and would probably stay there all day. Stella and her mother were real close, even though her mother didn't approve of anything at all in her life. That was what Stella told him. He couldn't tell how her mother felt about anything. She didn't talk a lot to him. They were probably at mass right now.

Having done his duty, Cesar went out to collect the Sunday *Enquirer*. The sun was up, but the heat hadn't set in, and it felt good outside, so he sat on the front steps to take a first look at the paper. The only hot action was the big guy still working on that old arms-for-hostages explanation. It didn't seem fair to Cesar that Ron had to do all that explaining. The guy was old and he forgot stuff. Cesar forgot stuff all the time. They should give him a break.

A photograph at the top of the front page caught his eye just as he was getting ready to find the Sports section. The picture was one of those little bitty ones the papers had taken to sticking up at the very top of the page to get you to look inside, and it was a face he recognized but didn't know very well. He stopped looking for the Sports section and read the lines beside the photo. "Ratings success to lead to success at the polls? See today's Metro section and tune in to the latest on Channel Three's resident genius." Rick Albers. That's who it was.

Before looking at today's Metro section Cesar took another look at the front page, this time hunting for word of the death of Dr. Don Poe. Nothing. So, despite Mrs. Poe's loose lips, the word had not gotten out about how he went. Surely that would have been a front page item.

When he finally found the Metro section under the eight thousand coupons for Cool Whip, he got his first look at Dr. Poe, who looked a lot like a light bulb to Cesar. Under the picture it said, "Local Dermatologist, Runner, Suffers Fatal Heart Attack." Cesar read through the brief article and found no mention at all of Dr. Poe's interest in cocaine research. There was, however, quite a bit about what a hotshot runner he was and how he had usually placed among the first finishers in his age group in the Physicians' Crosstown run.

The article referred readers to the obituaries for more information.

Cesar took the paper inside, separated the Sports and Metro section, and went upstairs to the bathroom, settled in, and read the obituary. He learned that Dr. Poe was thought to be hot stuff in the world of dermatology, a specialist in tattoo and birthmark removal. He had had a couple of articles in *Modern Dermatology* and got more calls than anyone last year on the medical call-in program. He was a Cincinnati native. In addition to the usual college information, the obit told about his going to St. Jay and what a hotshot he had been there, even mentioning his being a senator. His father was dead. His mother now lived with his sister in Cleveland. Normally the paper called someone in the family so they could get a quotation about how the dead person had been a really family-oriented kind of guy and how he lived for baseball, but either they hadn't been willing to pay for a toll call to Cleveland or his mother and sister wouldn't talk to anyone, because the quotation about what a great guy he was was from fellow former St. Julian senator and current news anchorperson Larry Wilmot. Larry Wilmot said that Dr. Poe was a great guy and lived for the sport of running. Cesar went back to the front page to look at the picture of Dr. Poe again. With the high, bald dome, hairless face, and pencil neck he really did look like a light bulb. A bright one, but still a light bulb.

On the other side of the page was the promised article about Rick Albers. "News Director May Make Leap to Politics" was the headline. The picture showed Rick Albers looking easygoing in shirtsleeves as he stood talking to a couple of very serious high school boys in suits and ties. This was the first Cesar had heard of Albers as a political type, although he wasn't surprised. The guy was very, very smooth, and he had that way of looking at you that suggested a fast and accurate calculation of your price that marked the powerful politician. Cesar read with interest.

"The man behind the scenes of the successful drive to put Cincinnati's Channel Three news team at the top of the heap may soon make the transition from news observer to news maker. Richard F. 'Rick' Albers, Channel Three's highly respected news director, has recently begun to make a series of public appearances, shedding a reputation as an invisible genius. Friends of the St. Julian and University of Cincinnati graduate say that he is studying a possible move from broadcasting to public service. 'My friends talk a lot,' says Albers in a weak denial. 'I've got loads to do here at Channel Three. We've got a lead, but we haven't had it all that long and we want to consolidate it. I'm a newsman. That's it."

Blah blah blah.

Cesar had read all he needed to be convinced that Albers was getting heavily into politics. He kept on just to torture himself. "'One of the most fascinating things I've learned from these kids,'" the article continued, "'is that there's a lot of interest, real solid interest, in some kind of national youth service. These kids almost seem to want to bring the draft back again. And they're bringing me around to their way of thinking.'" Great. Just great.

"So serious is Albers about national service that he has done something he didn't have to do when he was draft age. He's joined the service. 'Back then, during the Vietnam war, I didn't want to. It was partly the politics of the thing, but mostly that I wanted to finish my education. Then I got hit with a low draft number and thought 'This is it!' But as it turned out, I didn't have to worry. My size fifteen feet kept me out." Cesar nearly fell off the toilet reading that one.

Having read more than he wanted to, Cesar folded the newspaper section, tossed it to the other end of the small bathroom, and stared at the crazed but surgically clean tiles on the opposite wall. He wondered who was so interested in Albers that he would rate such a big feature, and then he measured Rick Albers against the other politicians he had had to meet and deal with or politicians he was affected by. He had to admit that, even though Albers talked the same sort of crap they all did, in person he was a lot easier to take. He didn't seem to be quite as openly hungry at any rate.

It would be nice. He had to admit it. It would be nice to have a little pull with a politician. Truth be told, it was more than nice. It was important. Important if you didn't want to get frozen at the same level forever. Or even if you just wanted to be listened to on those rare occasions when you had something worthwhile to say. Just having the people you work with know that you know somebody who swings a little weight can make things go just enough smoother to be worth it. Cesar certainly knew who in the homicide squad did and didn't know somebody worth knowing, somebody who would make Lt. Tieves think twice about being too rough.

Should he hook up with this Albers guy?

Cesar heard a sharp knock coming through the sound of the ventilating fan. Lillian was up early. "I'll be out in a minute," he called. She was there, waiting in this year's chenille robe when he opened the door. "What are you doing up so early?" Cesar asked his mother. But she just growled and went into the bathroom, banging the door behind her. He took his sections of the paper back downstairs, started a fresh pot of Mr. Coffee, and failed again to reach Stella on the telephone.

"Can you clean the porch today?" were the first words out of Lillian's mouth when she came into the kitchen. Talk about single-minded.

"I've got to go to work," said Cesar.

"Are you getting overtime?"

"Whatever I'm getting, it's more than you pay."

"Fred says we ought to enclose it anyway. I don't know. I never go out there, but I don't think I want it enclosed. What would we use it for?"

"He just wants you to do that because his mother did."

"Where are you going? People aren't going to like talking to you on Sunday, you know."

"Then they shouldn't kill people on Saturday."

Lillian's lips got thin. She didn't have much of a sense of humor when she first got up.

"I'm going to the hospital, anyway. Everybody always likes to talk there. They don't care what day it is. They just love to talk."

8

Boy, was that the truth about loving to talk. As soon as he walked into Baptist Hospital, the first person Cesar laid eyes on was Mrs. Esperson, who lived on the street behind the Francks and loved to talk about as much as anybody in the world. Lillian Franck was pretty good at listening to just about anybody go on about anything for as long as they wanted as long as she got her turn later. But Mrs. Esperson was a special case. When she wandered over into the backyard and started in about what she called "the colored," Mrs. Franck would say, "Well, I have to go in now," right while Mrs. Esperson was talking. As far as Cesar knew, Mrs. Esperson was the only person who ever got interrupted like that. A lot of the problem had to do with her voice, which sounded like a fluorescent light bulb going bad.

"Well, hi, Cesar! What are you doin' here?" asked Mrs.

Esperson. She was wearing a red dress like the one the lady behind the information desk was wearing. They both had blue and white scarves tied around their necks, suggesting that they were in some sort of uniform. Cesar read Mrs. Esperson's name tag, which said Welcome! I'm a Baptist volunteer! Callie Esperson. No truth in labeling. Mrs. Esperson was Catholic. Cesar didn't think he had ever known her first name in all the years she'd been chasing his mother out of the backyard.

"Hi, Mrs. Esperson. I'm sort of in here on business."

"Oh, gosh! You're not going to make an arrest, are you?" Mrs. Esperson let out a dumb laugh. It was no joke. She could get really irritating really fast.

"I'd like to talk to a couple of employees if they're in. I think I know where I can find them. Nice to see you."

"Have you been here since the new addition?" asked Mrs. Esperson as Cesar started to edge back toward the elevators. He shook his head no. "Then I have to come with you. You could get lost."

"I think I can find it. Thanks a lot." He was walking backward now. Mrs. Esperson was sticking tight.

"Oh, you have to have a guide, Cesar. That's a rule."

"It is?"

"That's my job. We don't want anybody getting lost. It's real easy. Now, where did you want to go?"

"The personnel office. I've been there before. I know where it is, Mrs. Esperson."

"Oh, Cesar, Hahahahaha." Mrs. Esperson laughed as if Cesar had really said something funny. He groped around for an up button by the elevator, keeping his eye on his neighbor. He wondered if she was a little crazy. "It's moved, honey. The personnel office is moved. I told you, you can really get lost here now. I'll get you there, though."

Cesar followed her down a short hall to the new personnel office, which was right next to the old personnel office, which Cesar had found several times by himself. He thought for half a second about pointing this out to Mrs. Esperson but thought better of it. He said thank you.

"You know you can call down to the desk when you want to leave, hon. That's a service too. But you don't always get me. You can ask for me, but I have to be available."

"Thanks, Mrs. Esperson."

"Good luck with your arrest! Hahahahaha!" Mrs. Esperson was still shaking her head over that one as she rounded the corner and went out of sight.

The new personnel door was locked. Cesar knocked on it, but nobody came. He knocked louder and at last the old personnel door opened. The girl who opened it was the same girl who had been there the last time Cesar had to talk to them. He pointed questioningly to the new door. "We don't use it," she said. She didn't think it was funny.

Fifteen minutes later Cesar was down on the BB level of Baptist Hospital waiting for Rosetta Macalaster to get her eighteen pineapple upside-down sheet cakes to a stopping point so she could talk to him. Rather than get mixed up with Mrs. Esperson Cesar had asked the personnel clerk how to get to the dietary area.

Mrs. Macalaster had probably talked to detectives before and she had certainly made a lot of pineapple upside-down sheet cakes, and she wasn't going to rush, which was okay with Cesar. She walked back and forth from counter to oven at the same deliberate pace, hefting the big sheet pans around and sliding them into the oven without once changing expression or grunting or spilling any of the batter. She was probably in her fifties, too big, but not obese. She listened to him without changing expression, stopped just once and briefly to look at his ID, and just barely nodded to show that she had heard and would get to him. He understood.

When all the cakes were at last in the oven Rosetta Macalaster deliberately rinsed and dried her hands and then went to a locked drawer for her purse. She stood at the drawer and looked at Cesar, who looked back at her. At last he figured out that she was waiting for him to get his white ass over to where she was, which he did, a little faster than usual to make up for having been so slow on the uptake. She led him at the same pace she used to move cakes around until they reached the dietary lounge, a room with a big window looking back out into the kitchen. There was only one other person in the lounge, a woman older than Mrs. Macalaster. She looked at Cesar and at Mrs. Macalaster, sized up the situation, and got up from her chair.

"You don't have to go no place, Alice," said Mrs. Maca-laster.

"That's all right. I was just fixing to go. I wasn't doin' nothin' but thinkin'. You want me to watch the cakes?"

"If I ain't out. I don't know how long this man wants to talk to me."

"Not long," said Cesar. "Shouldn't be."

Alice, deciding that Cesar was harmless, smiled one of those long sweet smiles that came from the south with her generation, and left the room, closing the door behind her.

Rosetta Macalaster reached into her bag, pulled out a leather cigarette case, shook out a Marlboro, and lit up. She sucked in a big lungful of smoke and blew it out, and at last asked Cesar, still without looking at him, "What's he done now?"

"Ma'am?"

Rosetta Macalaster at last turned a tired and cynical gaze on the policeman. "Devon," she said, "What's he done now?"

"Ma'am, I'm sorry. I don't know who you're talking about."

"I'm talking about my nephew, Devon Perry. I thought you came here to tell me something about him."

"No, ma'am."

Cesar remembered Mrs. Harris telling him not only that Rosetta Macalaster was devoted to Mrs. Harris's husband Dr. Harris to the point of baking him special cakes, but also that Mrs. Macalaster was devoted to a nephew normally in residence in the penitentiary at Lucasville. Maybe he was out for a while."

"Well, that's good," said Mrs. Macalaster. "So what you want then?" Between the two sentences her attitude changed from defense to defiance. As in so many similar cases, the rotten nephew was almost certainly the one blot on her record, so if it wasn't about him, she was in the clear, and she would make sure that Cesar knew it.

"I'm here about Dr. Don Poe. I'm with the homicide squad. I understand you knew Dr. Poe."

"That's a lie." She blew out a cloud of disgusted smoke. The policemen these days were pitiful. Pitiful.

"Did you know who he was?" asked Cesar.

"Well, of course," she said with continued disgust. "Everybody gets to know who he is real quick the way he always comes around and looks at things." She made looking at things sound pretty goddamned stupid. It could be.

"Did you know he died yesterday?"

"I heard that."

"Had you heard anything about how he died?"

"Officer, I got my work to do. Doctors come and they go and all I do is try to stay out their way so I don't have to hear them fussing. So I don't know nothing about how he died and I don't much care. But I guess he had a heart attack. That's what usually gets them when they're skinny like he was. How old was he?"

"Forty."

"Well, I'm fifty-two. And I'll tell you what. About the only time that skinny little man ever talked to me when it wasn't to give me what for for feeding one of his patients without calling up to see just exactly what he wanted them to eat, it was to tell me that I was too fat and that I was going to die of a heart attack sometime soon. He said it was his responsibility to tell me that. Oh, and the other thing he said was that cigarettes would probably kill me before being fat did." She stopped talking to put out her cigarette and light another. "So I figure he died of some kind of heart attack."

"Well, he did, sort of."

"That's real sad," said Rosetta Macalaster.

Mrs. Macalaster was turning out to be a tougher nut to crack than he expected from having talked to Mrs. Harris. He had thought that since she was into baking chocolate cakes for Dr. Harris she would be a little more like Alice, the nice dietary lady who left when they came in.

"My boss is kind of that way, too," said Cesar. Mrs. Macalaster looked at him out of the corner of her eye to see where he was coming from. "In fact, I had to go out and see him at his house yesterday and he told me out of the blue that I was too fat." He looked down at his stomach and then back to Mrs. Macalaster with a wounded expression. She didn't give over, but she looked a little softer. "He gave me some bottled water to drink. That's what he was drinking. At five-thirty on a Saturday."

Cesar thought Mrs. Macalaster was starting to loosen up, so he took a deeper breath and said, "I was talking to one of Dr. Poe's neighbors. That's how I heard you might know something about him." Mrs. Macalaster, back on the defensive, looked at Cesar. "You know a Dr. Harris?"

"Yeah," she said, knocking the ash off her cigarette. "Did he say something about me?"

"I didn't talk to him. I talked to his wife. She was bragging about your cakes." No reaction. "She said that you had told Dr. Harris that Dr. Poe was a cocaine user. Is that right?"

"Maybe."

"Well, it seems like you were right. From the way things have come out, it looks like that was what caused his death. It got to his heart."

"Is that right? Well. That's too bad."

"So what I'm trying to find out is where he got his cocaine

because it looks like that's probably going to tell us something about how it happened."

"Well, he sure didn't get it from me, if that's what you thinking."

"No, ma'am."

"And he didn't get it from Devon, neither."

"I didn't—"

And Rosetta Macalaster did start to talk. "You know, it's a shame the way people around here say things. They always saying things about Devon, blaming him for this and that when he couldn't even do half the stuff they talking about since he's in Lucasville so much."

"Does he work here?"

"When he can. He got a bad back. But anytime he's not feeling too bad I get him on here so he can get him some money. He's a good worker. He just got problems. But no matter what kind of problems he got, he don't never sell no drugs. No way. He just don't do it. Now, if you want to find someone selling drugs, you ought to take a look at some of these foreigners they got here. Some of those Indians."

"Do you know a former employee named Chester Patel?"

"Sure do. That's one of the ones I'm talking about. 'Course he ain't even in Cincinnati no more. He gone back to India. They sent his ass back. His uncle is suing the hospital trying to get the job back for his nephew, but he ain't gonna win. No way."

Cesar crossed Chester Patel off his list.

"But what really makes me mad is that some of the biggest drug dealers in this place is people you wouldn't think would ever have anything to do with anything like that."

"Who do you mean, ma'am?"

"I mean people like nurses. Everybody thinks nurses are just like the nurses on the stories on television, all goody goody, but they got some here that's as bad as anybody you want to meet. Some of them doing drugs and some of them pushing drugs and some of them doing both."

"Do you think any of them might have been involved with Dr. Poe? As far as drugs?"

"That's right. You better say what you mean. That man couldn't keep his hands off some of the sisters even after he got married."

"Nurses?"

"Mostly nurses. LPNs. Just so long as they good-looking and black."

"Would one of those be a Miss Robison?"

"Who told you about her? Mrs. Harris?"

"No."

"Yeah. Well, she's one of them for sure. She as bad as anybody you going to find in this place. I don't know how she keep her job. Well, maybe I *do* know."

"Drugs?" asked Cesar.

"I ain't gonna say for sure. I don't want her mad at me 'cause I think she's mean as a snake, but anybody who see her with Dr. Poe know that those two was tight. And that's all I'm gonna tell you except that she's on duty today. I seen her coming in when I did."

Cesar had already checked about that with personnel.

"You watch your step with her, though. Like I say, she's mean."

9

I hate this hospital," said Elaine Robison. "I can tell you why you're here. You want me to do that? The reason you're here is because somebody at this hospital told you something nasty about me that made you think I'm some kind of drug-dealing dope fiend. Am I right?"

Cesar was slow to answer, and when he did open his mouth to talk he flubbed a little. Lulled by the warmth of Rosetta Macalaster's kitchen, he was unprepared for nurse Robison's testy outburst. Waiting impatiently for an answer, the mother of Dr. Poe's child tapped her fingers on a white steel cabinet as the policeman tried to collect his wits.

One thing had cleared up for Cesar. He understood what had attracted Dr. Poe enough to entangle himself with a woman of another race and caste. Elaine Robison was powerfully sexy. Tall, with straightened hair pulled back into a bun, she exuded strength to match and excel that of Christa Poe. And she was prettier. She had enormous, slightly tilted eyes and a long, complicated nose over a wide, ripe mouth. Her unblemished walnut skin carried Cesar's gaze from a long, smooth neck down until it disappeared behind the white of her uniform top. Cesar blinked and shifted his gaze back up to those angry and contemptuous eyes.

"I'm really just looking for some information, Miss Robison. I'm with the Cincinnati homicide squad, and I—"

"Oh, *great*. That was the one thing that *hadn't* been going around about me. See, they said everything else you can say. That I'm a prostitute. That I'm a pusher. That I'm a liar. That I'm a blackmailer. I guess it was just a matter of time until they got around to calling me a murderer. Who's the victim? Wait! Let me guess. It's that humanitarian dermatologist himself, Dr. Don Poe. Am I right?"

"Really, ma'am, at this stage all I'm doing is looking for information. We're not even saying Dr. Poe was murdered at this time. All we know for sure is that he died after inhaling cocaine that was very pure. We've been told that he had been using cocaine with some regularity and that it probably wasn't as strong as this last stuff."

"That's for sure."

"But that's all we know."

"So you're here to find out if I sold him some bad coke. Am I right? You figure if he bought bad coke he bought it off of that all-around bad woman Elaine Robison, right?"

"Ma'am, I'm not accusing you of anything. Believe me. All I'm doing is trying to find out if anybody knows where he did get the stuff."

"But you come to me because I might know about stuff like that."

"I came to you because I had been led to believe that at one time you and Dr. Poe had been close. I thought if you had, you might have talked about that sometime. About the cocaine."

"Well, you're right."

"Ma'am?"

"We were close. Which is about the nicest way anybody in this hospital has ever put it. Can I take it you know about the paternity suit?"

"I had heard about it."

"I'm not surprised. It was the favorite topic of conversation around here for months. So you know how it came out."

"He took a blood test."

"That's right."

"And he wasn't the father."

"That's wrong."

"It is?"

"Who told you that? You didn't hear that here, did you? Most everybody here sounds like they read the settlement, which was supposed to be secret. Who got it wrong?"

"He was the father?"

"Let me show you something." Elaine Robison reached in her pocket and got a small billfold, which she opened to a picture of a little boy. The child looked as if he might be about two years old. He was just barely darker than Caucasian, with soft brown curls, and, although he was a happy-looking kid with an intelligent expression he had the distinct look of a light bulb about him. He looked like Dr. Don L. Poe.

"He made us go through the blood tests, can you believe it? With the way Anthony favors his daddy? Isn't that the meanest thing you ever heard of?"

"That's your son? Anthony?"

"That's my son and if you can't tell he's Don Poe's son you've got to be blind. Or maybe you never saw his daddy?"

"I saw his picture in the paper this morning. There sure is a resemblance."

"You want to know what's craziest about this whole business?" Cesar nodded an affirmative. "He *wanted* this baby. He *asked* me to get pregnant. That's right!" Elaine Robison was plenty disgusted. She was also, Cesar admitted, very, very pretty. "The only reason I got pregnant when I did was because Don begged and begged me to get pregnant. He said he wanted to have a son. So I did. I got pregnant and I had Anthony and I wouldn't trade him in for anything or anybody, but that child was born with the worst excuse for a father anybody ever had."

"I don't . . . I guess I don't understand," said Cesar. "If Dr. Poe wanted you to have the baby, how come you went through the paternity suit?"

"Because he changed his mind. Or more likely *she* changed his mind. When I was five months pregnant he started talking about how he wasn't sure the baby was going to be his. How he wasn't going to stick to his side of the bargain."

"What was that?"

"Money. He was going to pay for everything. Everything. That's the only way he got me to go along. He was going to take care of all the bills until Anthony was through college. And I was going to get an allowance, too. I was supposed to keep working, but I'd get something for my troubles."

"That's a pretty unusual arrangement."

"Well, he was a pretty unusual doctor. It took a whole lot of talking to get me to go along with it. I wasn't sure I wanted any baby by any white man even if he was a doctor."

"Why'd you change your mind?"

"I wanted a baby."

Cesar looked at Elaine Robison to see if she was kidding, but she didn't seem to be.

"I don't think a man can understand that, but it's the truth. I wanted a baby. I was getting close to thirty. And I didn't want to get married. You get married and think you're going to stay married and then the man decides he doesn't want to be married and there you are. That's the way it's been going. I just decided I wasn't going to go through all that crap, you know?"

"But why Dr. Poe? If you didn't want a white man?"

"Because he said he was going to pay. And he was a doctor."

"Did he?"

"Hell, yes, he did. He wound up signing an agreement. He made me and Anthony go through the blood test to make sure Anthony was his, though."

"Was this arrangement public knowledge?"

"It wasn't supposed to be. I sure didn't tell anybody. Not at first. He accused me of telling everybody, but that was stupid. Why would I want anybody to know I had a son by him? I just told everybody that the father left town. It wasn't until he got involved with that blood test and telling people he couldn't be sure who the father was because of my morals that I let the word get out about exactly what was happening."

"Do you think it's public knowledge now?"

"Officer, there are no secrets in this hospital. None."

"Where does Mrs. Poe stand on all this?"

"You mean about the baby? I suppose she knows. But maybe she doesn't if she told you I failed the blood test. I really couldn't care less about her. She's going to find out soon enough if she doesn't know already."

"How's that?" asked Cesar.

"When she sees the insurance. One of the things he had to do to get me to agree was take out a life insurance policy on himself and keep it up. But I'm pretty sure what he did was just change the beneficiary on one of the policies he already had."

More and more news. Cesar thought about Christa Poe and how she would take finding out she was a couple of hundred thousand poorer than she expected. Her wallpaper was probably going to fall off.

Now he had a question he didn't know how to put since it was so personal and since he thought that Elaine Robison was probably someone who could blow up nearly as hard as Christa Poe. Oh, well.

"Ms. Robison, would you characterize this . . . this

arrangement you had with Dr. Poe as . . . as completely businesslike?"

"What do you mean?" Elaine Robison set her jaw for action.

"I mean . . . what I mean is were you and Dr. Poe . . . were you friendly?"

"I don't know how you get any friendlier." She was not amused.

"I meant were you friends? Did you talk about things? What I'm getting at is whether you knew him well enough to know much about him."

"Like what?"

"Well, what it is I'm interested in—whether you knew about his cocaine use, for instance. And if you did, if you might have known something about where he got his stuff."

"And you were thinking we might have gotten into it together? Drug-crazed sex? Is that it?"

"No, ma'am. All I want to know is if there's anything you can tell me about where he got his cocaine." People were so touchy.

"Well, I'll tell you something pretty interesting. Dr. Poe was fairly famous around here for grabbing at the nurses. Like I mean *all* the time. Particularly black nurses. I didn't like him before we got involved and I didn't like him when we *were* involved. He just wasn't someone to like. But I got to say to his credit that he knew what he was doing when he got into bed. He was always real interesting. So carrying out the agreement wasn't too uncomfortable when you get down to it. We did spend a lot of time together when we were getting Anthony underway, and then for a while later, since it turned out we were a pretty good team, he talked a little here and there. And then he made a lot of phone calls. He was always talking on the phone. He was the first man I knew personally with a phone in his car who wasn't a pimp. He had a beeper too, of course. So he did phone.

"And a couple of times he was talking about his drugs. I

know he was. Even though he tried to put it in language he thought I wouldn't get, I got it. Always talking *around*, but anytime you're talking around like that it's easy to guess why. And he'd always show up next time with fresh stuff, so I was sure. But he was funny. Most men use that stuff *before* they get into the sex, you know. But not Don. He was worried about what it might do to his chromosomes. So he'd do it afterward. That was before we were sure I was pregnant. After that he was just like everybody else."

"Did he ever tell you who he was talking to?"

"Hell, no. I told you he was always real mysterious when he was making his drug calls. Except when he was being bossy. Sometimes that would happen. I figure whoever was on the other end wasn't doing things exactly the way he wanted him to and then he'd start talking real cold."

"Like?"

"Oh, you know, nasty. Just a nasty tone."

"Saying what?"

"I don't know. He'd say something like, 'Of course I always retain documentation.'" She pitched her voice lower, and Cesar had the feeling that he was hearing a good imitation of the late doctor. "But he didn't use names even then. He must have just expected everybody to know his voice. He'd just say 'It's me.'"

"So you never got any idea who his friends were? They never left numbers or names?"

"They didn't call me, officer. They called his number and the answering service got the information. I'm sorry, but I don't think there's anything I can tell you at all about who or what or why. All he ever did was talk all that talk around about drugs and when it wasn't that he was talking politics."

"Politics?" That was news. Up to now the only interests he ever heard about were running, rugs, and black nurses.

"Just on the telephone with his friends. We didn't ever talk politics."

"What did he talk about?"

"Senators."

"You mean like Senator Glenn? Or Senator Kennedy?"

Elaine Robison nodded. "That's right. Only he wasn't talking about those two. Or if he was he didn't say their names. I just remember that he talked about senators."

"Was that the only kind of politics he talked about?"

"Man, I don't know. I just told you he would get to talking about senators every once in a while. Like I never heard him talk about Celeste or anybody like that."

"OK. Now, when he was talking about senators, who was he talking to?"

"He didn't ever tell me who he was talking to. He wanted to make sure I didn't know."

"What kinds of calls were they? Were they just, you know, talking? Was it just friendly stuff? Or was it when he was making one of those calls to what you think was his drug supplier?"

"I don't *think* it was his drug supplier. I *know* it was his drug supplier. So you got to let me think."

"Fine. You want something to drink? Can I get you a soft drink or something?"

The nurse shook her head and pursed her lips in irritation. "I'm trying to think," she said. "I can't think with you interrupting."

Cesar shut up and waited. He started to get up and walk and then thought that might be irritating so he stayed where he was. He had mixed feelings about the answer to come. If, as he thought might be the case, the senators in question were not the psychopaths in Washington or the con artists in Columbus or even the Texas Rangers before they moved and changed their name, but were in fact Dr. Poe's old Saint Jay high school chums, and if their names had come up when he was arranging his buys, then he at last had a little bit of a lead. At the same time, if he had a lead, he was back in the danger zone, dealing with the likes of Lt. Tieves. Cesar had a strong feeling that, in addition to Tieves and Albers and Wilmot, everyone in the group picture of the senators was someone who could make Cesar's life unpleasant. Unless, like Dr. Poe, they were dead. They were getting close enough to heart attack age that a couple of them might have dropped out. Also, they were the right age for the Vietnam war. Some of them might have been killed there. Except that they looked pretty much like an exempted bunch. Except for Lt. Tieves.

"It's hard to remember," Ms. Robison interrupted the reveries. "But I think. I *think*, mind you, that when he was talking about senators he was at least sometimes talking all secret-like, which means he was talking to one of his little drug friends. That's what I *think*. I don't think he ever, you know, talked to his patients or his staff about them. Did I tell you he checked in with his wife every now and then when he was with me? He used to call her and remind her of things she was supposed to do. He really had a lot of nerve."

Cesar gave Elaine Robison another twenty minutes, but the nugget about the senators was his only find. He got her to promise that she would call if she ever remembered anything else that might shed light on the identity of Dr. Poe's phone friends. But he didn't hold out a lot of hope. A wife maybe could have figured out more, but Dr. Poe would have known that and been more careful when making calls around Mrs. Poe.

He headed for the office, still thinking about Dr. Poe and Elaine Robison. He supposed he could believe the idea that Dr. Poe would deliberately get someone pregnant so he could have a child. He sure as hell believed that Christa Poe was the kind of person to say she wasn't going to do that sort of thing. Still. Even though with civil rights and equal opportunity and all it was pretty unusual to decide to have a surrogate baby with a black lady if you were a white guy. Granted, the surrogate mother was very good-looking and probably very intelligent, but people still seemed to stick pretty much to their own race when it came to having babies. Particularly babies by choice.

He wondered for a few minutes whether civil rights laws had any effect on adoption. And then he wondered about civil rights and sperm donors. And then he wondered about how long he had to live if he was going to get a heart attack every time he did anything more strenuous than pick up a hammer. And then he wondered if Stella was at home yet and, if she was, was she ready to blow a gasket over the mess in the dining room. And then he wondered how Stella and Kay Gallery would get along if they knew each other. And then he wondered about the senators in the picture with the future Dr. Don L. Poe.

Elaine Robison's vagueness about the references to the senators in Dr. Poe's phone calls was the real thing. He was sure of that. She just plain didn't know who they were or why. All she knew was that there were senators someplace. That fit in with the kind of relationship she seemed to have had with the doctor. No pillow talk. Just sex. They didn't know anything about each other except where the various controls, switches, buzzers, and bells were located and what they did. It wasn't the kind of relationship he could imagine a policeman having. They tended to get involved.

Senators. High school hotshots all grown up. Poe, Tieves, Albers, Wilmot. It was time to find out who the other guys in the picture were. Cesar hoped that wasn't going to prove awkward, since the logical person to ask about the picture was Mrs. Poe and he had lifted it from her wastebasket. Why did she throw it out anyway? And was it really possible that she didn't know the real outcome of her husband's dealings with Elaine Robison? Did she honestly not know she had a stepson?

Cesar continued to chew things over between the police parking lot and the homicide squad office, nodding to and greeting the cops he passed without noticing who they were. He was still deep in thought as he opened the office door and headed for his desk, so that he was mightily startled when it at last registered on his brainpan that he was not alone in the room. Sitting with his back to the door and the telephone to his ear, in the loudest of Hawaiian shirts, was Henry Chapman. Talking to a woman.

"That's right," said Henry to the woman on the phone. "That's exactly right. That's the way it is. . . . No. . . . It's no different. . . . No. Because that's the way I do it." Henry turned his head to show Cesar that he knew he was there and he let the telephone come away from his ear. Whoever it was on the other end had a lot to say. Henry's shoulders twitched—an expression of his growing restlessness. Cesar gave the woman two more minutes, Three, tops. He looked at his watch and sat down at his desk to wait. At two minutes and fifteen seconds, Henry cut off the squawks, saying, "I can't talk anymore. Someone's here." He hung up the phone without waiting for a response.

"What happened?" asked Cesar. "I didn't think you'd be back 'til Thursday at the earliest. Did your car break down?"

"No. I take care of my car." That was supposed to put Cesar in his place. Henry's Lincoln got whatever it needed. Unlike certain cars.

"Is your mother okay?" Cesar hoped she was. She had been sending some pretty good lunches through to him via Henry. She was always hoping Henry would spend more time with Cesar and less with his girlfriends.

"She's okay. My stepfather's sick, though."

"What with?" Cesar knew the family health situation well enough not to panic. Henry's stepfather was a moaner, but he never seemed to Cesar to be what you'd call really sick.

"Nothing. He just couldn't figure out how to work the microwave, so when my mother called he told her he was dying. She said we had to go back."

"So what are you doing here? Nobody knows you're back, do they. You could have goofed off."

"I know. I didn't want to use the leave time if I didn't have to. I got other stuff I want to do with it."

"Are you gonna give me a hand with this Poe stuff?"

"You don't have that cracked yet? What's taking so long? You could have been through with that by last night."

"Sure, if I'd had some help." Cesar hoped Henry was kidding. He wasn't even close to cracking anything. "I could have used some help today for sure. You wouldn't have believed this nurse I talked to." Cesar got comfortable in his chair and began to tell Henry everything he knew about Dr. Poe and his friends and family. He was glad to have Henry back, someone who had met Christa Poe and knew what she was about. It was also nice to be in the office with Lt. Tieves at home and Sgt. Evans at church and Carole Griesel doing whatever Carole Griesel did with her Sundays. Neither Henry nor Cesar had ever involved themselves in any way with Carole's off time. Of course, they hadn't been asked either. They leaned back in their city-issue desk chairs, putting the springs to tests not envisioned by the manufacturer. The sun was shining through the window, undoing most of the air-conditioning, so their short sleeves were necessary. Cesar was wearing a five-year-old Jack Nicklaus golf shirt. It stretched tight across his stomach and almost made him look fatter than Henry, who outweighed him by a lot. That was probably why the Hawaiian shirts were back.

Henry enjoyed hearing about Mrs. Harris and her theories concerning Christa Poe's romantic life. For all he fooled around, Henry was surprisingly straitlaced when it came to marriage vows. Christa Poe was probably condemned to hell now. She would certainly be Henry's number one suspect.

A nasty little smile played on Henry's lips when Cesar told him about the senators and particularly Lt. Tieves, even though the senators were Catholic. But the involvement of Larry Wilmot proved baffling.

"Larry Wilmot?" Henry was incredulous. "You're not thinking about him, are you? Not seriously? He's so . . . so—"

"So dumb?" asked Cesar.

"Right."

"I suppose. Did you talk to any of the Channel Three people? I get the feeling that Albers does all the thinking for Wilmot."

"That sounds more like it. What do you think about Albers?"

"Did you know he's getting into politics?" Cesar asked. Henry shook his head no. "It was in the paper this morning. He seems like a smart enough dude. I think you're right about him running Wilmot."

"So he's smart enough to plan a murder."

"I suppose so. Beats me why he'd try, though. He's probably pulling down a hundred thousand a year."

"So what?"

"And then, he's getting involved with politics. Murder's not something that goes over real big with the voters."

"What about the lieutenant?" Henry dropped his voice. Neither one thought there were bugs in the shop, but there was no reason to let the world know what they were talking about.

"You want to see what he looked like in high school?" Cesar pulled the photograph out of his pants pocket, smoothed out the crease, and handed it to Henry. "You see him?"

"You all can really look like a lot of doofuses, you know that?" Henry shook his head and clucked his tongue as he looked at the picture. "You never see brothers looking like that."

"Did I tell you I swiped that picture?"

"Yeah. Which one is . . . wait a minute. I see Wilmot. Okay. And that's Lt. Tieves. That has to be. Now which one's Poe?" Cesar pointed out Dr. Poe and then Rick Albers.

"Skinny dude," said Henry. "You know what his head looks like? It looks like a light bulb."

"His kid looks just like him. Just darker. I've got to get Mrs. Poe to tell me who the rest of the guys are," said Cesar.

"I don't know how to explain that I picked this out of the wastebasket."

"Don't explain. Just show it to her. Give her something to think about."

"You want to go out there with me?"

"Now?" asked Henry.

"Why not? You're pretending to work, aren't you? Come on out and protect me."

"I was gonna do paperwork. That's what I came in for."

"No you weren't. You never do paperwork. Come on out. Give me a hand. I need it with that woman."

"I'm driving," said Henry. He refused to be driven in the Camaro. He might be seen.

They pulled into Denmark Place to find it still empty of cars. Henry drove up as close to the house as he could. "Do you believe it?" asked Cesar. "Nobody here! This guy must have been really well liked." Henry got out of the car and looked up at the house. His mirrored sunglasses reflected the tops of pin oaks and a few puffy clouds. It was as quiet a place as you could find in the city limits.

Henry rang the bell. They stood there listening, but the front door was closed and they couldn't hear any chimes. Henry rang again. There was still no sound other than a soft scraping against the door. Henry aimed his shades at Cesar, a question in the angle of his chin. "Cat," said Cesar and Henry nodded. Cesar whacked the great bronze door knocker three times. They stood waiting, both men holding their hands behind their backs. But no one came.

"She's probably gone out to eat," said Henry. "Time for brunch." Cesar nodded. Now he didn't know what to do. He had spent so much time psyching himself to face Mrs. Poe that he hadn't considered the possibility that she might not be home. But really, you don't expect a house to go empty until the funeral. And even then everybody nowadays leaves somebody to watch the place. There was a tip in the *Reader's*

Digest thirty years ago about burglars reading the obituaries and everybody in the U.S. was hip.

"You want to see the back?" asked Henry. Cesar shrugged. He followed Henry around the house, wondering if Mrs. Harris had called the cops. Maybe she recognized the Lincoln from yesterday. He tapped Henry's broad back.

"She might be in the back sunbathing," he said.

"Okay with me," said Henry. A ghost of a smile touched his lips.

"Hello?" said Cesar as they approached the back of the house. He thought it was fair to give Mrs. Poe a chance to cover up if she wanted to. But there was no answer.

A little wind came through as they walked behind the house. It stirred up the branches and rattled the leaves and as it did so, a cloud that had been shading the place moved off and let the sun hit the scene.

What a place. Cesar thought that this must be what backyards were all about, a semicircular sweep of grass diving into a little ravine, trees surrounding the scene, a deck leading from the back door and continuing in a sweep out beyond the edge of the ravine, and at the end of the deck closest to the house, invisible from the upstairs windows, a hot tub. But of course. Henry and Cesar saw it at the same time, waggled their eyebrows lewdly at each other, and ambled over to check it out. Neither detective owned one, but they had heard plenty.

About fifteen feet from the hot tub it registered in Cesar's mind that the white stuff floating on top of the water was not soap suds. Neither was it a towel adrift. He began to trot over to the tub, Henry following him step for step, fearing the worse and finding it. It was a body. No. It was two bodies. The tops of two backs bobbed on top of the water, the heads submerged side by side, ear to ear, the arms near the top of the water, each person reaching for the body opposite for a final embrace. Christa Poe's hair and suntan were unmistakable. The two men stood by the tub for a moment and then Henry asked softly, "Who's the guy?"

Cesar remembered the broad shoulders and thick curly hair. "I think it's Gupta."

10

It was indeed Gupta. And the woman was Christa Poe. The two bodies lay naked side by side on the deck where the emergency medical technicians had laid them. Water from the hot tub still stood in puddles where it had not dripped through the gaps in the deck planking to the gravel below.

The heavy-duty extension cord that had been the agent of their deaths still hung over the edge of the hot tub, its business end dangling in the water. Henry, immediately seeing the problem, had run into the kitchen, following the cord, and unplugged it from the socket it shared with the Mixmaster. A ghetto blaster stood upright on the ledge built into the edge of the hot tub. The hot tub itself had been sunk to about half its depth in the deck for easy access.

Cesar had always wanted to try a hot tub. He and Henry

Chapman stood side by side and stared down into the water. Henry's toothpick was working its thoughtful way back and forth from one corner of his mouth to the other. Cesar, having no toothpick, stood motionless, his hands on his hips.

Both of the policemen smelled something wrong with the situation. But since Henry too was ignorant of the ways of the hot tub, they felt distinctly disadvantaged. The question they were both addressing, silently and privately, had to do with the cord in the water. What they wanted to know was how it got there.

It could easily have been an accident. Gupta and Mrs. Poe are in the hot tub, discussing the day's events, relaxing a little, when one of them, Mrs. Poe, no doubt, decides it would be nice to have a little music. Gupta, the gallant lover, fetches a ghetto blaster from one of the houses, maybe it's even already there, and reaches for the extension cord, intending to plug it in. His foot slips on the slippery bottom of the hot tub or perhaps Mrs. Poe gooses him, and the cord drops into the water, bringing the busy day to an abrupt end.

But if that's how it happened, why wasn't Gupta sprawled over the edge or crumpled up some way? Was Mrs. Poe the electrician? Okay, why wasn't she draped over the ledge? Was the crisp Mrs. Poe one to make an elementary mistake such as handling a live electric cord while standing in a tub of hot water? Didn't most people get instructed in the hazards of electricity mixed with bathwater pretty early on? Lillian Franck wouldn't talk on the telephone while sitting in the bathtub even though the cord was plenty long. She had that much respect for electricity. Cesar himself was in the habit of hitting the bathroom light switch with a dry towel rather than risk an embarrassing death.

Were they shitfaced? Stoned out of their minds? Cesar's eyes traveled to the two wineglasses on the ledge next to the ghetto blaster. One was empty, the other had a couple of fingers of white wine. Usually if you're going to get stinking or even if you're already stinking you bring a bottle along. There was none in sight. There was a little bit of ash, not a lot, next to the single small roach in the alabaster ash tray. Split between two robust adults, that was probably not enough to wipe them out.

Anyway, didn't all ghetto blasters run on batteries? Sure they did. How else could so many kids drive so many adults crazy downtown with their headsplitting cassettes? So what do you need a cord for? Ah! Dead batteries.

With that thought, Cesar started to reach for the power switch on the tape player. Henry's mind had apparently been on the same track, as he too was reaching for the switch. Henry got there first and flicked it on. The sound of cleaned-up jazz blared from the powerful but compact Sony, startling the paramedics who had been about to bag the bodies for the short trip over to the coroner's office in South Avondale. Cesar and Henry looked at each other and then back to the tape player. If you've got a full tank of batteries, you don't need a power cord.

Cesar walked over for a last look and a quick inventory of the jewelry. Gupta was wearing a gold chain. That was it. But Christa Poe had on what looked very much like diamond earrings. They were too small to be junk jewelry, and he couldn't see her wearing anything but the real thing anyway. She also had, on one index finger, a heavy gold signet ring, and on her ring finger an engagement diamond of at least one carat. He pointed the ring out to Henry.

"I saw that," said Henry. "Big one."

"You would think that lets out robbery," said Cesar.

"You would."

The two detectives stepped away from the bodies and let the paramedics step back in.

Mutual suicide? Without a note? Right when Mrs. Poe had shed what was beginning to sound like a fairly annoying husband? A husband who was almost certainly insured out of his mind? It sure didn't seem likely.

They stared at the plug and the unplugged tape player and the hot tub and the rest of the deck.

"I didn't hear any music. They weren't playing any music," said Cesar.

"Hunh?" asked Henry.

"When I came by here last night they weren't playing any music. I would have heard it."

"What were you doing out here?"

"I just came out. I wanted to see it again by myself. I was thinking about it. I don't think they were in the hot tub then. I didn't hear any spashing. They were —" Cesar's vernacular ran into an unwillingness to speak roughly of the dead. "They were engaged in sex." And then he added, "A lot of it."

"They were?" Henry looked askance. "Did you stay around to hear it all?"

"Give me a break," said Cesar. "I didn't say they were doing it for a long time. I just mean they were real enthusiastic."

Henry grinned at Cesar and Cesar looked back down at the hot tub. "But they weren't listening to any music. Not then."

"So what?" asked Henry

"I was trying to figure out what's wrong with the idea that one of them just accidentally dropped the business end of a live cord into the water. Do you believe they were that stupid?" Henry shook his head.

"So, are you thinking somebody threw the cord in with them?"

"Maybe," said Cesar, a little defensively. "We're supposed to think of everything."

"Why? Can't be the husband coming back and finding them buck nekkid in the hot tub. Too late for that."

"Does Gupta have a wife somewhere?" asked Cesar. Henry shrugged. They stared at the tub and they stared at the house. "That door was open, wasn't it?" Henry nodded. "What about the front door?"

"It could have been," answered Henry. "People been coming through there all day."

"Did you turn off the burglar alarm?"

"No. It must have been off already. Never made a sound. They wouldn't have it on, though. Not if they were in the house."

"I guess not," said Cesar. "What do you think, though? You think someone could get close enough to them to drop an extension cord in the tub without their noticing?" It was a good ten feet from the back door to the tub. The policeman stood on the deck and tried to imagine someone sneaking across it. "The lights were on. They're still on."

"All it takes is one good throw," said Henry. "You toss that cord right, and that's it."

"Still," said Cesar, "it's funny. I mean, if this is right, if one of these two," he aimed a thumb at the bodies, which were being carried away on stretchers, "didn't just drop the cord in, which is probably what happened, you have to figure that they either knew there was someone else around and didn't mind, which means it was someone they knew, or else someone was able to get in the house, see the situation, figure out how to take advantage of it, find an extension cord, plug it in, and pitch it into the hot tub on the first try. You see it any other way?"

Henry shook his head. "Was the front door open when you were here last night?" he asked. Cesar thought a minute and then shook his head. Henry walked toward the house with Cesar behind him, following the bright orange extension cord. They went through the back door and stood in the dark hallway for a moment to let their eyes adjust to the lower light.

They were under the landing of the big staircase, which made an unusually low ceiling. To the right was the kitchen with the orange cord running across the floor and up to a counter. To the left was a closed door. Cesar twisted the knob on the closed door and found it to be unlocked. He pushed the door open and found himself in the living room. He wondered how that had happened, since he couldn't remember a door being in that spot. He stepped through, closed the door, and saw that the door was flush and papered like the living room. Only the little brass knob and a faint outline gave it away. He pulled it open to find Henry staring at him. "It's kind of a secret," said Cesar. Henry, uninterested in the secret, opened the door leading from the back cross hall into the big stairhall that led to the front door and that separated the living room and office from the dining room. He went over to the front door and opened it to check the nightlatch, which was off. There was a big deadbolt for the real security.

"What do you think," asked Henry. "You think a woman would leave the front door unlocked like that. In Avondale?"

"Not if she was by herself. But she wasn't. She had her boyfriend in."

Henry's tongue clicked in agreement. Then he asked, "You know her?" Cesar looked the way Henry was pointing, out the door and across the yard. There in her own open doorway stood Mrs. Harris. She was waving vigorously in their direction. Cesar told Henry who she was. "I think she wants you over there," said Henry.

Cesar walked slowly across the grass, leaving Henry to watch him from the Poe's front door. Which might, Cesar thought idly, be Elaine Robison's baby boy's front door.

"This is getting to be a dangerous neighborhood," said Mrs. Harris before Cesar had reached her yard. "I don't even bother to watch "Miami Vice" anymore. It doesn't compare." He had to smile at that. "Are you going to tell me what happened?" she asked as he got to the front door. "I've got eyes. I saw two dead bodies being put in that ambulance. So who were they? One of them is Mrs. Poe, am I right? Come on in. I've got some fresh coffee. You want some?"

"No, thanks, ma'am."

"It'll just get thrown out. I made it for you. My husband won't drink the stuff and I've already had mine, so it's for you and your friend. That's the same man that was over here yesterday, isn't it?" Cesar nodded. "I knew I recognized that car. And speaking of cars—" Mrs. Harris had turned around and headed into the house, rightly confident that Cesar would follow. "Was that your car I saw parked out there last night?"

"Yes, ma'am."

"I thought so. I told Dr. Harris, but he thinks I can't tell one car from another. But that's not so. Sometimes I wonder how he can take living with someone he thinks is so dumb, but we've been married a hell of a long time, so it can't be too bad. I'm not too dumb, though. Not too dumb. Sit down." She had led him into the kitchen, a light room with yellow walls and six thousand Formica cabinets. "I'm going to pour you some coffee. I never heard of a policeman who didn't drink coffee. Now, what do you want in it?"

"Nothing, thanks."

"And I'll fix a cup for your friend when you go. Don't let me forget.

"That was Gupta with her last night, wasn't it?" Mrs. Harris could jerk you around like Mike Wallace when she wanted to.

"Yes, ma'am."

"Is he the other victim?" She watched Cesar closely. At last he nodded. She might as well know. "Am I surprised?" The question was rhetorical. "Even on the day her husband, God rest his soul, breathes his last. Was it another overdose?"

You really had to stay on your toes around Mrs. Harris. Cesar thought she would have made an excellent interviewer for the division except that she never could have met the height requirement. "It looks like they were electrocuted, ma'am. An accident."

"No! What kind of an accident? How do you accidentally electrocute two people?"

Cesar explained about the cord and the hot tub, with Mrs. Harris interrupting him to warn that hot tubs harbored some of the nastiest bacteria known to man. Cesar assured her that he wouldn't be getting in one for a while.

"But you know, I don't believe it," she said when he was through telling her about the cord. "And let me tell you why. Nobody is that stupid. Nobody. It's one of the first things you teach your children. Don't play with electricity around water. So I think somebody stuck that cord in the hot tub. That's the only way I can imagine it. And it wasn't the man who was in just before you got there, because you heard them carrying on still, so it must have been one of the people who showed up there when you weren't watching the place."

"Were there other people there?"

"Somebody was there before you got there. In fact it was just before you got there. It couldn't have been more than a couple of minutes between the time he left and the time you parked your car. I didn't leave the window. I was keeping an eye on the place. So there was him."

"It was a man," Cesar prodded.

"I think so. You know, these eyes are great, but they're not perfect. Who can see that well at night? But my impression is that it was a man. He had on pants and he walked like a man. So there was him. And then there were two cars that came after you left."

"Two cars? Were they together?"

"One at a time. One of them came not too long after you left and stayed for a while—"

"How long?"

"I don't know. Twenty minutes. Half an hour, maybe. Then he left and nobody came for about another half hour, so I got ready for bed. That takes some time these days. And then I was looking out the window and somebody else showed up."

"What time was that?"

"Oh, gosh. You know, I don't watch the clock too much anymore. It's too depressing. Let me think a minute. Dr. Harris had gone to bed by the time the last car got here, and he never gets to bed any later than midnight, even on a weekend when he's got a good book, and it wasn't too long after that, so I doubt that it was any later than twelve-thirty. But that's just a guess, you understand."

"That's fine. That's close enough."

"And you're going to want to know if both the other people were men, and I'm thinking." Mrs. Harris stood with her arms crossed and gazed into the distance. Cesar's eye traveled to the diamond on her left hand. It was twice as big as Christa Poe's, and there were a couple more rings flanking that one. One of the flankers had two rows of diamonds. The other had one row with a couple of red stones thrown in for variety. Mrs. Harris's fingernails were glossy with clear polish. Cesar pecked at his coffee and waited.

"I would like to tell you that I know. I know that would be helpful to you. But I would be a liar. I simply don't know. I'm thinking. I can remember how the cars were parked, and I can remember the doors opening and the lights coming on inside the cars . . . no, I'm lying right now. Only one of the cars had an inside light on. The other one stayed dark. The reason I can't tell you, Officer Franck, is that both of the cars parked in such a way that whoever it was stayed between the car and the house when he got out, and I never saw him really well. And that's sort of interesting, you know? They both got into the driveway and then backed around so that they were ready to pull out. That should have tipped me off to something happening, because nobody ever does that. I feel terrible that I didn't call you."

"You shouldn't."

"Well, it was my inclination. And if I'd been here by myself, I would have. But I wasn't. My husband was here and he's the voice of moderation. You don't call the police until you've got the PLO standing in your kitchen with machine guns aimed at your heart when Dr. Harris is making the decisions. So I didn't call. I'm sorry."

"This is really good coffee, Mrs. Harris."

"Thank you. Let me get you some more." She topped off his mug.

"How are you at identifying cars?" asked Cesar.

Mrs. Harris slid the carafe back into the coffee machine, put her hands on the edge of the counter, and dropped her head for a few seconds. Then she lifted her head. Shame was on her face. "You don't know what an embarrassing question that is for me. How could you be expected to know?" She shook her head sadly. "Don't ever let your children be this dumb. My father, God rest his soul, was a very brilliant man. He figured out how to make the power window just about trouble free, and he sold his design to General Motors. (Of course he wouldn't set foot in a Ford plant.) And, smart man that he was, he took his payment in General Motors stock. That was very, very wise, but he was a very wise man. And even though the idiots that are running the place these days are doing their best to ruin the company, it's still a good stock and believe me it's been a godsend for us. So you would think, wouldn't you, that having enjoyed so many benefits from General Motors, I would at least be able to tell their products when I see them?" Cesar shrugged. "Well, I can't. It's embarrassing, but it's the truth. My children think I'm hopelessly dumb. My husband thinks I'm blind, but I can't tell a Buick from a Nash Rambler, which they don't even make anymore."

"That's not such a big deal," said Cesar. His own mother couldn't tell one car from another except to tell you when one was a deathtrap and the other was nice, but she didn't ever apologize for it. Of course, the only stock she owned was some Federated Department Stores that she got through profit sharing. And she could sure tell Lazarus from Elder Beerman.

"So I can't help you with the cars. And if ever there was a time that it would be useful to be able to identify one, this is it. But I can't. So there it is."

"It's okay, Mrs. Harris. No problem."

Mrs. Harris reached over and patted his hand where it lay on the counter. "I knew you were a good boy when I first saw you. A mother knows these things." The diamonds flashed wildly in the afternoon sun. "And I can tell you this, if it's any help. None of the cars was like yours. I can tell yours. Not what kind it is, but I recognize it. And none of them was a station wagon. As a matter of fact, they were all sedans. Probably about the same size although I couldn't guarantee that, since they were never next to each other. And I don't think any of them was a Jap car. Can you believe we're letting them do that to us? Oh. One of them might have had some writing on the side."

"Which one?" asked Cesar.

"The middle-sized one."

"Could you read it?"

"I wish I could. I really wish I could. You know, we had to fight to keep these gaslights we've got here. They tried to get rid of them during the energy crisis and we raised such a stink along with the people in Clifton and Hyde Park that they left them in. It's because they're so charming. And they really are. But they're not worth a damn when it comes to giving off enough light. I mean you might as well have nothing as what we've got. So no. All I can honestly say is that I think I saw some writing."

"Did all of these people go to the Poes's house?"

"All of them."

"Did they go in? Did Mrs. Poe let them in?"

"You know, I should be embarrassed that you know you can ask me questions like that. It means that you think I'm someone who would watch the neighbors like a hawk or in other words that I'm the snoop of the year. But I'm an old lady and I don't care. Do you want some more coffee?" He didn't. "Everybody went in the house. I can tell you that. What I can't tell you is who let them in. I can tell you that they went to the front door and that they went in the house, but I actually couldn't see if somebody answered the door or if they just let themselves in."

"How long did they stay?" asked Cesar.

Mrs. Harris thought about that. She rocked back on her high heels and looked at the toes of her shoes. "I'd say fifteen to thirty minutes. Fifteen minutes for the first one, the one that was there just before you, and maybe half an hour for the others. And maybe there was ten minutes between the last two visits."

Which was pretty helpful. It was a shame about not being able to recognize the cars, though. Try as he might, giving what he thought were pretty good descriptions of cars, he couldn't get Mrs. Harris to commit to anything that would help sort the models out. Of course a lot of that was General Motors's fault since they were the ones that started making all their cars look exactly alike no matter how much they cost. But he didn't want to make her feel any worse about her stock than she already did. Mrs. Harris tried to get him to drink the whole pot of coffee. He said no thanks and she steered him to the downstairs toilet without his even having to ask. There was a paper towel dispenser in the bathroom with purple paper towels from the hospital. Dr. Harris's touch. When Cesar got back to the kitchen, Mrs. Harris was putting the top on a large Styrofoam coffee cup. "Cream and a lot of sugar, right?" she asked. She was right, but Cesar didn't have the faintest idea how she had guessed what Henry took. She escorted him to the front door. "You know, I should be worried about being next," she said, "but I'm not. I'm gonna get calls all day from everybody telling me I'm living in the most dangerous neighborhood in the city, but that's nothing but a lot of crap. Of course I can't tell them that. Not that way. But this is family business, don't you think? This isn't some sort of mass murderer."

"I don't think so, ma'am. But you still want to be careful."

"I'm always careful, officer. Don't worry about that."

* * *

Cesar carried the coffee across the lawns and crossed back through the Poe house. Henry wasn't out in back. There were only a couple of forensic guys looking for prints just for the record. Cesar went back in the house and looked from room to room. At last, upstairs in one of the bedrooms, he looked out the window and saw Henry crossing the front yard from the direction of the street. Cesar met him at the front door and handed him the coffee, which Henry began to drink without question.

"Where've you been?" asked Cesar.

"Talking to people," answered Henry, wandering back out to the doorstep as he sipped the steaming coffee.

"Neighbors?" Henry nodded. "Find anything out?"

"Not a lot. These folks back here don't have much to do with anybody that isn't their type." Which was no surprise. "But they know who lives back here. Lived." Cesar waited as Henry drank some more. "They saw you, man. Described you perfectly."

"Me or my car?"

"Your car. They said it was 'a old broke down Camaro with a dude inside looked like the police.'" Henry loved that. He grinned over the coffee.

"There were at least three other cars that came back here around the time I did. I don't suppose they noticed as much about them?"

"Don't get your feelings hurt, Ceez. People just know these things."

As it turned out, they had noticed quite a bit, and Henry had done his usual thorough job drawing them out. The car that preceded Cesar was a Buick Century driven by a white man. The car after Cesar was a Channel Three Celebrity driven by a good-looking white woman. The car after that was another Buick Century driven by another white man. Henry said they were all good solid identifications of the cars, if not of the people.

How come Kay Gallery had come back? Cesar was unhappily sure that it was she. There were other women at Channel Three, but she was the one who was interested in the story. But it was funny that she hadn't said anything about going back to the Poes when she and Cesar were drinking coffee. He felt a little put out.

"There's one other thing," said Henry. "One of the ladies on the block saw somebody running that way later on."

"What kind of running? You mean like a runner?"

"Just some dude running. White dude."

"But running? Like a jogger? In running shorts? One of those?"

"She couldn't tell. He was in long pants and a T-shirt. And he went by too fast to get a good look. The lady says he stayed out from under the street lights. She only knew he was a white dude from seeing the back of his arms on his way down the street."

"What time was that?"

"She thought it might have been as late as one o'clock. She wasn't watching the time. It's not that odd, you know."

"Did she think he was just a regular jogger or what? Was he running from something?"

"She didn't know. She watched for a couple of minutes after he was gone to see if anybody else turned up, just in case he was being chased. But nobody else came through."

"Did he come back out?"

"If he did, she missed him. She was up for maybe a half hour longer and then she went to bed. She didn't see anything. She didn't think it was any big deal. Saturday nights you see a lot of things you don't think about."

"Is there a back way out of here?"

"The kids say there's a path down at the bottom of that ravine that goes through the back yard. It comes out on Washington Avenue."

"What about the other direction?"

"Vine Street."

"Oh, shit!" said Cesar. Not about the path. That was pretty interesting. It was the arrival of the Channel Three news team that bothered him. The 4WD led the way, followed by a Celebrity. "We've got to make sure they don't trample through the house. In fact, let's keep them out there at the driveway." Henry set his coffee cup down on the doorstep by a porch column and the two policemen set out to meet the medium.

Before they were halfway to the cars, an eager beaver cameraman had hopped out of the 4WD and aimed a minicam at them. "Hold it there," said Henry. The cameraman, a different weasel from the day before, stopped in his tracks and then started edging forward, sneaking a few inches on them. Cesar started to say something, but Kay Gallery and Larry Wilmot had gotten out of the Celebrity. The two policemen held the news crew at the end of the sidewalk while the frustrated cameraman kept walking around them and filming.

Larry Wilmot was not happy with the policemen. "This isn't right, you know. You have to have a pretty good reason to keep us from getting in there." He pointed to the house.

"They have a good reason, Larry," said Kay Gallery before Cesar could open his mouth. "It's the scene of a crime. Isn't it?" She looked to Cesar for confirmation. You really had to be careful around her the way she was always coming through the back door with stuff. It didn't matter that they had had what you might call a date last night. Today she was working. Even when she seemed to be controlling Larry Wilmot she was looking for a story.

"There's still an investigation going on," said Henry. "Until we're sure we've gotten all the evidence there is we can't let anybody in there. You wouldn't want to disturb anything." He stared straight at Larry Wilmot, who had responded wonderfully to Henry's official tone. His expression had changed from outrage to awe. Cesar looked at Kay Gallery, who was trying not to laugh at Wilmot.

"We sure wouldn't," said Wilmot. He turned to Kay with

a new and serious expression on his face. "They're looking for evidence," he said, as if she might not have understood. "We're going to have to go back to the studio."

Kay Gallery put her face in her hands for a second and then took a deep breath. She explained to Wilmot that they could wait a bit and see what was shaping up. He listened earnestly, and before too long she had him out of the way, standing under a pin oak and talking seriously to the camera. Having found something to keep Wilmot busy, Kay came back to Cesar. He blurted out his question before she could start worming information out of him.

"Did you come here last night? After you left the coffeehouse?"

She was taken aback. Surprised? "Yes. Yes, I did." The surprise changed to reportorial aggression. "Why? Did you?"

You really had to stay on your toes with her. "You were seen. Were you driving that car?" Cesar pointed to the Celebrity.

"Maybe." Was she trying to be a jerk? Cesar gave her what he thought was a pretty tough stare. "We have three of them. They're all just alike. You just grab a key off the board and take one. I just took one."

"What did you come back for? I would have brought you."

"I was working. I wasn't working when I was with you."

"I'm glad to hear that."

Henry had been listening, unnoticed, but he backed away when it sounded to him as if things were getting a little personal. Kay and Cesar turned for a moment to watch him go. "We've embarrassed him," said Kay.

"He'll be all right."

"Did I do something wrong? Coming back like that?"

"Depends on what you were looking for."

"I was looking for a story. I wanted to talk to Christa Poe. I thought she might open up a bit."

"Did she?"

"I didn't get to talk to her. I tried. The lights were on and I rang the bell, but no one answered."

"She was probably still out back," said Cesar. He told Kay, who had only heard that there had been an accident, what the accident was.

"How awful," she said when he stopped. "I feel responsible." That was not what Cesar wanted to hear. "I could have done something. I know CPR. I should have checked. You're sure they were alive when you were here?" He nodded. "What were you doing here?" she asked. Trying to slip another one past him. She never took a break.

"Did you hear anything?" he asked, having decided that it was his investigation and not hers. "When you were here? Like any music? Or any talking?"

"No. Nothing."

So, if that was true, and if she had come right after he did, which was the way he had things put together from Mrs. Harris's story, then Mrs. Poe and Mr. Gupta were either dead or having a cigarette when Kay was ringing the doorbell. Cesar wasn't one hundred per cent sure that he believed Kay Gallery. She was a good reporter. Was it possible that she hadn't gone around to the back? Maybe. Would he himself have gone around if he hadn't heard all that shrieking? Maybe not. Cesar asked Kay if she had seen anybody else at the Poes. She had not. Had she seen anyone arriving as she left? She had not. Had she by any chance seen a Buick coming in Kerley while she was driving out? She had not. All right then, had she seen anybody out running while she was in the neighborhood?

"Running?" she asked. "What does running have to do with anything?"

"One of the neighbors saw somebody running this way last night. I need to know."

"Just somebody running?"

"No. A runner. You know. A jogger."

"I know what you mean." Kay sounded a little annoyed. "Who would be out jogging that late?"

"My boss," said Cesar, before he knew what was coming out of his mouth. The words shook him up, as though he had unleashed some sort of evil spirit. The truth was that from the time Christa Poe had first mentioned Lt. Tieves in her late husband's study, Cesar had just zapped all thoughts of Lt. Tieves as a suspect before they got started. He had only allowed himself to think of the lieutenant as being an interested and frightening but peripheral figure, somebody who could make things unpleasant if Cesar wasn't terrifically careful.

But this. Cesar realized that Kay Gallery was looking at him intently. He wondered how long he had been been silent. "You don't think your boss is involved, do you?" she asked.

"No. You asked me if I knew anybody who would be out running that late at night, and I just remembered that my boss is out at all hours. I guess it depends on when he has the time. He seems to run real long distances."

"So does mine," said Kay.

"He does?"

"A lot. He thinks we don't know about it. He's funny. One of the very few runners I know who doesn't make a fuss about it. Does Lt. Tieves?"

"You know him?"

"I know who he is. I see him from time to time. You know he's a friend of Rick and Larry's."

"Sort of."

"So what would he be doing over here running in the middle of the night?"

"He wouldn't. Or I don't think so. Or he couldn't. Could he? He lives over in Westwood. You wouldn't run over here from there."

"But he could. It's not that far." They stood squinting at each other, trying to read each other's minds. For all it seemed to be a ridiculous conversation, it wasn't. Two people were dead, quite possibly the victims of an intentional electrocution. They were not the victims of robbers. A white man had been seen running down a black street into this little subdivision and had not been seen running back out.

"Where does *your* boss live?" asked Cesar.

"Hyde Park," answered Kay.

"Can he run that far?"

Sure," said Kay. "But then who couldn't? It's only a couple of miles."

Was she being cruel? Or was he the last person in Cincinnati who couldn't run a marathon before breakfast? Cesar casually turned his body away so that his stomach would be out of Kay Gallery's line of vision. "It always seems a lot farther," he said. "I guess it's having to go through Norwood." Cesar referred to the little industrial city that separated Hyde Park from North Avondale. He stayed out of there as much as he could. Norwood police were as dumb as it was possible to be and still drive a car.

"I know what you mean. Anytime I run that way I get through faster than I do driving. But, you know, I never see anyone I recognize."

"You run through places like that? By yourself?"

She nodded. Her eyes seemed to be laughing at him.

"That's not always a safe thing to do," said Cesar. It was his responsibility to give the warning, no matter how fussy it made him look.

"Why would anybody want to kill them like that? Was anything missing from the house?"

"Doesn't seem to be. VCR's still there."

"Is that your acid test?"

"It's a pretty good check," said Cesar.

"For burglary."

"Isn't that what we're talking about?"

"It's not the only thing that ever gets stolen."

"No. But it's usually the first thing. You can just about count on it."

"I'm not arguing with you, Cesar. Don't be so defensive. I'm just suggesting that maybe sometimes people are after something other than electronic equipment."

"Well, of course, there's a lot of silver that—"

"No, no, I mean things like letters. Files. That sort of thing."

"Oh. No cash value. We don't see a lot of that."

"But it happens."

"It does. It's possible."

"You got anything in mind?" Cesar had already decided that the electrocution was deliberate and planned and had happened because the two victims were fooling around, and he had begun some preliminary groping toward a connection with Dr. Poe's death so he had a little trouble shifting gears. Frankly it hadn't occurred to him that there was something else mixed up. He would have gotten around to thinking about that, though. It was just that she got there a little ahead of him.

"I don't know. Medical records? Doctors always have a lot of information you wouldn't want spread around."

"I think that sort of stuff must have been at his office. I don't think he did any work here."

"But you're going to check, aren't you?"

"We check everything," said Cesar. "Excuse me." He turned away from Gallery and strode a little extra firmly into the house to check everything.

At first glance the house seemed to be untouched. Still, Cesar wished he had paid a little more attention to what was supposed to be where when he was here before. Of course he hadn't spent any real time in the living room or dining room. He stood in the middle of the living room and looked around, remembering that there never had been much in the way of ornaments or pictures. There were only two framed prints hanging on the walls, but that was all he could remember positively from yesterday. He thought that all the furniture was still in the room.

Cesar stuck his head into the dining room. There, on the center of the starkly modern, bleached oak dining table, stood four thick, modern, silver candlesticks. Any burglar who missed heavy sterling silver had to be pretty dense. And it couldn't have been kids. Kids *always* went for the VCR. It was a rule.

He walked back into the big living room and stood in the center, wondering what it was that felt faintly wrong about the place, couldn't figure it out, and went to the hall where he slowly began to climb the stairs, still as clean as they had been after Christa Poe's thorough vacuuming.

All the exercise equipment was still in place. Nothing had been moved. Cesar stepped out into the hall, heard no one, and went back into the gymnasium. He climbed awkwardly onto the stationary bike and began to pedal. Since he hadn't even touched a bicycle since he was sixteen, he had forgotten that there was a certain amount of wind involved, and by the time ninety seconds had passed, Cesar was wiped out. He let the contraption coast to a stop and got off, puffing and dizzy. He looked around the room, watching the black spots rather than checking for signs of burglary. He couldn't believe he would have so much trouble riding a bike.

The bedroom looked the same to Cesar. That was one room he did remember. Easy enough, since there was so little in it. He went over to the chest of drawers. He didn't know what had been in there yesterday, but it sure as hell didn't look as if anything had been disturbed. Ever. Every article of clothing was folded, similar articles being folded exactly the same way so that there were perfect stacks of identical underpants and undershirts, knit shirts and dress shirts (Poe used a laundry for them) all lined up, nothing out of place. Two of the drawers were cedar-lined and held what Cesar suspected was about two thousand dollars' worth of sweaters.

He left the bedroom and roamed the hall, opening doors and checking closets and unused bedrooms. Order reigned everywhere. There was not the slightest indication that anyone had disturbed even one article of furniture or linen anywhere.

There were back stairs opening off the smallest bedroom, a chamber somewhat hidden behind an angle in the hall. Given the stairs and the tiny, very plain bathroom that served the room, Cesar figured he was in the servants' quarters. He groped down the staircase, which was lit with a twenty-five-watt bulb, and opening the door at the bottom found himself back in the kitchen.

Nobody had stolen the Cuisinart or its attachments, all of which were sitting out on a countertop. Nobody had stolen the three-inch Sony portable television perched in plain sight on the breakfast table. Nobody had taken the brown bean pot full of coins (no pennies) sitting beside the TV.

Cesar went back into the living room and stood in the center, thinking. He turned around slowly, wondering what it was that was different about the place. Finally he decided that what was missing was Christa Poe. That was all he could remember that was there yesterday but wasn't today. Maybe.

The den, Dr. Poe's office, the room in which he had been interrogated by the late Mrs. Poe, was definitely different. As soon as he went in, Cesar knew something had been changed.

He sat down in the same chair he had used the day before, thinking he'd get his best perspective from there.

Actually more than one thing was different. The frame was there, the little one that had sat on Dr. Poe's desk holding the picture of the St. Julian senators. It was back on the desk but pulled apart, the glass and backing stacked on the empty frame. Cesar remembered that Mrs. Poe had dissassembled the frame yesterday, but she had put it back together after throwing out the photograph, and then she had taken the frame out of the room. And she had looked at the pieces one by one. He realized now that she was not just after the photograph, she was looking for something else. And she, or somebody, had fooled with the other picture, the little print that used to hang under its own special light on the wall opposite the desk. That was gone from its spot. Cesar got up and began to look for it. What he found was the disassembled components of the frame stacked on top of one of the bookshelves. He couldn't find the little print.

Cesar wished he knew more about art as well as more about the Poe family. All he could remember about the picture was that it was a little sketch. It wasn't in the wastebasket. Valuable? Who knows. Maybe it was a Picasso; maybe it was a Don L. Poe. He strained his brain trying to remember what it was a drawing *of*, and drew a complete blank.

The books looked a little different. He *could* remember that. Yesterday they had been in perfect order, spines aligned a uniform half-inch from the edges of the shelves. Since that time, they had been messed with. There were no obvious gaps to indicate missing volumes, but the backs of the books were no longer in perfect harmony.

Cesar sat down in Dr. Poe's swivel chair and thought. It did not take more than thirty seconds to decide that someone, at some time, between his two visits, had been looking for something small, probably paper, which could have been secreted in a picture frame or in one of the books. Who and what? Not kids. Kids didn't stack things neatly when they were through taking them apart. Ever. And he had never in his life heard of a teenage thief who went after pencil drawings. But it didn't have to be a thief at all. The person who had taken the first picture apart was Mrs. Poe. Maybe it was she who took apart the little drawing. But if she did, what did she do with it? And why? And why would she pull the photograph frame apart again? And what would you look for? What kind of paper? How big? Document? Documentation? Where did that come from? Somebody was talking about Don L. Poe's documentation. Did somebody come for documents? Christa Poe said she was going to go through her husband's papers and then act. Act? Did her husband's filing system include picture frames and books?

He rested his chin on his hands and tried to let his mind go blank so he could free-associate the way the psychologist from U.C. had told the homicide squad they ought to do when they were getting nowhere. The psychologist was another goofball idea of Lt. Tieves's. He liked for the squad to spend at least five hours out of every month in classroom work, something different every time. He always had more money in his budget for training than any other lieutenant in charge of anything.

Cesar was not getting any ideas. He was starting to nod off. But quite suddenly his eyelids snapped up. There *was* something else different. The floor had changed. It was flagstones. It wasn't flagstones yesterday. It was a carpet. No. Not carpet. A rug. An oriental rug. And it was gone.

In something of a daze, Cesar pushed back the swivel chair and peered under the desk as if the rug might somehow have worked its way out of sight. But it hadn't. He got up, circled the desk, squatted, and put his hand flat to the cool flagstones, wondering. No doubt about it. That sucker was gone.

Cesar almost ran into the living room. He sure as hell didn't want to be the last to discover that the rugs were gone from there too. But he slowed to a stop. There was still a great big red patterned rug in the middle of the room. Yet there was also more of the floor showing. How much more he didn't know. He tried to remember the floor yesterday. It seemed to him that there had been several smaller rugs overlapping the big central carpet, but that was all he could recall. He should have paid better attention. Who was going to know what was missing?

Cesar resigned himself to having to dig around for the insurance policies to find out if the Poes had carried an itemized rider on the rugs. Maybe he would get lucky and find out something about that pencil drawing, too.

He ran up the stairs and back into the Poes's bedroom to see if the rug he and Henry had examined together was missing, but it was still there. He checked all the upstairs rooms quickly, looking for holes where rugs might once have been. But the upstairs looked untouched. All of the floors seemed well covered, with rugs overlapping in many places.

Cesar went back to the bedroom and stood in the doorway thinking. Christa Poe had said something about rugs. Something about somebody wanting one of the rugs real bad. Which rug? Who? He checked his notebook. Victor Imwalle. A man named Victor Imwalle had wanted something that Cesar had had to spell out phonetically as "ooshack" that was in the living room. Too bad he didn't know which rug was an Ushak and if it was one of the missing rugs. Who the hell knew anything about rugs? Stella.

Cesar turned around, hoping to find Kay Gallery, and found Henry Chapman, still holding the Styrofoam coffee cup from Mrs. Harris's kitchen. "There's some rugs missing," said Henry.

"About time you noticed that," said Cesar. Henry gave him a funny look back.

"What do you think?" asked Henry.

Cesar shrugged. "I guess they could be at the cleaners. It's possible. But I don't think so. It's Sunday."

"How valuable are they?" asked Henry. Cesar assumed, correctly, that Henry wanted to know if the rugs were so valuable that somebody might commit murder to get them.

"Beats me," said Cesar, answering both questions.

They were worth thousands. Henry and Cesar leaned over the desk together staring at the itemized list on the attachment to the Poes's homeowners' insurance policy. Cesar was again sitting in the swivel chair behind Dr. Poe's desk. Henry stood next to him, bent over the blotter, his elbows on the table, his toothpick traveling furiously. There were over thirty rugs listed and priced on the rider. No rug was listed as being worth less than $300. The most expensive rug, a Kuba approximately four feet by eight feet, was worth $16,500.

"You suppose this is for real?" asked Henry. "You suppose this is what they're really worth, or is this just to make out on his insurance? I can't really believe any rug is worth sixteen thousand dollars. Not a four by eight. You could carpet this whole house for that much."

Cesar wasn't really thinking about rugs right then. He was too busy reading the item about the pencil sketch by Renoir that was valued at $35,000. He looked up at the spot where the sketch had hung and tried again to visualize it, but it was no good. He hadn't looked closely enough when it was there. It just looked like a sketch. He realized that Henry was staring at him, waiting for an answer. "What?"

"I said, do you think this is two different cases?" said Henry. "Yesterday and today?"

"No."

"Why not? Yesterday was a drug overdose. Long distance stuff. But this looks like a burglary."

"No, it doesn't." Cesar hadn't meant to be blunt, but he was thinking hard about why he had answered no so quickly. Henry, quick to feel hurt, glared at Cesar. "It's one day," said Cesar. "Everything happens within one day."

"Early this morning for them," said Henry.

"Yeah, but really the same day. They were still up and awake from Saturday. Less than twenty-four hours."

"But all these rugs," said Henry.

"It's not just the rugs. There used to be a picture there. According to this," Cesar pointed at the insurance policy, "the picture was worth twice as much as any of the rugs."

"No shit?" Henry read the description. "But that's even more reason," he said.

"Maybe she sold it," said Cesar. "She could have called a dealer and sold the picture and all the rugs. Or just moved them. Maybe she's just packing up the valuable stuff to send to the bank. People do that, you know."

"And then she went swimming with her boyfriend and pulled the extension cord in with her. What are you talking about? This is maybe fifty thousand dollars' worth of stuff missing that you could put in the trunk of a car. Worth a whole lot more than some rinky-dink VCR."

"I know," said Cesar.

"So? You don't think that stuff is missing for a reason?"

"You don't think two murders in the same day in the same house don't have something to do with each other?"

"They don't have to," said Henry. "You sure can't assume that they do."

"Yeah, but—" Cesar looked back at the wall. He wondered if the little sketch was something hard to fence or easy to fence, besides being easily portable. He knew what Henry was getting at. Basic burglary. And it wasn't impossible. The word had gone out on television about Dr. Poe being dead. "But whoever got these rugs knew what he was doing."

"So?" Henry was still sore.

"So how could it be someone just hitting a target of opportunity? If you wanted to do that, you'd get in, take the first six rugs you came to, and then split. Somebody's been shopping. There's a rug gone from here and a rug gone from there. They're missing from several places. And then there's the picture. They knew what to get. What kind of a burglar knows how to recognize a Renoir? Do you? I sure don't." Cesar added the last hastily. It was true, but it was mostly necessary to keep Henry from sulking. He hated it if you said he didn't know something. "Don't you think somebody would have to know where everything was to come in here and get it?"

"Maybe she packed it away to sell." Henry and Cesar agreed that Christa Poe would be the type to sell anything that wasn't nailed down in order to keep the Robison baby or anyone else from getting it.

And then Henry asked, "What was in that? A Rembrandt?" He was pointing at the empty frame on Dr. Don L. Poe's desk.

"That's what the picture was in. But I can't figure out what it's doing back in here. She took it out of here. She took it apart and looked for something and then put it back together, and then she took it away somewhere and left it. She didn't bring it back."

"Maybe she did. What's it matter?"

"Well, she checked it real thoroughly. Looked at every part of it real closely and then she put it back together. So I don't think she'd take it apart again. No need to."

Henry wasn't very impressed with Cesar's reasoning, so Cesar added that the books had been checked through. Henry pulled apart the desk blotter while Cesar talked, something Cesar had not done. There was nothing hidden away, not even any eraser dust or paper clips. Either Dr. Poe didn't ever use the desk for anything or he was the neatest man in the world after Lt. Tieves.

"Let me see the picture again," ordered Henry.

Cesar pulled the photograph from his pocket, where he had been pretending it didn't exist. Henry shook his head in silent comment as he again looked at the dudes from long ago. Cesar didn't know whether Henry was noting the haircuts or the absence of black senators. There probably were black guys at St. Julian's then. They just weren't in the picture. Henry turned the photograph over. The back was covered with writing. Cesar had never looked at the back. He had been too interested in the front.

The writing was very small, done with the fine tip of a fountain pen. Though it was very neat, it was hard to read. The two policemen wound up with their heads pressed together about six inches from the photograph. Someone, presumably Dr. Poe, had written the names of everybody in the photograph in the same order as the picture. For each entry there was also a number and, for most, a word or two in quotation marks. After Don Poe was the number 1 and "Doc." "I guess those are nicknames," said Cesar. Henry just grunted. Larry Wilmot's nickname was "Doof," Rick Albers's was "Bigfoot." One of the boys was "Smeg," another "Pist," and one was "Nasser." Cesar and Henry must have landed on Lt. Tieves at the same time, because they both started laughing in the same way. He was "Brownie."

"What are the numbers?" asked Henry. Cesar didn't know and wasn't even close to figuring out. He thought it might be some sort of code about their position in the picture, but Henry found and pointed to a line at the bottom. "# = class ranking." So Poe was first, Albers was third, Tieves thirteenth, and Wilmot thirty-second.

The telephone rang, badly startling the two policemen, who knocked their heads together and nearly tore the picture in two along the crease. They looked at each other as the phone rang a second time. Henry shrugged, and Cesar picked it up.

"Hello?"

"Who is this?" asked a woman.

"Who's this?" asked Cesar.

"I want to talk to Christa Poe. Is she there?"

There was something familiar about the voice.

"She's not available," said Cesar. That was true. "Who's calling?"

"Well, is she there?"

"She can't come to the phone."

"She better come to the phone. I have some important things I want to talk about with her if she knows what's good for her. You tell her to come to the phone."

"Miss Robison?"

"Who's this? How you know who this is?"

"This is Detective Franck. I talked to you this morning."

"Oh. What are you doing there? Are you going to let me talk to that woman? We have to talk about some money for my baby."

Cesar sat there with his mouth hanging open for about five seconds. He had gotten himself in a little bind, playing coy with Miss Robison, not telling her that the party she was trying to reach was as unreachable as it was possible to be. Now he was going to have to tell her. Or shouldn't he? Because Elaine Robison, as the mother of Dr. Don L. Poe's son and heir and therefore the probable trustee of the very minor child, automatically went to the short list of suspects in the murder of Dr. Poe, maybe Mrs. Poe, and incidentally Mr. Gupta.

"She's dead."

"Say what?"

"Mrs. Poe is dead." Cesar held off on the explanation to see what Elaine Robison's reaction would be. There was a silence on the line.

"Are we talking about the same lady?"

"Dr. Poe's wife. Yes," said Cesar.

"Dead? Well, that's just great. That's just real great. You know she's supposed to give me some money? Now how am I supposed to get that? You tell me that if you know. This is a real problem. I have this baby and there is no money to take care of him, if you know what I mean. You tell me what I'm supposed to do about that. This is just great. Did she get into the cocaine too? I bet she did."

"No."

"How'd she die, then?"

Cesar thought he wouldn't answer that for a while. "I'm

not a lawyer, ma'am, but I would think your baby is probably going to inherit something. Just so long as there's some sort of official recognition of paternity."

"Oh, I have that all right. But that doesn't pay anything right now. I need money right now. This boy's got to eat."

"Well, I'll tell you what, Mrs. Robison. As soon as we can find out who's Dr. Poe's attorney we ought to be able to find out where you stand. There's probably some way he can get you some money if everything's straight."

There was a bit of indignant squawking, but he was eventually able to ease off the phone.

"That lets her off, then, don't you think?" asked Henry.

"Maybe for Mrs. Poe. Not necessarily for Dr. Poe." He looked down at the picture of the senators, which was lying on the desk. Nothing had changed since he first looked at it. There were no new clues to be seen in the expressions of the short-haired seniors. There was certainly nothing to indicate that any of them would be doing cocaine twenty years down the line. Or fathering illegitimate children. Or, for that matter, planning to be chief of police.

He turned the photograph over to look at the back again. Henry leaned in with him. This time a new name caught his eye. Mike Gallery. "Red." Fifth in the class. Cesar counted the names from Donald Poe's own spot to figure out where Mike Gallery would be in the picture and then he turned it right side up. He should have spotted it without having to read the name. The resemblance was strong and obvious. Mike Gallery looked as much like Kay Gallery as it was possible for a boy to do. Even with the white sidewalls and crewcut. He had to be her brother.

"What you looking at?" asked Henry.

"Who does that look like?" Cesar pointed.

"Everybody else in the picture."

"Smartass."

"Okay. It looks like that reporter outside, the one you've been checking out."

"I haven't been checking her out. She's on the story."

"Okay, man." Henry didn't believe him. That was going to be a problem. He was a big fan of Stella's and sort of a prude when it came to everybody's love life except his own. "So was I right?" Henry flipped the picture and found Gallery's name. "Did she tell you about him?"

"No."

"Maybe she didn't know. You don't know everybody in your sister's class. Do you?"

"Hell, no. But my mother does. Or did. Anyway, if somebody in her class got killed and it happened here in town we'd know about it within five minutes. The phone lines'd be burned out. You know how it is. Besides, she's a reporter. They're supposed to pick up on things like that."

"Not if it has to do with them. They for sure find out if it's somebody they want to get. Somebody on the council. Somebody black."

There it was once again, the old complaint. But this time it was probably valid. Both ways. If you were going to be black and at the same time be on the city council or municipal court or anything where you were in the public eye, you had to really be on your toes. One little slipup and the reporters would be on you in a microsecond. Although it was Cesar's theory that the reporters never found out anything on their own, since they could pretty much count on people ratting on their colleagues. But the other side was that you never heard much about reporters turning up at orgies or gay bars or after-hours clubs.

Why hadn't Kay Gallery told him she had a brother who went to school with Dr. Poe and Cesar's boss and her own boss? It was one of those things that you would expect to come out pretty quick.

Cesar immediately started working out reasons why it might be OK, even though he should have been outside asking her just why the hell she'd kept it a secret. Maybe she and her brother were raised separately. Maybe her parents had died and they were orphans raised by different aunts and didn't even know they lived in the same city with each other. Or her brother was a convicted felon and had been locked up in Marion, Illinois, since 1972. Or she thought Cesar would be embarrassed talking about Catholic schools since he hadn't been lucky enough to be born Catholic and get on the fast track at Elder or the faster track at St. Julian's.

Naah. It was something bad. It had to be.

Cesar sighed and told Henry he was going outside to see about something.

"She's going to know what you want as soon as you go out that front door with you looking like that," said Henry.

Cesar glared at him, pissed off that he had read the situation so quickly and so accurately, but as he headed for the front door, he made a conscious effort to put on a poker face. Since he couldn't feel any change, he had to wonder if it was the poker face that had given him away to Henry. He slid the folded picture into his shirt pocket.

Kay Gallery was standing outside the front door talking to her cameraman. She saw Cesar and smiled a big beautiful smile that went up past her eyes and made Cesar feel as if he had been smashed by a detonating airbag.

"Is it okay to come in now?" she asked with a throaty, kidding little laugh.

"In a minute. Could I talk to you about something?" Cesar choked a little on his words, and Kay, who was no dummy, saw that something was up. The smile stayed on, but the lights went out in her eyes.

"Sure." She sent the cameraman back to his truck and turned back to Cesar, waiting for him to say something.

"I was—" Cesar stopped, wishing he had taken a few minutes, maybe even a few days, to prepare. "Do you have a brother?" he asked at last.

If Kay Gallery had been expecting him to ask something, that wasn't it. She shook a little as if she had been hit by a sudden gust of wind. "I have a sister," she said. "Is that OK?"

"Sure," said Cesar, wondering if she was going to be really pissed off at him without saying why. "You don't have a brother?" Maybe everything was going to be OK. A lot of Irish people sort of look alike. He'd read that somewhere. "I was wondering about a man named Mike Gallery. 'Red' Gallery. He's not related?"

Instead of answering, Kay just looked at him. Cesar waited.

"Did you know him?" she asked at last.

Did? "No."

"How do you know about him?"

"Who is he?"

"He was my brother."

Oh.

"He's not alive anymore."

"I'm sorry," said Cesar. "And he was.

"I'm curious. How did you know about him?"

Instead of answering, Cesar slipped the photograph out of his pocket and handed it to her, straightening it first. She took the picture and looked at it, holding it down near her waist so that she had to bend her head over. She was near tears when she looked up. "I hadn't seen that picture," she said. "It was a surprise to me. I thought I had seen every possible picture of him. I thought I had them all. I know them all so well. So it's like . . . I'm afraid it's a little bit like a sign of life. It's very surprising, Cesar."

"You don't have to explain that," said Cesar, who was close to tears himself without knowing why.

"Anyway," Kay said, starting in afresh, with the slightest shake to her voice, "you guessed right. This is my brother Red. Mike. Michael. And, as you can see, my brother went to school with Don Poe and he was also a senator, which is what these boys are. Oh, God, they're such boys." The last just kind of rushed out and the tears got out of control for a second and then she sucked in her breath and buckled down again. "Have you figured out who the other boys are?"

Cesar nodded. "It's on the back."

Kay turned the picture over and read a few items, but they were no surprise to her. She was starved for the sight of her brother, and she returned to the picture.

"The reason I didn't say anything about him is because he was killed in the war in Vietnam and it's not something I talk about very much, but I should have told you. It's something you would want to know. Where did you get this?"

"It was in the house. It was in Dr. Poe's room."

"I don't suppose I can have it."

"I'll get you a copy."

"I can't believe I haven't seen it before. I'm surprised that Rick doesn't have it hanging in his office."

"Is he real active?"

"As an alumnus? No. No, I guess not. He doesn't even talk about it. You'd think he would, wouldn't you? Running for office?"

"I didn't know he was, for sure."

"It's not official. But he is. That's your Lieutenant Tieves, isn't it?" Kay was looking at the picture again, and she pointed correctly to the doofus-looking future policeman. Cesar nodded. "You know, out of all of these, he's the only one besides Mike who was in the war. They all got out of it. Can you believe it? Mike and he were the only ones who went . . . Even if you don't like him, you ought to respect that."

"Nobody else got drafted?"

"Drafted?" She made an acid sound. "Saint Julian boys don't get drafted, Cesar. If they serve, they're officers. They either go through R.O.T.C. or go to one of the academies. They're real big on the academies. Or, if they're like Don Poe, they don't even have to do that. All he had to do was finish med school and he was an instant captain. He didn't even have to leave Cincinnati. He just stayed here and gave physicals."

"Did your brother go to West Point?"

"No," she snapped. And then, softer, "He wasn't the type. You didn't know him. The ones I know that went to the academies were either kind of nerdy—airplane worshipers— or hard-chargers, and he wasn't either of those. He was," she stopped to take in a deep breath, and Cesar wished that he had never had to hurt her, "He was the nicest boy God ever put on the earth." She laughed. "I don't believe in God anymore. Except for that." She looked at Cesar in frustration. "That sounds wrong. I mean, he wasn't a saint. Not at all. He just hadn't a mean bone in his body. He was big and handsome and all he ever wanted to do was make everybody feel the way he did all the time, which was great. He was seven years older than me, but he made me feel like I was his twin. I swear it. All of my friends used to bitch about how mean their brothers were to them and how they hated their guts and how they thought boys were slime, and for years I thought they must all be nuts. Or lying. I just didn't know how different he was. I'm rambling. I'm sorry. It's the picture. I'm really sorry."

"Was he drafted?"

"He enlisted. Right in the middle of everything, right when the war was starting to get ugly, he enlisted."

"He didn't go to college?"

"He started. He did two years at Notre Dame. And then he dropped out. It was the first screwy thing he had ever done that anybody could remember. And he wasn't failing. He was getting good grades. As and Bs all the way. But he just called home one night and said that he was coming home at the end of the semester and that he wasn't going to go back to school."

"Ever?"

"He didn't say that. He just said he wasn't going back to school. My parents didn't know what to do. They didn't know what to say. They hadn't ever even discussed anything like dropping out. I mean it was the last thing in the world they would have suspected. I think I was the only person in the world who wasn't surprised."

"Why not?"

"He gave me a hint. I guess I was the only one. Or the only one who listened. Or got it.

"We went on a walk when he was on spring break. I forget what for. To get something at the store, maybe. And I asked him if he was going to take French next year. At one time he had planned to. I was going to take it if he was and I thought it would be so neat if we could talk to each other in French at the dinner table in front of everybody and be the only ones to understand. And he said no without any explanation and I got a little indignant and started complaining and asking why and he said he just wouldn't. I needled him some more, but he wouldn't say anything more and finally I let it drop because of his expression. He looked about ten years older and a little sad. And that was the first time in my life I had ever seen him look anything like that. I was so shocked I just shut up, and we didn't say anything more about it. And then he cheered up in the grocery store and I forgot about it until he said he wasn't going back to school." Kay stopped looking at Cesar and went back to the picture. Cesar waited, but she seemed to have forgotten he was there.

"What was the matter?" he asked. Kay looked up at him as if she were surprised to find him still there.

"I don't know. I guess," she said after a moment, "that it wasn't fun anymore."

"School?"

"School. Notre Dame. Anything he was doing. I don't know what happened. Maybe nothing happened. Maybe he just outgrew being happy all the time and it was too much for him. Maybe he found out that his friends were nowhere near as nice as he was and it was too much for him. I don't know. I just know that he came home with all his stuff and nothing my parents could do would get him to change his mind. He stayed at home for three weeks listening to them go after him about Notre Dame and the 'future' and then one night at supper he said, 'I joined the army.'"

"Just like that?"

"Just like that. My mom nearly fainted and then started crying. And so did my dad. So Mike, of course felt really terrible and had to spend the rest of the night trying to make it up to them. He couldn't. It was the first crummy thing he had ever done, and they weren't prepared for it. He was over there for six months and stepped on a mine.

"I was supposed to be an aunt by now."

OK.

"Mike was supposed to have married somebody and had four children so I wouldn't have to, since I wasn't going to get married. I told him that about a thousand times. I always knew I was going to work."

"What about your sister?"

"It's not the same. She married an accountant. I don't like their kids. I was going to love Mike's kids.

"Don't you hate it?" she asked. "Doesn't it bother you how nobody went to Vietnam? Nobody you know?"

"I don't know," said Cesar.

"Well, his friends didn't. None of them. Except Tieves, and Mike used to make jokes about him. Just to me. Never to him. The others just didn't go. And they didn't want anything to do with Mike when he went. Or before he went. He came home on leave after all his training and started calling them up, and after three calls he stopped. They were all avoiding him as if he had AIDS. Except there wasn't AIDS then. But you would have thought he had some horrible sort of communicable disease. They just wouldn't come near him. They were afraid."

"Of him?"

"Of him. Of the war. Of getting off track. I think he scared them all by dropping out like that. That was before anybody respectable dropped out, and they didn't know what to do about it. I hate them, Cesar. I really do. I hate their guts."

There was an awkward silence.

"And the final thing," Kay said at last. "Not one of the bastards, not *one* showed up at his funeral. None of them. Because they were scared shitless by the situation. I know that was it. I saw Larry, the stupidest man on the face of the earth, a few days after the funeral, and I asked him why he didn't come. I was so angry I didn't even stop to think about how much older he was or what a rude question or anything like that. I just asked him right on the street. He said it was too emotional for him. I was supposed to think that meant he cared so much for Mike that he just couldn't take it, but I didn't believe it. He was too stupid to be able to hide how scared he was. *That* was the emotion. He was scared. They were all scared.

"I've got to run."

Cesar must have looked confused, because Kay started to laugh and said, "To get out of the state I'm in. I'm ready to stab somebody."

Jesus.

"You want to come too?" she asked. "Do you run?"

It was one of those decisive moments. Of course he didn't run. Not only did he not run, he didn't want to run, hadn't considered running, wasn't ever going to run, and he had a whole lot to do to get to the bottom of three homicides. So he said, "I've been thinking about it."

Weeks later, when he was trying to sort things out, he could only conclude that it had to do with Kay Gallery's mental state more than it had to do with taking advantage of a situation that would have him wearing a lot fewer clothes with her wearing a lot fewer clothes. She was distraught and it had been his clumsy handling of things that had put her in that state. And also she was indicating the possibility of committing a homicide so he had to check that out.

"Seriously?" asked Kay.

"Sure," said Cesar. "I've got to do something about this." He patted his stomach, which he had been sucking in, on the chance that she might say he didn't need it for *that*. But she didn't.

"Have you got anything to run in?"

"Sure, I've got some stuff in the car."

"Running shoes?"

"Gym shoes."

"Better let me see them," said Kay. And she made him take her to the Camaro and stood there while he opened the trunk. Christ. What a mess. He hadn't really expected to have a lady looking at his personal stuff, and the trunk of his car was in bad shape, nothing like his room at home which was always in perfect order. She could have dropped into his bedroom and checked out his drawers any time. Any time. But the trunk.

Cesar popped the lid. The springs whined about how they hadn't had any oil since the warranty ran out, which was about 87,000 miles ago. The trunk gave off its own special smell of unwashed gym clothes, golf shoes, motor oil, spare tire dirt, apple, newspaper, unredeemed pop bottle, and rust. The gasket on the trunk lid hung on in a few spots, but it was really just going along for the ride, and the rains had been finding their way in. None of the stuff that had been white or light colored had escaped the rust. He hoped to God there were no cockroaches in there. Cesar rummaged through the debris until he came up with first a left and then a right high-top gym shoe. He held them up with a weak grin.

"These do it?" he asked, ready to drop the trunk lid on the disgusting scene.

"They'll kill you," said Kay. "Haven't you got something else? Even a tennis shoe." Cesar wasn't ready to admit that he thought tennis was as dumb as running, so he rooted through the mess, pretending there was something to look for.

"I guess not," he said dropping the lid, wishing he were under it.

"You can't use those, Cesar." Kay pointed to the Converses as if they were wooden spoons or light bulbs. "You really can't. Follow me."

"Where?"

"We've got to shop. It'll just take a minute."

"Look, this isn't such a good—"

Kay looked at him. A little of the panic she had suppressed showed in her eyes. Cesar didn't know if that was on purpose or if she was really about to crack, but he didn't want to put it to the test, so he found Henry and told him he had some business to take care of and that he should mind the store. Henry looked over Cesar's shoulder in the direction of Kay Gallery. She was in her car with the engine running. He pursed his lips to let Cesar know that he was thinking about Stella Hineman, which was totally outrageous since Henry was never without at least three significant relationships. But he just nodded.

She led him to O'Bryonville, where she took the last open parking spot on the block, forcing Cesar to rumble through the shopping district until he found an opening in front of a nursing home. He walked as briskly as he could past the wine and art and real estate shops back to where she stood smiling on the sidewalk. His shirt was soaking.

"Come on," she said, taking his arm. She led him toward a store with brown awning that said the Fast Track. "Have you ever been in here?" He shook his head. He hadn't been in any of the O'Bryonville stores even before they got cute, except for the time he stopped in a delicatessen and ordered a sandwich that turned out to cost five dollars and gave him gas like he wouldn't believe. Strategically located between two overpriced neighborhoods, O'Bryonville was for people who weren't police.

Like the Fast Track. Too late to turn around and go home, Cesar realized that the Fast Track was for Serious Runners, not for policemen who couldn't say no to a pretty newsperson. Sucking in his gut, Cesar wondered why the hell she couldn't have gone to a mall where it didn't matter how much you weighed. There were three skinny salespeople helping four skinny customers. Kay detached herself and said she would be right back, and Cesar began to wander around the store, thinking again about bolting, until he came to a display of photographs of people in running clothes. Labels under the pictures told what races they were taken at. He saw Lt. Tieves right off. He wasn't the subject of the picture. The subject was the winner of some race. Lt. Tieves stood in the background soaked in sweat, looking like he was about to puke. Cesar didn't think he had ever seen the lieutenant looking so bad, and it made him feel a little better. He looked at a lot of the other pictures but he didn't see any police, just a couple of judges and a guy from city hall whose clock Cesar wanted to clean.

Cesar felt a cool hand on his elbow, and he turned around to see Kay Gallery. She had gone somewhere in the back of the store and changed into lavender shorts and a white top and pinned her hair up in back. For a moment he was kind of blinded by arms and legs. "I'm going to run while you shop," she said. He started to protest. What was the point if they weren't going out together? "I'll run with you after you get some shoes." Kay waved to one of the salespeople, a blonde woman who weighed about eighty pounds. "Take care of him, OK?" The woman nodded without speaking as she laced up an Adidas on a woman in a three-piece suit. "Wait for me, Cesar," said Kay. He nodded and she left the store.

Cesar stood on the edge of the sales floor wondering whether death could be worse than life. Death was a distinct possibility. Ron Schwetzenau, a guy Cesar's age who had gone through Cesar's recruit class with him, had had a major heart attack very recently, due to putting in an air conditioner when he wasn't in shape for it. Cesar began to wonder if he would fail to collect his life insurance if he had a heart attack trying to run when he was supposed to be at work. Before he could solve that one, his saleswoman approached him and led him, his heart sinking, to a chair.

Half an hour later he knew for certain that it would have been better to die. The little saleswoman, after asking him sixty embarrassing questions about what his running goals were, had sold him the most expensive shoes he had ever bought in his life. They were, the woman had explained, the right shoe for someone at his weight level, someone who needed extra heavy support. He was so shaken by the experience that he had let her sell him a pair of polypropylene shorts and an undershirt that together cost as much as his winter coat. And then he had agreed to put them all on in the changing room in back.

So there he stood, all geared up, waiting for Kay to get back. The saleswoman, having relieved him of over a hundred dollars in plastic, left him alone with nothing to do but look again at photographs. This time he got interested in a posterboard with a collection of pictures of people shopping at the store. He recognized a councilwoman and two of the lawyers everyone on the force loved to hate for the way they got their clients off. Everybody got his picture taken in new shoes. He started to move on when he spotted the gang from Channel Three. There were Wilmot and Albers, and there was Kay, and a fourth person who looked familiar. The weather man. They were in a chorus line, all kicking their new shoes. Kay was the only one who looked cute. He looked around, hoping she had shown up, but she hadn't.

He caught sight of himself accidentally in a full-length mirror and broke out in a cold sweat. What a freak! His legs were as white as the underside of an Icelandic codfish. His stomach, which he had forgotten was supposed to be under compression, was instead putting the fabric of the singlet to the test. Panicked again, he spun around and in the process knocked over a display. A heart attack would be real mercy.

The salespeople, all still engaged with skinny customers,

looked at Cesar as if he were a Martian. He said "Heh-heh" in the best fake unworried chuckle he could manage under the circumstances and started to reassemble the display, an unstable and top-heavy pedestal holding up what turned out to be the largest and smallest shoes available at the Fast Track. The big one was a fourteen in the same brand Cesar had bought, which made him wonder if he had bought special freak shoes that would be instantly recognizable to everybody in the city even though it was several sizes smaller than the Bozo special in the display. He heard the door open and was overjoyed to see Kay.

Kay looked a lot better. She was smiling now, and her color was back, along with a healthy coat of sweat. She bounced over to meet him, never letting her legs rest. "Ready?" she asked. "You look terrific."

Cesar peered at her to see what was up. He looked no more terrific than he looked athletic. She didn't *look* like she was teasing him, but she wasn't blind either. He wondered if maybe she hadn't gone a little crazy. Maybe seeing her brother's picture was more traumatic than either one of them had realized. Or maybe she was just unbalanced. He followed her out of the store, ignoring the other customers and salespeople who were going to laugh their asses off as soon as he was out of earshot.

"Now, we're going to take this really easy, Cesar. You probably feel you can do more than you actually can. That's just adrenaline. We're going to do just a nice easy jog here and any time you feel like walking, you just say so, OK? You're not trying to prove anything."

Cesar's infatuation for Kay Gallery, and that's what it was, there was no getting around it, was being put to the test. He had reacted pretty strongly to what he felt was her instant understanding of how he had felt over the past couple of days, and he sort of thought she might have felt the same. But now. Now she was saying things like, "You probably feel you can do more than you actually can," and "You're not trying to prove anything." These statements were actually what you would call bullshit, he was sorry to say, since he for a while there he had thought she was incapable of dealing in bullshit. Because he didn't feel like he could do *anything*. In fact he was pretty sure that this was going to be really embarrassing. He was going to tell his legs to run and they weren't going to do it. It was also bullshit that he wasn't trying to prove anything. Why the hell did she think he was standing out here on Madison Road in next to nothing? Because he *enjoyed* it? Oh Christ, no!

Cesar's reflexes tried to throw him into a darkened doorway or alley as he spotted what he knew without a doubt to be Detective Carole Griesel's BMW slowing to a halt alongside him. The reason he didn't throw himself anywhere was because Kay Gallery would think he had gone insane. "Let's go." He choked out the words and started jogging in the opposite direction to where Carole Griesel had been driving, hoping against hope that he would get past the car before she recognized him.

"Are you all right?" asked Kay, gliding along beside him.

"Fine. I'm—"

"Cesar! Is that you? Oh, God, I can't believe it! God, somebody call the news crews! Oh, God, you look so funny! Cesar! Stop."

"Who is that?" asked Kay. Cesar didn't answer. He wanted to save all his wind to get as far from Carole Griesel as he possibly could.

"This is great!" he managed to spit out, hoping it would distract or at least confuse Kay Gallery so she wouldn't ask him any more about Carole.

"I knew you'd love it," said Kay. "Who was that woman who knew you?"

"I don't know," Cesar found it hard to get the words out. They seemed to be going a little faster than a jog, but that was OK. He wanted to get away.

"Is it your girlfriend? Do you have a girlfriend?" He

looked quickly at Kay and then back at the hill that was looming ahead of them. "Her? Carole? No! Hell, no!"

"So you do know her. She's very attractive." Even in his confused state, Cesar recognized "very attractive" as fighting words. Kay already didn't like Carole, which was all right with him.

"It's," he huffed, ". . . she's a woman—"

"I know." He didn't think this was the time for teasing.

"Woman," he said, ". . . detective."

"Oh," said Kay. "Like you."

Not exactly. He thought for a second about explaining but realized he wasn't going to have the breath, so he just didn't answer. He looked around to see if Carole had made a U-turn so that she could follow him and embarrass him to the point of throwing himself into traffic. That was the kind of thing she wanted to do to him, he was pretty sure. But she had whipped the BMW into a parking space and seemed to be headed into the Fast Track. He could tell she was looking at him, even at this distance.

With the immediate danger gone, Cesar wondered about maybe slowing the pace a little, since he was beginning to see dots floating in front of his eyes. He wasn't ready to walk yet, though, since they had only gotten about a block from the store. He tried slowing down gradually, hoping Kay wouldn't notice what he was doing, but as soon as she realized she was four feet ahead of him, she turned her head. She was smiling in sympathy. This was the worst thing that ever could have happened. Why did he lie? Why did he say he was thinking about running? What in God's name had led him to spend more than a hundred bucks on gym shoes and a track suit?

Cesar became aware of his belly as it slopped around in its bearings. The movement of what he had to admit should truthfully be called beer gut seemed to be even more exaggerated at the new slower speed. He tried sucking it in, but that meant he had to remember to do two unfamiliar things at once, running and sucking, and he was afraid he would fall.

"You're doing *great!*" said Kay. Christ. She was talking to him the way everybody talked to kids nowadays no matter how terrible they were at whatever it was they were doing. Positive reinforcement. It made her less attractive, since he started thinking she might say it to him in bed when he was actually pretty ordinary. She wasn't ordinary. As she was running a little ahead of him, he got to get fairly familiar with what was as cute a butt as he had seen running down a sidewalk.

Looking at Kay's backside, Cesar forgot to watch where he was going, and the thick sole of his new running shoe caught the edge of a sidewalk block where it was heaving out of the ground. Starting to fall, hoping to recover, he whacked along in great loping bounds, bent nearly double. Kay, hearing the peculiar thuds of his footfalls, looked around in time to see Cesar launch into a flying forward roll off to the side, coming to rest with his feet propped up on an iron fence. She ran back to him and squatted by his side. "Oh, gosh," she said, "Did you hurt yourself?"

He wished he had. It was the perfect excuse to stop. But, except for the feeling of something cold and sticky on the back of his left knee, something that he knew without a doubt was going to turn out to be dogshit, he was fine, so he levered himself up, sneaking a peek at the possible disaster, which turned out to be a wet tissue. He flicked his leg and the tissue fell off.

"Are you OK?" she asked.

"Fine. I don't know what happened."

"Ready to go?" Kay asked.

Say no. Just say no. "Sure."

"I know how that feels," said Kay. She was setting a pace a little faster than they had been going before.

"You—" Cesar was back to huffing, ". . . you . . . fall down . . . a lot?"

"Well, I can't remember that I've actually fallen down," said Kay. She was not huffing at all. In fact, Cesar couldn't hear a trace of heavy breathing. This run wasn't really a run as far as she was concerned. "But I've gotten off balance." She smiled over her shoulder, and Cesar tried to smile at back at her, but he couldn't keep it on. It wasn't just that he was having such a rough time, although he was. He was trying to think. Something about the fall had jogged something in his memory. But whatever it was was only partially dislodged. So he was trying to think and run at the same time, and it wasn't easy. Perhaps his face showed his effort to concentrate. Kay was leaving him alone for a change, making no effort to chat. Cesar noticed to his surprise that they had passed through the cool leafy tunnel of East Walnut Hills and had reached DeSales corner. Kay turned the corner at Woodburn and headed toward William Howard Taft road, leading Cesar past at least six bars known to him to be drug supermarkets. He had viewed corpses in two of them. But he was concentrating so hard on dislodging the stuck memory that he wasn't even bothered when he spotted a guy he had helped send up after the man had knifed his brother-in-law. The guy had gotten manslaughter and was probably on parole. Cesar waved, and the guy, either forgetting or failing to recognize, waved back.

It had something to do with his new running shoes, which, by the way, really made a difference in how the pavement felt. Cesar's old low-tech high-tops had all the cushion of a pair of socks, but these new babies felt like clouds. He sneaked a peek at the new shoes to see if they looked fast. Actually what they looked was big. The salesperson had had to go a size larger than Cesar was used to in order to give him enough width and toe room, so the shoes extended nearly an inch past the end of his toes, turning his feet into unfamiliar objects.

Cesar looked back up in alarm. He hadn't meant to take his eyes off the road as long as he had, but everything was cool. Kay looked over her shoulder and smiled again but didn't say anything. His concentration must still be showing. Somehow the big sneakers had jogged his memory further. It had something to do with shoe sizes, and, Cesar realized, the memory had started before they even began to run. Back in the shop, maybe.

"Let's walk for a minute," said Kay. Cesar's concentration lapsed.

"I'm doing . . . OK," he panted.

"We'll walk," she said, slowing down. He didn't argue. He hadn't the breath. And for the next few minutes he had to listen to a scientific lecture about oxygen intake, and being anaerobic, and hemoglobin, none of which really registered. He was overjoyed to be walking, but the lecture was keeping him from recovering what seemed to Cesar to be an important item in his memory. "I can run," he told Kay, hoping she would stop lecturing him. But all he got was more breathing theory for a whole city block. Then she startled him by stopping and gently picking up his wrist. He hadn't thought he was getting that far with her, and since the hemoglobin lecture he wasn't 100 percent sure that he wanted to, but her fingers were cool and slim and he let her hold on if that was what she wanted to do.

"I did this all wrong," she said. It seemed all right to Cesar, and he said so, smiling what he thought was a fairly sophisticated smile. "Your pulse is way too fast. I let you run too fast too far." Well, if he had to err, he'd rather err on the manly side. Too fast. Too far. "We'll walk a little farther," she said, dropping his wrist. "And for heaven's sake, don't try to impress me. This is supposed to be for *you*." Cesar felt chastened and less impressive. They walked along, silent except for the roar of Cesar's breathing.

"Are you ready?" Kay asked after another block. Cesar nodded, and she began to jog at what Cesar knew was just barely more than a walking pace for her. He felt his belly slopping around again and then deliberately ignored it. "Kay?" he asked. "Do they always sell you such big shoes there?" He realized after getting the question out that he had done so without stopping for breath. Kay noticed too. "That's great," she said. "You should be able to carry on a conversation while you run." Jesus. She couldn't let up. "It's a useful test, even if you're by yourself. If you can't talk, you're going too fast. You're getting anaerobic." Cesar recalled from a safety lesson that botulism was something that occurred when things got anaerobic. He shuddered.

"If you can sing," Kay went on, "you're not going fast enough." And then, to prove her point, she started to sing. It sounded like she had a pretty good voice, sort of operatic. Only she was singing "Leader of the Pack." Cesar was a little embarrassed, and he wished she would stop. They had turned off William Howard Taft onto Victory Parkway, and he felt pretty exposed. He saw a police car overtaking them in the corner of his vision, and turned his head away from the street. This was just the sort of thing that guys liked to discuss for about six years. He just prayed to God nobody recognized his backside. Kay stopped singing when she saw that he wasn't laughing. "Why?" she asked. Why what? "Are your shoes too big?" Oh. She was answering his question.

"Well, they're a size bigger than I usually wear," he answered. "I think that's why I tripped. But the salesgirl said I had to have the room."

"It depends on the brand. Panthers run small." Cesar was wearing Panthers. He had never heard of them before today, and now he had a pair that cost enough to feed most of Haiti for a month. "Now, I've got Nikes, and they're the same size as my street shoes." Cesar began to tune out. He was reminded of Carole Griesel and Lt. Tieves when they got over in a corner and started jabbering about running. He couldn't believe it was happening to him. ". . . has the same kind you do, and they're a size bigger than *his* street shoes."

"Who?" asked Cesar.

"Rick Albers. Is this too fast for you?"

"I'm talking."

"Is it easy?"

"It's OK."

"Try singing."

"Naah," said Cesar.

"I'll step up the pace," Kay threatened.

"I don't know any songs."

"You're embarrassed."

"I'm not."

"You're having too easy a time of it," said Kay, and she stepped on the gas a little. "Can you still talk?"

"Sure." As long as he didn't have to deal with more than one syllable. Kay kicked in a little more speed and Cesar's belly stopped rocking. Now what he felt was his legs starting to throb and his knees starting to pop. He also began seeing those little spots as his breath started to come in heaves.

"Still talk?" asked Kay. Cesar couldn't see that she was breathing any harder than she did standing still.

"Sure," he said. A lie. He could barely get out the one word. They kept up the pace, following Victory Parkway as it turned back towards O'Bryonville and the safety and sanity of Cesar's car. Kay seemed to be sneaking the speed up a little more. Did she hate him that much? Now his breath was coming in great ragged gasps. And then he stopped. Some safety circuit somewhere in his system finally tripped a switch, and a message came through loud and clear: "Stop or die."

Cesar pulled over to the side, fighting for his life with huge, wracking, involuntary gasps of warm and sticky air. Sweat began to pour from his scalp and his ears and neck, draining into his armpits and soaking the speedy-looking new racing singlet. His stomach was heaving, and there was the distinct possibility that he might throw up. Cesar was barely aware that he was standing in the spiffy little front yard of an insurance company. He simply knew that he did not want to throw up on himself or his expensive new shoes, so he bent where he stood, over a neatly trimmed hedge that lined the insurance building under a large plate-glass window. His stomach churned and heaved as he waited. In his agony he sensed someone watching him, and he lifted his head to come eyeball to eyeball with a horrified secretary standing in the insurance window. She flicked the backs of her hands at him the way she might shoo away a dog dumping on the grass. Cesar, with superhuman effort, clamped down on the spasms and got off the grass. Kay Gallery was nearly a block away and had just noticed that she was alone. She was turning around and beginning to walk back. Cesar found a tree and leaned on it with one arm, clutching his stomach with the other. He bent over and waited, but the crisis seemed to have passed. Someone honked long and loud. He looked up to see Detective Carole Griesel driving slowly down the street watching him. "Are you all right?" she shouted, without coming to a stop. He nodded weakly. "You look like you're dying," she said. Cesar mustered enough strength to flip her a bird and she peeled away. He knew she was laughing like a hyena, and he knew that she would talk of nothing else for days.

"I'm sorry," said Kay as she reached him. "I got carried away. Are you going to make it?" Cesar nodded feebly. "Come on. We'll walk for a while." Kay laid her cool hand on Cesar's bicep, which was vibrating like an off-balance refrigerator, and she began to steer him back toward O'Bryonville. "I know you feel awful." Kay looked for forgiveness in his eyes, but he was far from ready to send any message other than acute distress. "It's too hot. You're not acclimatized." Something new to have to worry about.

The immediate dangers of vomit, stroke, and heart attack began to recede as Kay and Cesar walked slowly along. In their place came alternate waves of panic and rage and embarrassment and new sensations of pain, disorientation, and breakdown. His biceps continued to shake, and somewhere in the backs of his thighs he felt rats gnawing at muscle fiber. His knees throbbed. A blood vessel in his neck suggested that it might be about to burst, spewing blood into his esophagus and drowning him.

"Feeling better?" asked Kay.

"Yeah," said Cesar. "I just got kind of winded there for a minute." Why was he lying? What had happened to his sense of self-preservation? If he didn't handle this right he might give the impression that he would consider running with her again sometime.

"It won't be so bad next time," said Kay. "I promise."

12

Cesar and Kay walked slowly in the shade of the big trees on Madison Road until they reached a little park where Kay turned off the sidewalk and led him to a bench where they sat side by side. Cesar's breathing was back to normal and he no longer felt like vomiting, but his clothes were soaked with sweat and he suspected that he was glowing beet red.

"I'm sorry I did that to you," Kay said.

"It's OK."

Kay picked up Cesar's wrist again, and even though he knew why she was doing it this time, he felt his pulse and blood pressure pick up. "Still a little fast," said Kay. "The more you run, the slower it'll get." She kept hold of his wrist and then slipped her hand into his, and he started to breathe heavily again. Now that his vision was clear and he was no longer concentrating on his pain and terror, Cesar was once again aware that he was in a state of undress next to a beautiful reporter in equal undress. His pulse picked up even more. He hoped she couldn't feel it.

"How are your shoes?" she asked. He wondered if they were now never going to talk about anything except running.

"Great," he said.

"You need to sort of break them in for a while. Not too many miles a day."

"For sure." He had no plans to ever run again.

"You should wear them to work. They'll get loosened up."

"I'm afraid I'll trip over stuff. Can we talk about your brother?"

"OK." She pulled her hand away, but he got it back.

"Was he friends with Dr. Poe?"

"Not really. They were very different, you know. And Don was ahead of Mike in school."

"How come he's in that picture?" asked Cesar. He had assumed that everyone was the same age.

"Mike got into the senators early. They wanted him. And actually Don Poe probably wasn't in school anymore when that was taken. He left early, too."

"Left where?"

"Saint Julian. He left after his junior year. He had enough credits to graduate, so he went on to college and finished there in three years too. He was a fantastic student." Kay's expression showed a low opinion of fantastic students. "He wanted to get into med school as quickly as he could so he could start making money."

"Did he?"

"Oh, he got into med school all right. He had terrific grades in high school and college. And he apparently did really well in med school too, even though he was two years younger than everybody in his class. But he didn't start making money as fast as he wanted to. He had to do time in the army. Mike said he had gotten some sort of scholarship, something that meant he had to put time in. His family didn't have any money. I guess now he could have gotten out of it, but it was different then. There was still the draft. Of course his service time was a lot different from Mike's."

Cesar looked to see how she was taking this, ready to stick in a different topic if necessary. But she seemed to be all right.

"He spent his time doing physicals right here in the city at the AFEES station." She didn't explain what AFEES stood for, but Cesar knew, since he had been through it. The Armed Forces Entrance Examination Station. "You can imagine the kind of danger he was in," she said drily. "Are you ready to go back?"

Cesar, who had been thinking about his own draft physical, had to think for a moment to take in her question. The mention of the AFEES station had triggered all sorts of memories. Not painful, just long unviewed. To this day he didn't know what all the doctors and nurses and corpsmen had been looking for as they had him and the other assorted felons, morons, and wiseacres stoop, bend, cough, spit, and bleed. And there hadn't even been AIDS to look for back then.

"Sure," he said, heaving himself off the bench, hanging on to her hand. "But this has been great. It really has." Kay laughed as she let him pull her up. It was like lifting a feather, she was so light and so well coordinated. She bumped easily against him, but she didn't stay around. She headed for the sidewalk, which tripped Cesar as he followed her. "It's these damned shoes. Are you sure they're OK? I feel like Herman Munster. They're so thick."

"Yes, they're fine. You just have to get used to them. Believe me, Rick Albers wouldn't wear anything less than the best."

*   *   *

Cesar changed back into his clothes in the Fast Track
dressing room. He had let Kay go first, and there had been an
awkward farewell in the shop area when she came out in her
unwrinkled reporter's clothes while he stood in his soaking
wet shorts and singlet. She said she was going home for a
quick shower and then back to the Poe house. He said OK.
They stood looking at each other, wondering what was next.
Cesar said he'd better get dressed and she agreed. He said
he'd see her on the job and she said OK. He said it had been
a great run and she laughed. He went into the changing room,
sticking his head out to say good-bye, but she was already
striding toward the front door.

Cesar nearly fell over trying to put dry underwear on his
wet sticky body. He couldn't remember the last time he had
felt like such a human scumbag, and wondered why the Fast
Track offered no shower. He couldn't wait to get out of the
oppressive dressing room with its collection of posters of the
lean and fastest. The posters might have been bearable if
there hadn't also been a full-length mirror to offer cruel
comparison. Snatches of conversation reached his ears from
the sales floor, where clerks and customers discussed miles
per week and minutes per mile. Without Kay there, the place
no longer made any sense to Cesar and he wanted nothing
more than to get clear of the shop and never return.

Dressed at last, he made his way out, nodding and
mumbling to the smiling clerks, holding his wet clothing and
running shoes in a dripping bundle that started to disassem-
ble as he grappled with the door. One of the clerks jumped
up, grabbed a plastic Fast Track bag, handed it to Cesar, and
politely held the door open as Cesar picked up the damp
socks and shirt from the floor and stuffed them into the bag.
"Heh-heh," Cesar said, wishing the door would close on the
clerk and kill him.

Cesar opened the trunk of the Camaro, unashamed now
that he was alone, and threw his expensive new clothes into

the middle of the rotting mass in the trunk. The ripening smell of the running clothes mingled with the musty odors kicked up by the impact and slid into his nostrils like the fumes from an August corpse. He slammed the trunk lid down and promised himself to trade the car in without ever opening it again. He got into the Camaro, an oven in the midafternoon sun, rolled down the windows, and started the engine. But he turned the engine off before putting the car in gear. There was something he wanted to check.

Cesar went back into the Fast Track. "Forget something?" asked one of the clerks. Cesar shook his head and mumbled, heading for the display he had knocked over earlier. He stood for a moment looking at the gigantic and tiny versions of his own new shoes, and then went farther back in the store to look for a moment at the photographs. Mumbling again at the clerks, he left the store for good.

"Gus, did you take a shower today?" Lillian Franck stood about six feet behind her son as he squatted on the floor. He was going through the stack of newspapers.

"Yeah," he answered, discarding an Elder Beerman insert in distaste. A healthy lad in a sweat-free running outfit grinned cockily up at him. He covered the boy with a Swallens section.

"Well, what have you been doing?" Lillian sounded as if she didn't believe Cesar.

"Working." He flipped through a sports section even though he was pretty sure that what he wanted was in the Metro section.

"Well, Gus, I hate to have to put it this way, but I don't know how else to tell you. You don't smell too good." Cesar's reply was a noninformative grunt. "I just thought you ought to know. It'll be in your clothes." Another grunt. He had found the Metro section, and he stood up, rereading the article he had sought. "What did you do to make yourself sweat like that?"

"Ran," he mumbled.

"You did?" Mrs. Franck was not happy with the answer. "Why? You don't run."

"I know." Cesar continued to scan the article.

"They say that's the worst thing for you, you know. That guy who ran, he's dead. Did you see that?"

"I'm the one who told you about it." Cesar finally looked up at his mother in exasperation.

"Not him," said Lillian, getting testy. "I'm not talking about Dr. Poe. That other guy. The one who wrote all those books about running and then dropped dead."

"I don't know what you're talking about."

"Just like that. Without any warning. So what are you doing running? He was in good shape."

Cesar thought things must be pretty bad indeed if his own mother was suggesting that maybe he wasn't in the best shape. "Yeah, well, it was just this one time and it was sort of in the line of duty. I won't be doing it anymore."

"Good." Lillian was more or less satisfied. "Although I just read that they say exercise is for sure the reason whether you die or not."

"That makes a lot of sense."

"I'm just telling you what I read. If you exercise, you're going to live longer."

"You just told me I shouldn't be running. What do you want me to do?" Cesar, clutching his newspaper, started to edge from the kitchen, wondering if his mother was starting to fray a little at the edges.

"Your father didn't exercise at all. That wasn't popular back then. We were eating the wrong things." She shook her head and stared thoughtfully at the toaster. "Of course it was what he wanted to eat. Meat and potatoes. And cabbage. But I tell you, Gus, I read this stuff and sometimes I start to feel like a murderer."

"Well, ma, that's crazy." Cesar didn't want to hear any more dietary nonsense. If anybody in the family knew murder when he saw it, it was him, and he didn't think his mother had intentionally packed his father's blood vessels with cholesterol. "I'm going to take a shower," he said over his shoulder, making his escape to the bathroom.

"Make sure you use the Dial," was Lillian's last advice.

Thirty minutes later, clean and freshly clothed, Cesar was back in the Camaro and on the way to Ezzard Charles Drive where the police division had its headquarters. He wanted to sit at his desk in an empty office. If he stayed at home he would fall asleep. The newspaper sat next to him in the passenger seat, and he had transferred the photograph of the St. Julian senators to his clean shirt.

But the office was not empty. Although all of the desks in the outer office were vacant, there was a light on in Lt. Tieves's room. Knowing that he would have to reveal his presence sooner or later, Cesar opted for sooner, to have it over with, and he stuck his still damp head into the lieutenant's immaculate chamber. "Evening, lieutenant," he said in what he hoped was a casual voice that would get him out quickly.

"Where have you been?" asked Lt. Tieves, causing Cesar to go cold. The question told him that Lt. Tieves was not there just to dust and polish. He was there to deal with Cesar. "I'm working on those cases in North Avondale." There was always the hope that depersonalizing the Poes would keep the lieutenant off the subject. No such luck.

"Cases?" asked Lt. Tieves, accentuating the plural.

"Yes, sir. It seems that Dr. Poe's wife and her—"

"I know what you're talking about. What I don't see is any paperwork on a second and third homicide. What I haven't heard is any oral report on a second or third homicide. So what I want to know now is why? Is there some reason you want to keep me in the dark about what is most assuredly my business?"

"No, sir. I didn't—"

"If it weren't for the fact that I happen to know a couple of persons from the Channel Three news organization, I wouldn't know anything more than I did the last time I saw you. Is that the kind of communication I've encouraged?"

"No, sir."

"You're damned right it's not. Now can you confirm whether I've heard correctly? Was Mrs. Poe found in a compromising position?"

"Well, she was found deceased, sir." Cesar hadn't meant to be flip, just accurate. But the already irritable lieutenant narrowed his eyes and flexed his jaw muscles, so Cesar hurriedly added, "But you would have to say that she was deceased in a compromising position. That's pretty clear. She and a male Caucasian who was also her neighbor, and according to another neighbor, her boyfriend, were deceased and undressed in her hot tub."

"That's incredible. Incredible," said Lt. Tieves, shaking his head. Cesar knew that the lieutenant had seen a lot stranger things, and wondered which aspect was giving him trouble. "There's Don, still on a slab in the morgue. Dead less than twenty-four hours, and she can't wait a decent interval to get into the sack with someone else. Disgusting." Technically it wasn't the sack, but Cesar didn't think he'd correct his boss. Tieves was a little moody. "So what are you doing about the burglar? Does this MO match up with anyone we're looking for?"

"Burglary?" asked Cesar.

"Yes, burglary," snapped Lt. Tieves. "No thanks to you, I happen to know that there are some valuable objects missing from the house."

Cesar wondered how he knew. It seemed unlikely that Henry would have volunteered information. He counted on Cesar to negotiate with the lieutenant, an arrangement that suited the lieutenant just as well. "Sir, I know there are some things missing, specifically some rugs and a picture, but that's not necessarily a burglary." Lt. Tieves glared at Cesar, unhappy to be contradicted. Cesar hurriedly suggested that Christa Poe might have been getting things ready for the cleaner and maybe even ready to sell. Lt. Tieves looked increasingly disbelieving. Cesar started to explain his theory about Mrs. Poe's possible plan to keep anything of value out of the hands of Dr. Poe's baby, which sounded worse in the telling than it did in the thinking, but it got quite a reaction from the lieutenant. "What the hell are you talking about. What baby? Don didn't have any baby."

So Cesar had to explain the whole business of the dermatologist's biracial baby and then the lieutenant wanted to hear about Christa Poe's binational boyfriend. It was an hour before he finally set Cesar free, an hour in which Cesar became increasingly sure that Lt. Tieves had something else on his mind. And whatever it was was gnawing at the man. Cesar, who wanted to make Lt. Tieves happy so that he could get out of there, had no way of knowing whether the something else was something having to do with the homicides at hand and, if it was, whether it was something Cesar could help with. Did he know something the lieutenant wanted to know but couldn't ask? Or was it that the lieutenant knew something that Cesar wanted to know but didn't know enough to ask. Whatever it was that was eating the man was still at work when he at last dismissed Cesar.

Cesar didn't have to be told twice to leave, but as soon as he was out the door he had a feeling he should have stayed and helped his boss out. So instead of leaving, he went to his desk and pulled out report forms and started writing, hanging around for a while just in case.

And a few minutes later, Lt. Tieves came to his door and stared over at Cesar. Cesar smiled nervously and went back to his forms. "Detective Griesel says she say you out running today," said the lieutenant.

She probably got on the first telephone she saw. Hell,

she could have put it out on the police radio. Someday she would die.

"Yes, sir."

"While you were supposedly investigating these homicides."

Oh, shit.

"Yes, sir."

"That's good. Good. Keep it up. You'll drop that pot in a month."

"Oh, that would be great, sir." Worse and worse. Not only was Cesar sure that this was just a preamble to something else, something troubling, but he felt he had just committed to further running to please the lieutenant. Would it please the lieutenant if he suffered cardiac arrest?

"Who were you with?"

"Sir?"

"When you were on your run? I understand you were with a woman."

"Yes, sir." Something in the Tieves's voice told Cesar that they were now onto the subject that had been lurking since the time he walked into the office.

"Anyone I know?"

"I don't know, sir."

"Damn it, Franck, who *was* it?"

"A reporter, sir. Kay Gallery." The reporter business was in there to depersonalize the situation. But it seemed to make it worse.

"That's what I heard, but I didn't believe it. How could you do something like that?"

"Sir?"

"Fraternize with a reporter. In the middle of an investigation."

"She was upset, sir."

"So fucking what! What's that got to do with anything?" Cesar now felt like he was somewhere out in the middle of a quaking bog, where any step he might take could lead to his doom. Lt. Tieves normally made it a big point never to swear or use profanity since it didn't fit in with his image of the fittest, fastest-rising cop in Ohio. But he was as close to out of control as Cesar had ever seen him.

"I felt responsible sir. I was the one who upset her."

"Oh, you did? And what the hell did you do? And who the hell cares what the fuck you say to a goddamned reporter?" Lt. Tieves was leaning in over Cesar's desk, forcing the detective to lean back farther than he liked in his crapped-out chair. He hoped there was not going to be one of those stupid accidents.

"Sir, I accidentally reminded her of her brother who had been killed in Vietnam, and she wasn't prepared for it. They were very close." Cesar got it out as fast as he could.

Lt. Tieves turned white. He stared at Cesar. "Who. He's not . . . she's not . . . is her brother, is he Red Gallery? Mike?"

"Mike Gallery. Yes, sir. I guess . . . I guess you know him. Knew him?"

"Knew him? Yes, I did. I can't believe I didn't know that was his sister. She's the one on Channel Three?" Cesar nodded.

Cesar sat without moving, trying to read his boss's face, crazy to survive. Fortunately the lieutenant seemed to be decompressing, leading Cesar to hope that he would live another day.

"You're sure about that?" Tieves's glare bored into Cesar's eyes and Cesar nodded, not a hundred percent sure it was safe to talk. "In that case—" Tieves's voice sounded tentative. He almost looked as if he had forgotten what he had been so angry about, straightening up and staring out over Cesar's head. Cesar found that he was still leaning back in his dangerous chair and let himself back down as quietly as possible, not wanting to annoy. But even when a spring somewhere in the chair let out a grinding squeal Lt. Tieves seemed not to notice.

By the time the chair was upright Cesar had figured out that the reason he was no longer in trouble for talking to the reporter was because she was the sister of a senator, and wasn't that some shit? Not for the first time, the detective cursed the fates that had denied him a Catholic family or, at the very least, a black family that could have gotten a scholarship to St. Julian's.

He leaned forward in his chair in an effort to get completely out of Lt. Tieves's sight. As he did so, he noticed that the chair was not completely on an even keel, having landed on a pencil or something. Still trying to be invisible, Cesar tried a little sideways pressure to bring it all the way down, but the chair wasn't quite read to roll. Cesar looked down and found that he had somehow managed to land on the edge of the lieutenant's mirror-polished Johnston & Murphy bluchers. A nauseating web of tiny scratches where the foot of Cesar's chair had scraped the many layers of Kiwi stood out like Gorbachev's birthmark.

Jesus.

You can do anything, but lay off of them spitshined shoes. Was it possible to get out of this? Did the lieutenant know? Was it too late to change careers? Cesar looked up in time to see that the lieutenant was starting to move his head down to see what Cesar was staring at.

"FWWWAAAHHHHBBAH!!"

Desperation had driven Cesar to try to fake sneeze while simultaneously leaning his chair back, but in one of those lucky coincidences the sneeze turned real in midstream, so he had a real legitimate reason to yank open a desk drawer. He needed a tissue bad. Fortunately there was a wad of Frisch's napkins back in the drawer containing his pretty good collection of fast food condiments. He had ripped off a good handful the last time he had a cold.

Cesar began blowing his nose with an apologetic upward glance. Bad news. The lieutenant was staring down at his shoes. Cesar followed his glance.

And then, as he stared at the ruined gloss, something that had been nagging at his brain for hours at last came in to focus. He stared back up at the lieutenant, his mind working furiously, his jaw hanging stupidly slack.

"Excuse me, sir," he said, and he stood up at his desk, absentmindedly sliding the condiment drawer home.

"Cesar—" the lieutenant began.

"Excuse me, sir," Cesar interrupted, backing away. He needed to get out of the room and away from the impending blowup to a quiet place where he could make some sense of the sudden dump of new information into his consciousness, and he continued to back away from the flabbergasted Lt. Tieves until he was near the door, whereupon he turned away and bolted into the hall, heading for the front lobby.

Ten minutes later, Cesar was driving west on River Road, thinking. He had left District One in something of a fog, the suddenly synthesized information screaming for his total attention. He was just enough aware of his place in the universe to stop at the soda machine and get a can of Coke and then, considering how much he had to consider, another. The first Coke now sat with its top popped in the plastic rack that hung from the door near his left knee. The second rode in the passenger seat as the car twisted through the endless curves and lumped through the endless bumps of the nearly empty highway. From time to time he eased the Coca-Cola from its holster for a long, thoughtful swig, but he never took his eyes from the road. He cruised along a little under the speed limit, obeying the traffic signals without really seeing them.

So far he had figured out that he needed to break into the city personnel office and peek at some files. If this realization of his was sound, and every instinct told him that it was, he was going to have to have some paper to back it up. And if there was going to be any paper that would back him up that he could get to without getting a search warrant or running up against the bureaucracy of the United States Department of Defense, that paper stood the best chance of being found close at hand in city hall. It would also, since this was a weekend, be locked up tight as a drum. What a pisser. He drove along, rejecting possibilities. The maintenance crew was incorruptible. He couldn't go through Lt. Tieves. He wasn't ready to submit to the grilling Sgt. Evans would make him undergo. And he didn't have a girl in the personnel department.

But Henry did. Sure. The only city department with which Henry had not been able to establish at least one ardent relationship was purchasing, where for some reason they hated his guts.

Cesar pulled into the nearby empty parking lot of Al's A&C Inn and went into the tavern to use the phone. The skinny, greasy-haired bartender, who might have been Al but was probably Rudi, was watching "Soul Train" by himself. There wasn't a customer in the place. When Cesar asked where the phone was, the bartender pulled out a desk set from under the bar and set it on the counter without taking his eyes off the screen.

It took some calling around, but Cesar finally reached Henry at his cousin Dorothy's house in Silverton. When Henry at last came to the phone, Cesar walked out to the end of the cord and stood in the middle of the empty tavern so he could mumble into the phone without being heard. With his back to the bartender he got Henry to admit that he did in fact know a girl with whom he had some influence in the personnel department. Once that was established, Henry made Cesar explain every last detail that had led him to make the request he was now making, and that took some time. Cesar stood holding the telephone and praying for cooperation while Henry considered the matter.

"Job applications?" Henry asked in the middle of a silent stretch.

"Right. I'll bet you five bucks."

"No bet. You're probably right. You all apply for anything."

Cesar didn't answer that. He didn't know for sure that it wasn't true.

"Right now?" asked Henry. "Why can't you wait?"

"Come on," said Cesar. "Will you or won't you?"

"Not up to me," said Henry. "I'm not the one to get in the office. That's up to Leila, and I got no idea if she's even in town."

"But you'll try?" Cesar kept the natural begging whine out of his voice.

"I don't know," said Henry. "I'll see."

Cesar thanked him a lot and told him he would call back in twenty minutes to see what Henry had come up with. He handed the phone back to the bartender.

"You want to wait here to call back?" asked the bartender. It took a minute for Cesar to realize that the man had turned off the sound on the television where the "Soul Train" dancers now writhed in silence. He was leaning on the bar where he had been frankly listening for God knows how long.

"No, thanks," said Cesar. He couldn't be too pissed. It was a public place. Still, he wondered how much the guy had heard.

"You on the police?" asked the bartender. Cesar nodded. "You know an officer named Mike Diehl?"

"Sure." Not well. But he knew who he was. Kind of dumb.

"He's my nephew." Cesar waited to hear anything the guy might want to say about his nephew, that probably being the price for using the phone, but the bartender turned away from him and turned the sound back on the television without saying anything. Maybe all he was looking for was proof that his nephew wasn't lying about his occupation. You never knew.

Cesar spent the twenty minutes he had allowed Henry in an antsy drive up and down River Road and over the ferry to Kentucky. The first phone was at a scabrous marina with a driveway that dropped like a rock and clawed away several pounds of rust from the bottom of the car. Cesar dialed Henry with considerable excitement, reading the numbers and initials gouged into the enamel on the sturdy prebreakup phone without comprehension. The telephone rang and rang at Henry's house. Not even the answering machine was home. Finally he remembered that Henry was at his cousin Dorothy's. Cesar rummaged through his pockets until he came up with the pink message slip holding what he believed was Cousin Dorothy's number.

Henry answered on the second ring.

"She'll do it," he said.

"Great." Cesar breathed his relief.

"It'll cost you."

"A lot?"

"Could of been worse. You know what Joy is?"

"Who?" asked Cesar.

"I didn't think you would. It's perfume. I told her I'd get her some. A lot, if she'd get moving and get down to city hall. She's on her way, so you better find yourself a bottle of Joy."

Cesar could not believe what had just happened. He had just spent more on the little bottle of Joy in his hand than he had spent on any date he could remember until the night he talked Marge Froschauer into spending the night in Louisville, and even then he had steered her toward coffee shoppes. The clerk at Lazarus considered the purchase important enough to read the name off his charge plate, which had happened only once before in his life and that was because the lady in small appliance repairs had been smart enough to catch the resemblance to his mother.

Gripping the shit out of the perfume box, he walked from Lazarus over to the side entrance at city hall, where he found Henry standing on the sidewalk chewing a toothpick.

"Have you got it?" asked Cesar. Henry waggled the toothpick to indicate that he had not. "Is she here?" asked Cesar. The toothpick went up and down. "Can we go in?" asked Cesar.

"What for?" A question the toothpick could not ask.

"I don't know. To see what she's doing. Maybe she needs help. Don't you think she might need help? Are the files in the basement? Maybe they're boxed up."

"Relax. She knows what she's doing."

"OK," said Cesar, although he did not want to relax. He wanted to have the application forms in his hand. He wanted to know they existed for sure. He wanted to see what he knew had to be there.

"Is that the Joy?" asked Henry, with a glance at Cesar's hand.

Cesar had forgotten the costly little package. He lifted it now and looked at it as if trying to figure out what it might be. The bag had gotten crumpled and sweaty.

"Did you get it gift-wrapped?" asked Henry.

"No. I forgot."

"Give it here." Henry took the tired little bag and pulled it away from the box containing the perfume bottle. The box was covered in platinum colored foil. Maybe it actually was platinum. God knows it cost enough. Henry stuck the box in his shirt pocket, pulled the charge slip out of the bag, read it, whistled softly, smiled, and returned the bag and slip to Cesar.

"What about the perfume?" asked Cesar.

"That's for her," said Henry.

"I know. I want to give it to her."

"No. She thinks it's from me."

"She does? Does that mean you're paying for it?"

The toothpick waggled from side to side.

"Any of it?" asked Cesar, who knew the answer. Henry just smiled.

Before Cesar could tell Henry what a cheap son of a bitch he was the door opened at the top of the granite stairs and the lovely Leila slipped out. She wore an orange blouse, tight black pants, high heels, and a turban, and in her left hand she held a file folder.

"You better take a look at this and make sure I got the right stuff, Junebug. I don't want to have to come back here again until it's time to go to work." She handed the file folder to Henry and smiled coolly at Cesar. Henry opened the folder, but he didn't know for sure what he was looking for, he had to hand it to Cesar. Just as Cesar started to look, there was a sharp squeal from Leila, who had opened the platinum foil box and found the Joy. She hugged Henry and planted a big kiss on his forehead, which was where her lips reached if she didn't bend over. Cesar looked back at the application.

Leila had done her job correctly. He was holding a Xerox copy of the application he had requested. He read it through slowly, not coming to what he had hoped to find until he had moved from the application to the supporting documents. There was the statement. And it was signed by Dr. Donald Poe.

Cesar read it through once again to make sure that he had seen what he had seen. He had. He looked to tell Henry that they had scored, but Henry was not there.

Soft squeals sounded behind Cesar. He looked around to see that Henry had maneuvered the delectable Leila around to the driver's door of her Prelude where she more or less stood, having wrapped herself comfortably around the corpulence of Cesar's partner whose ear she was now chewing. There was another, sharper squeal as Henry tickled her, which made her let go long enough for him to slip her into the car. She made him give her a big kiss through the window before pulling away in the direction of the expressway. Henry walked past his big Lincoln on his way to rejoin Cesar.

"This is it, Henry. She got the right stuff. We're in business," said Cesar.

"I know. I watched you read it. Now what you gonna do with it?" asked Henry.

And Cesar told him.

13

don't know, Cesar. I've got to see where I stand with this thing before I tell you about it." Kay's voice on the telephone was heavy with what sounded like grief. "I've been thinking so much about everything. About Red. About Don. I just don't know. Or maybe I know too much."

"Are they still there?" Cesar asked her.

"I guess I just want to be alone for a while. I have to think about this some more. I know you don't want to hear this but I think I have to sort of run it out."

"You're right," said Cesar. "I'm hurting."

"I mean that I just have to put in some miles by myself," said Kay.

"Can you stay on for a while? He's not—"

The door behind Cesar opened to admit Lt. Tieves, who looked curiously at his detective.

"Evening, lieutenant," Cesar said over his shoulder.

"That's good," said Kay.

"You working?" asked Tieves, glaring.

"Yes, sir. Be right off, sir." Cesar returned his attention to the telephone. "I can't get away," he said. "I don't think you should be running there by yourself, Kay. It's dangerous. I don't think there's any part of it that's safe. Especially not by the lake."

"I just know that if I can put all this information in my head it's going to drop into place," said Kay at her end.

"I don't care how many people are there," said Cesar. "Those aren't people who can help you. They're dangerous."

"It's just the idea that a doctor would *lie* like that. For something so important. I guess that's really naive, isn't it? Are you surprised?"

"So what," said Cesar. "I don't care how many times you've run through there. There's gonna be a time when somebody wants to do something to you and you're not gonna be able to stop him. You've got no protection at all."

"No, I don't know how Red got hold of it. Or why. Or why he kept it."

"Kay, the park police don't count for nothing. It's the truth. Especially in Eden Park."

"All I can figure is that Don sent it to him as some kind of insurance," said Kay.

"I know. I wish I could. But I already promised, and she would know. I've got to be there. Just run in place, OK?"

"No. I've told you all I'm going to tell you. When I know what I want to do about it, then I'll tell you who it is. You'll just have to wait."

"Do you have a whistle? Carry a whistle, then, all right? And run fast. I know you can do that. All right?" Cesar smiled stupidly over the telephone at his boss.

"I promise. You'll be the first person I tell. I won't do anything without telling you first."

"Just remember what I told you, Kay," said Cesar.

"Of course," answered Kay, answering Cesar at last, "I'll be very careful."

"I hope so, Kay. No shit. I really hope so."

"I'll talk to you later, Cesar."

"Yeah. Good night."

Cesar hung up the phone feeling somewhat smutty. He had found it easy but uncomfortable to pretend concern when he was plenty worried but in a way he didn't want to show. He looked up at Lt. Tieves, who had been listening openly. Lt. Tieves probably thought himself pretty much of an actor, but he was unable to disguise the intense interest that lit up and narrowed his eyes.

"Was that Kay Gallery?" he asked Cesar.

"Yes, sir."

"Were you trying to keep her from going out?"

"Yes, sir. She's what you'd call serious. I mean she's a serious runner."

"But she runs alone at night? That's extremely dangerous."

"I know. I tried to tell her, but she seems to think Eden Park is pretty overrated as a trouble spot. She runs there a lot. I guess I should have dug up some of the statistics for her."

"You probably wouldn't have convinced her."

"I would have felt better."

"You did what you could. She's not going out real late, is she?" asked Lt. Tieves in his version of a casual voice. Cesar thought the lieutenant might lose the circulation in his knuckles permanently if he leaned any harder on Cesar's desk. The long fingers had gone white all over.

"After she gets off work. About eleven."

"She'll be all right. As long as she sticks to the sidewalks and doesn't try any short cuts. The vehicular traffic is still heavy at that hour. Are you through here?"

In lieutenant talk that meant that Tieves wanted him out of his sight.

"Leaving now, sir. Just checking over some stuff about the Poes."

"Great. Give me a full report in the morning."

Get your ass out of here before I throw it out.

Cesar swept the notes from his desk top into the kneehole drawer and locked up. They were mostly messages from Henry's friends, but Cesar thought it looked like work to any but the most skilled eye.

As he left the room he turned his head far enough to confirm that Lt. Tieves had made a beeline for the phone in his office, where he was now talking with his back to the door. Cesar slipped on out.

"Chirrrupp!" sang the fake bird. Or frog. Cesar, reared in the city and never one for nature walks, did not know enough about wild life to be able to say what he was supposed to be hearing. "Chirruppp!" Maybe it wasn't supposed to be a bird or a frog. Maybe it was supposed to be an insect like a cricket. Whatever the perky chirp was supposed to sound like, it didn't take a team of Audubon experts to know that the chirp was a fake chirp. For one thing, the warbler was throwing way too much expression in. Or emotion. The guy sounded like an old-fashioned cartoon bird the way he was carrying on.

Now the fake bird or frog that was throwing out *his* chirps from the bush about twenty feet to the other side of Cesar was doing a better job of it. At least he was if he was supposed to be sounding like an act of nature. He didn't seem to be throwing too much message in. And he actually had a pretty authentic-sounding warble when he really got going. What Cesar didn't know was whether authenticity counted in this particular game.

It had taken him too long to figure out that it was a game.

According to the deal he had set up with Kay Gallery, a deal that had gone from seeming sort of hotshot to seeming pretty solidly half-assed in record time, he was sitting in the dark under a bush near the mirror lake in Eden wearing nylon shorts, a T-shirt, and his new gym shoes, the ones that cost more than a night in a good hotel, waiting for Kay and possibly someone else to come running past. Now, between chirps, it was dawning on him that instead of being who they had in mind, the someone else could just as easily be an uninvolved axe murderer unaware of Cesar's theory that he and Kay could get their suspect to bridge the gap between an embarrassing lie in the suspect's buried past and several recently committed murders if he would correctly overhear and interpret a staged telephone conversation, feel threatened, and seize an opportunity presented in that bogus discussion to remove Kay and her knowledge of evidence sent by the late Don L. Poe to Kay's late brother. Well, they'd just have to handle the axe murderers on an ad hoc basis.

The immediate problem was in the spot they had picked for their athletic sting. Cesar had parked his car in the closest allowable spot, which turned out to be farther away than he had planned. He had jogged from the car, his leg muscles screaming all the way, until he turned off the sidewalk and onto the footpath leading into one of the many groves of trees that studded the park, at which point he had given up all pretense of being a runner and had started to trudge. And as soon as he stopped running and started trudging, he started picking up these chirps, which he took at first to be authentic sounds of nature. He might have believed a little longer if one of the chirpers hadn't coughed in the middle of a chirp. Also, it seemed to him that in your usual natural kingdom, the creatures of the woodland shut up when Mr. Man came around, but Cesar's presence seemed to be setting off the warblers like a lot of oversensitive burglar alarms.

He was probably so slow on the take because he had his mind on Kay and what he had set her up to do. He wondered if he was about to kiss his career good-bye. You never knew. If it worked, he would be all right. If it didn't . . . anyway it at last registered that there was a hell of a lot of pedestrian traffic, which was not something he or Kay had planned on.

And they were all guys. Well, you wouldn't expect women out in the park in the dark the way things were. And not only were they all guys, but they kept giving Cesar these funny looks. Really intense—like they thought they recognized him, or maybe like he might hit them. Geez, he was the last guy to want to mug somebody. And then he started to pay attention and it finally dawned on him that there had been an unusual concentration of earrings, tight shirts, and tank tops on the strollers.

Cripes.

Of all places to pick out for a rendezvous. It was a homo hotspot. It had to be.

It was.

As soon as he realized what he had wandered into, Cesar tried to figure how to wander out. But there was no way to reach Kay, who was probably on her way here. She might even be in the park. So he had gone off the path to find a place where he could watch everyone going past without getting confused with the shoppers. But as soon as he stepped off the path there was a big "CHHHIIIRRRUPPP?!" right at his elbow that about scared the shit out of him so that he fell back a step. And then the chirper stood up and revealed himself as a skinny guy with glasses and a tank top who looked like he thought Cesar might possibly kill him.

So Cesar said, "How's it going?" thinking it might defuse the situation, and the guy said, "Great" in what you would have to call a gay voice no matter what the human relations counselor said, so Cesar charged on past like he was on his way to work or the bathroom. He could feel the guy's eyes on the back of his neck as he strode vigorously along the path, banging his feet on the exposed roots of the surrounding trees until he executed a manly right-face into what he hoped to God was an empty spot where he could hide unmolested.

So, wouldn't you know, now he had to take a leak. It was the coffee he had last thing before he set out, thinking it would give him that competitive edge. What it had done was put an edge on his paranoia and terminal pressure on his bladder now that he was in a spot where exposing himself to take a leak would expose him to a misunderstanding of epic proportions. Christ.

Cesar squatted there in the gloom in increasing agony for what seemed to be hours. From time to time he pushed the light button on his cheapo digital watch to find that only a few minutes had passed. But the few-minute intervals began to add up, and as time went, the chirping around him diminished. Dispirited rustlings in the shrubbery told him that his companions were giving up and going home. He began to feel more alone than he wanted to. Soon the only sounds in the night were the background hum of the city and the occasional swoosh of a car driving somewhere through the park.

The need to take a leak had now become paramount and inescapable, but Cesar was afraid to leave his spot lest he miss Kay. Finally he had no choice. Backing through the bushes, keeping an eye on the path as long as possible, Cesar hunted as quietly as he could for a private spot.

Relieved at last, he had barely completed squaring himself away when he heard the sound of fast footsteps somewhere near and getting nearer. A wave of panic crashed over Cesar as he at first assumed the approach of one of his brother cops charging in for a roundup of the local deviates. How the hell was he going to explain his presence at this hour?

But the panic left as quickly as it had come, replaced by a huge surge of adrenaline as his senses simultaneously registered the fast lightweight footfall of a woman's running stride and the sharp, rhythmic grunts of a woman trying to call for help as she fled. It had to be Kay.

Cesar spun around, trying to fix her position on the path. Unused to the traction on his new running shoes, his feet stayed planted where they were, and he tumbled on the spot. He felt something give somewhere in his left leg at the same time that the soft underside of his arm connected with a vicious knob on a low-lying branch, and then his chin connected with the ground. His twisted legs had slipped underneath a yew limb so that as he tried to scramble back to his feet he was unable to pull them back into position and he crashed again to his stomach. The running steps were nearly on him. He twisted onto his side to look down the path in the direction of the noise and tried again to pull his feet out from under the yew.

"Kay!" He tried to call to her, but since he had knocked a fair amount of wind out of himself it was a strangled and unintelligible cry. Yet she must have heard. As she rounded a mammoth maple and scrambled up the path toward him, Kay looked right at Cesar. Her eyes were huge with fright and she was panting heavily. Cesar couldn't tell whether she knew him or not. She ran right past him. "Kay!" he tried again to yell, but it still came out strangled. He kicked furiously at the tree branch, wedging his feet in tighter. "Think!" he told himself. "Think!" The sound of new running feet began to register in his confused mind. Kay's pursuer.

Cesar tried once more to pull his feet out from under the tree, straining until his eyeballs felt like they were about to pop out of his head, until all of a sudden his left arm slipped from under him so that he fell flat on his back, a maneuver that suddenly untwisted his legs and allowed him to slide his sneakers back to the right side of the tree. He scrambled at once to his feet and gasped for breath, turning to see if Kay was still in sight.

WHOOMP.

Sacked from behind. Kay's pursuer, momentarily forgotten, had charged along the path and thrown a block that knocked Cesar a good five feet and landed him once again on his stomach.

He was stunned. His chin had connected with something on the way down and his head was reeling. There was a sudden understanding of birdies and knockout victims and then there was blackness.

Cesar came to with no idea how long he had blacked out. He scrambled again to his feet, as quickly as his addled and battered condition allowed. This time he looked behind him to make sure there was not another maniac coming through. He was alone.

What to do? Had it been hours? If so, his stupid plan might have meant the end of Kay Gallery at the hands of her pursuer. If it had been seconds she might be running along believing Cesar was hot on her trail and expecting him to save her.

Another shot of adrenaline hit his bloodstream at the thought of Kay under attack, and Cesar began to limp off in pursuit.

Somewhere ahead of him he thought he heard a strangled cry. Cesar broke into a fresh sweat and pushed his limp into a lumbering stride that accelerated as he hit a slight downslope. "Jeez!" he thought out of nowhere. "This is fast!"

And maybe he was getting fast, because now he thought he heard someone running ahead of him. Could he actually be gaining on someone? Was it possible?

The path suddenly emerged onto a narrow lawn surrounding one of the small artificial lakes in the park. Cesar swung his head, searching frantically for his quarry and his quarry's quarry. And there, at the other side of the lake, he saw them. But just for a moment. Kay had about ten yards on her pursuer before she disappeared into the dense wall of trees across the water. "Stop!" Cesar tried to shout. But he couldn't yell and run at the same time. All that got out was a "Stahg" sound. But it was enough to make the attacker look across the pond at Cesar for a moment before charging into the woods.

Who was it? Christ! Why were the lights so bad? If it had been daylight he would have known who he was after instead of just suspecting. Cesar tried to drive himself faster, leaning into the curve at the end of the lake like a track star. But he no longer felt quick. He felt like a heart attack. A big one.

Still, he had to hang on. And he did, making it around the lake and plunging into the woods where he was pretty sure the others had gone.

His night vision had been screwed up back there in the open space, and he couldn't see the path, if there was one. He began banging into trees. Was he lost? He stopped, listening for the sound of running feet. What he heard was thrashing in the underbrush somewhere in the distance. He aimed his heaving chest at the sound and tried once again to run.

He stopped once more. Footsteps ahead? Footsteps behind.

WHOOMP . . .

Once again he was on the ground. Once again he did not know how long he had been knocked out. For five seconds he lay flat on his stomach, chin in the dirt, wondering. His eyes cleared and so did his memory. He had been hit from behind again. Did he have any wind? He sucked in air with a great wheezing gasp and figured out that if he had been without air any longer than two minutes he would have been dead. Maybe he was lucky. Maybe he had just been out a couple of seconds. He traded the first wheeze for another groaning gasp and pulled himself to his feet. What was he supposed to be doing?

"Help! Oh, God, Help help help!"

That was what he was supposed to be doing. Kay was alive and she was not too far off and she was screaming. Cesar forgot his agony and crashed off in the direction of the cries.

"Help!"

"I'm coming!" shouted Cesar. "Where are you?"

"Oh, God! He's bleeding!" cried Kay from somewhere ahead of Cesar.

"Who?"

"Hurry!"

"Where are you?"

"Here!" A new note of hysteria rang in Kay's cry. It drove

Cesar faster until he at last crashed into another small clearing where, under the statue of a leading abolitionist, Kay sat astride the inert body of a man. Cesar rushed to her side. Blood streamed from her nose and spilled onto her white singlet. "Look!" she screamed. "Look!"

Cesar looked down at the face of the man on the ground. There was just enough green light from a fixture off at the edge of the clearing for him to realize that Kay had subdued and possibly killed Lt. Tieves.

"You're all right!" he shouted in Kay's face. Her eyes were open wide in what he was afraid was hysteria. "He can't hurt you." Cesar's hands groped around his body in an unconscious search for handcuffs.

"No!" shouted Kay.

"You're all right!" Cesar said in the firmest voice he could muster. His wild run was beginning to catch up with him and he was straining heavily for breath. He also thought he might puke. "You're all right!"

"No!"

"I've got him!" he told Kay, and he grabbed her shoulders in a clumsy effort to steer her away from the body of Lt. Tieves. She continued to sit on her victim.

"He's dead!" she sobbed wildly.

Cesar felt for the pulse in the lieutenant's neck and found it, slow and steady. "It's okay," he said with a big reassuring smile that fought with a new terror. What the hell was he going to do when his boss woke up? How would he arrest him? How would he charge him with murder? How could he? "You didn't kill him!"

"What?"

"You didn't kill him, Kay. You just knocked him out. Do you have a stocking?"

"No! No! I didn't. It was him! Oh, God! Where *is* he?"

It had been too much for her. She was talking nonsense. He shouldn't have confused her about the stockings. He just wanted something to tie up his boss with.

"You've got to get him!" Kay said urgently. "Now!"

"No, Kay. It's all right! you've got him! Look!"

"What? No! No, no! Cesar, that's Tieves."

"Right! You got him!"

"No! Oh! You . . . oh, no. Cesar, not *him*! He saved me! No, no, no. It was somebody else! They had a fight!"

"A mugger?"

"A runner. He was running. He caught up with me. Where . . . where were *you*?" Kay asked suddenly and with more than a hint of accusation.

"Here. I got knocked down. I got knocked out. Let's take a look at him." It seemed like a good idea to change the subject. He started to peel back Lt. Tieves's eyelid but jerked his hand back as the eyelid started to flutter and then open under its own steam. There followed a long and horrible moment as Lt. Tieves's eyes gathered focus and began to bore in on Cesar. Anger registered, and then hate, and then pain.

"Aghh!" grunted the lieutenant.

"Are you hurt, sir?" Cesar asked in a loud firm voice.

"Off!" said his supervisor.

"Sir!" said Cesar.

"Off!" said the lieutenant. And then "Aghh!" His agonized eyes raked the confused detective. At last he realized that his knee was resting on the lieutenant's chest, pinning him to the ground. He jerked it back and then realized that Kay, too, was causing pain. He grabbed her upper arm and pulled her off.

"Aghh!" said the lieutenant. One of his hands shot to the small of his back.

"Oh, God!" said Kay. "His back's broken! We broke his back!"

"Don't move, sir. Wait!" shouted Cesar. The lieutenant was now writhing and snaking a hand underneath him.

"I did!" said Tieves.

"Sir?" said Cesar.

"I got it!"

"Yes, sir." Cesar did not know what was happening but thought that the lieutenant's mind might have become unhinged when his spinal cord snapped until Tieves's hand began to pull out from under him, and Kay and Cesar gasped. It was not a spinal cord injury. It was a running shoe.

"Oh!" said Kay with a gasp. "Oh! You got it! It's his!"

"Sir. May I have it, sir?" But as Cesar reached for the shoe there was a crashing in the underbrush. He yanked the shoe away and interposed himself between the noise and Kay, holding the shoe as a weapon. Kay clutched at the stretched elastic in the waistband of his shorts.

A new figure stumbled into the clearing.

"Where the hell have you been?" asked the lieutenant.

14

Henry Chapman didn't answer. He looked at his lieutenant and his fellow detective and the television newsperson, who stood and sat in their running wear, panting and out of breath. He stared at the extra shoe that Cesar held for a moment. "He got away," Lt. Tieves answered the unspoken question. "Where were you?" he asked again.

"Right where you told me to be, sir. But I was expecting to find you where you said you would be. Was that wrong?"

Lt. Tieves ground his teeth as he pulled himself up from the grass. Cesar was afraid of a nasty scene. "We can get him now, sir," he said. "All we need is a warrant."

Lt. Tieves swung his angry glare from Henry to Cesar and back again. "And a ride, sir. We need a ride to our cars," Cesar added. "I'm sure Henry can help us with that." Henry gasped at the thought of three unwashed and sweaty bodies touching the butter soft leather of his Continental, but before he could say no, the lieutenant asked "Where is it? We've got to move out." He grabbed Henry's plump arm and began to steer the policeman in the direction he thought the car should be. Cesar took the opportunity to grab Kay's arm and follow them, carefully avoiding Henry's indignant glare.

Judge Hebenstreit had been nasty about the warrant. He didn't like having Cesar show up on his doorstep in the middle of the night and he had actually started to slam the door in Cesar's face until he recognized the still woozy Lt. Tieves. Of course, the judge was a senator, too. Not from Tieves's years, but there was still blood brother atmosphere as thick as driveway sealer once the word *senator* was mentioned. And the atmosphere got thicker when the judge learned who it was that the policemen were after. "Wasn't he—?" asked the judge, and Lt. Tieves nodded grimly. It was probably about the worst thing that could happen short of finding one of the senators at a pentecostal church.

It also didn't exactly thrill the judge to have Cesar plunk a great big sweaty running shoe on his desk when the subject of evidence came up. Cesar just wasn't thinking. He was tired and fired up at the same time and he had swung the sneaker right smack into the center of Judge Hebenstreit's pristine desk blotter. He thought Tieves was going to start screaming at him, but the lieutenant merely picked up the offending shoe and handed it back to Cesar while explaining to the judge why there was a good case for finding the mate or at least others of the same size in the closet for which they were headed. Even if the owner had had the presence of mind to throw away the mate, they were sure they could find some blood or sweat or foot powder that would effectively determine ownership. When the judge at last signed the warrant, Cesar knew that it was not because he had bought the Cinderella theory but because he trusted his fellow senator.

Not for the first time, Cesar thought about the possibility of becoming a Mason and wondered if it cost a lot.

Cesar threw a quick glance at Lt. Tieves as they rolled up the curving driveway in Hyde Park. If the lieutenant was having any second thoughts, they weren't visible in the stern expression on his lean profile. He stared dead ahead across the long hood of the Ford Cesar was driving. The police van that had been parked and waiting on Bayard Drive followed in their wake. They pulled up behind another squad car that sat empty in the drive, its uniformed team guarding the front and back of the house. By now the neighbors would have all called each other. They were sure to be watching, even though there had been no sirens or flashing lights. Cesar *felt* watched. He was glad that there were no children in the big stucco California cottage. He didn't see how children could get over something like this.

He followed the lieutenant to the door, which opened to reveal news Anchor Larry Wilmot before Tieves could push the doorbell. The anchor peered out from a well-lit hall and then flicked on a switch beside the door.

"I have a warrant, Larry," said Lt. Tieves, holding the paper in front of him.

"Oh!" said Wilmot. He managed to pack about five emotions into the single syllable. The only one Cesar believed was confusion.

"We're coming in."

"Can't you wait?" asked Wilmot.

"No." Tieves was all business.

"It doesn't seem—"

"Where—?" Tieves interrupted in irritation and Wilmot collapsed completely.

"Upstairs. In the bedroom."

Wilmot stood at the bottom of the curving staircase and stared at Cesar and Lt. Tieves as they took the stairs two at a time. Cesar looked back and saw that Wilmot's mouth was hanging open. Then he followed the lieutenant into Rick Albers's bedroom, where they found the broadcasting executive sitting on the floor, leaning against the end of his kingsize bed, still in his running wear, still wearing one shoe, the mate to which was outside in the car that the police had driven to his house. A small fortune in unoccupied sports shoes was piled up beside him on one side and a larger fortune but smaller stack of street shoes on the other. He smiled an intelligent and curious smile up at his fellow senator, but found no like response. The light in his eyes faded.

"They were all size thirteens, except some of them were even twelves and twelve and a halfs," said Cesar, spitting little bits of plaster as he spoke. He wiped his mouth with his sleeve, getting even more dust into his moustache and onto his lips. "He was going to burn them all."

"But you said he was just sitting there," said Stella. She might have gotten him a damp cloth. Normally she would have. But she was still a little angry about Cesar's long absence and the mess he had left.

Which wasn't exactly fair, given the messes she had made herself and let sit around for a lot longer.

And something about the way she was talking indicated to Cesar that her powerful woman's emotional radar had picked up dangerous signals about Kay, even though he hadn't made a big deal about her. Maybe he hadn't been able to control the eye movements or pupil dilations. That was possible. Or maybe he put out some sort of treacherous smell. But she was on to him.

"He was just sitting there because he realized there was no way he *could* burn them. You'd have to have a coal furnace."

"Why didn't he just burn the one he had on? Wasn't that the one that tied him to being in the park?"

"FSPTTTFF," said Cesar, spitting again. He had also got a chunk the size of a telephone in his left eye. If he touched it with his hands he would go blind. So he stood there blowing away bits from his lip and winking like some sort of demented lecher. Stella let out a disgusted little sigh and went to the kitchen for a damp paper towel. She handed it to him with an expression that said, "This is not because you deserve help. I just want to hear the story."

"He wanted to burn all of them *because* they were thirteens. That's the kind of guy he is. He knew that it was going to come out that they were thirteens, and that he had never worn a size fifteen shoe in his life," said Cesar after he had picked the boulder out of his eye.

"Even though that was supposed to be the reason he hadn't been in the army." Stella pursed her lips in disapproval.

"Right."

"Does that really keep you out?"

"Having feet too big?" Cesar shrugged. "Beats me. I never heard of anybody else getting 4-F for that, but I guess it's possible. Maybe they weren't making jungle boots that big. But it doesn't matter. That wasn't what kept him out. Which was what he knew was going to come out."

"Would it have?" asked Stella.

"Hell, yes," said Cesar. "I told him while we were there that I had read about his shoes in the newspaper, so even if nobody else picked up on it, I would have told somebody. Pissed me off. And I'll tell you, this guy, I'm pretty sure, is more worried about that than the homicide charge."

"But it *is* the homicide charge," said Stella.

"No, Stell. All his shoes are is the evidence. That was what made me go looking up his city job application, which was where the bullshit hypertension excuse from Dr. Poe's draft physical turned up. The whole business about the shoes is something he cooked up as a reason for not being in the service now that he's gotten interested in politics. See, he could point to his feet and then nobody would go looking for the fake physical."

"Which is what kept him out of the service."

"Right. He lied. Or his senator buddy Dr. Poe lied for him."

"And why he was blackmailing him. I told you doctors were all crooks. I tell you that all the time, but you're always saying they're so great."

"He's the first one I've ever seen blackmailing," said Cesar.

"And blackmailing for cocaine." Stella laughed a victor's laugh, which stopped suddenly as a thought that had been percolating for a while came bubbling up, catching Cesar by surprise. "But the reason you got to thinking about the city application and the phony physical was because of this newswoman you don't care anything about. Am I going to get to meet her?"

"Because of her brother. Right. I didn't . . . I don't care that much about the draft, but we were talking about her brother and he seemed like a pretty nice guy and all, you know—" Cesar snuck a peek to see what he was going to get away with. Not much. "So I guess that when we talked about how her brother got killed and when she said that Dr. Poe was doing those physicals, it started me thinking about what a stupid reason big feet were for getting out of the draft, and then I just had to figure out some way to prove that that wasn't the whole story. Or the real story."

Cesar stropped trying to work on the ceiling and let his neck flex back to normal. "Apparently he was a really mean son of a gun." He was pretty sure he had deflected the Kay questions for a while, but he wanted to be sure.

"Rick Albers?"

"Poe. You *know* he could have afforded to buy cocaine. He was a doctor. But he was mean. He got a kick out of keeping Albers under his thumb and making him do his shopping for him. And he didn't have to pay anything, so he had money for his rugs."

There was a knock at the door. "It's unlocked!" yelled

Stella. The latch rattled, but whoever it was didn't know that you had to turn it to the left, which was Stella's only security against invasion. Stella, exasperated, opened the door. It was Kay Gallery.

"Would this be where I would find Cesar Franck?"

"I know you," said Stella. She didn't sound friendly.

"I'm Kay Gallery," said Kay, holding out her hand. Stella had to shake it. She pointed to Cesar's feet on the ladder. "There he is."

"May I come in?"

"Sure."

Cesar looked aloft and wondered if he had enough upper body strength to pull himself up into the ceiling and stay there while the two women sorted things out. "Good to see you again," he said with what he hoped was not too much enthusiasm.

"Why don't you get down?" asked Stella. Cesar climbed slowly down.

"I hope you don't mind. I called your office and they said you might be here. I wanted to thank you for the tip about the footprint," said Kay to Cesar. "You didn't have to do that."

"What didn't you have to do?" asked Stella, putting out cool air like a window unit on max.

"It was another thing about those running shoes," said Cesar. "The lab got a couple of good prints at the Poes's and I let her know about it."

"They're from the night Rick Albers ran over to the Poes's house. Or that's what they think," said Kay, smiling at Stella and taking in her stained sweatshirt and Levi's at the same time. "And they're the same shoes we played Cinderella with."

"Can you believe that?" Cesar asked, a little too eagerly. Stella was checking out Kay's pristine sweatsuit and he was afraid things were going to get out of hand. "Albers ran all the way over from Hyde Park."

"I might have believed it if you had told me," said Stella.

242

"I thought I had. What we think happened is that he ran over there and that he's the one who threw the cord in the hot tub that electrocuted those two."

"That's why he ran over?"

"He's not telling—"

Kay interrupted. "But I know he went over there to look for the documentation that—"

"That this Robison woman who had Poe's baby was talking about." Cesar stepped in quickly before Kay started blabbing about how she and he had cooked up the business about her having documents she didn't have when they were trying to flush Albers. He hadn't told Stella about that, since it would sound like he had been spending even more time with Kay than he had actually told her about so far. "This Ms. Robison said that Poe used to hint to whoever it was that supplied him his coke that he was 'keeping documentation.'"

"What of?" Stella was asking him, but she had her eyes on Kay.

"Well, this is kind of stupid, but I thought he must have had some kind of receipt for cocaine or something that you don't actually get for that kind of transaction. But we think it was the postcard we found at Albers's house. He wrote to Poe from Florida saying it sure beat Vietnam and thanking him for the help."

"And what Cesar thinks is that Christa Poe actually found the postcard and called Rick about it."

"He thinks that?" asked Stella unpleasantly.

"She said she was going through his things and that she was going to act if she found something. If she did phone him, you can bet he wanted to do something about it. He must have thought he could run in and out and get the card. But then he saw the chance to do even better with the extension cord. Of course that's not going to get anywhere in court—"

"But I'm using it in my story," said Kay. There was a brief silence as Kay and Cesar independently thought about the risk they had taken in inventing even more documentation in order to suck Albers in. "I love your house. Can I see that quilt?" Cesar's head started to swim when he couldn't follow the transition.

"Help yourself."

"These stitches are fantastic. They're so small. Is it antique?"

"I did it."

"Jesus, you're good." Kay peered at the stitches.

Cesar thought it might be warming up a little.

"I hate the pattern," said Stella.

"But the fabric's so wonderful."

"Cesar, why don't you make some tea," said Stella.

"I'd love some," said Kay, somehow undoing the good she had done, if Cesar read Stella's face correctly. Probably too pushy.

"I still don't get why he didn't just take the card," said Stella.

"Believe me, if Christa had figured out that he was the cocaine connection, she would have told," said Cesar. "She was that kind of a person."

"Or blackmailed," added Kay. "And you *can* believe it about him. You have to have the guts of a burglar to be a really good news director. And he was."

"But you can't prove it," said Stella.

"Not yet. But we can prove he was there. We've got a good footprint. And Henry's going to work the neighborhood with a picture of him now to see if some of those people who saw a runner that night might remember a little more. Anyway we've got the evidence from the draft physical. And the lab is analyzing cocaine we found at Albers's to see if it's from the same batch of pure stuff that killed Poe. That's going to be the case that goes to court probably."

"Are you going to fix the tea?" asked Stella. Cesar excused himself, wormed through the plastic flap into the kitchen, and fired up the kettle. There was a murmur of voices for a few minutes as Kay and Stella discussed Cesar's dining room project, and then a little silence. Cesar sped up rinsing the cups so he could get back in.

"They found the rugs, and the Renoir by the way," Kay called from the living room.

"No kidding? Where?"

"At Gupta's. All tied up and stacked in the living room. I was out there when this little man from Louisville showed up with a pickup truck to claim them. He said she had called him and he had bid over the phone and she had told him where they would be."

"Why?" asked Stella. Which Cesar, coming back into the living room, also wanted to know.

"My guess?" asked Kay. Stella had to nod. "I think she was trying to cut the baby out of the estate. I was trying to think like she would, and I'll bet that's it."

"What a bitch!"

"That's just a guess," said Cesar.

"Yeah, but I know she's right," said Stella. "That's got to be it. Are you going to get that?" The kettle was starting to shrill.

When Cesar hustled the steeping mugs back into the living room, they seemed to have finished with Mrs. Poe and had moved on to Dr. Poe and how he had the goods on Kay's boss.

"Would he have told?" asked Stella.

"Who knows? He was mean enough to do anything. But Albers couldn't take a chance. He was getting ready to run for office. Apparently he thought there was enough of a chance that Poe would give up the free coke for the thrill of telling the world about Albers," said Kay. "And if Albers got elected, he might not have been able to get any more, anyhow." Stella looked at Cesar and he nodded.

"But Poe would go to jail," said Stella. Cesar could tell that she thought Kay knew too much and was showing off.

"No, no. He wouldn't tell about the coke. He'd tell about

the army physical," answered Kay before Cesar could jump in.

"He'd go to jail for that too," snapped Stella. "He's the one who signed the false report. He'd lose his license, wouldn't he?"

"You don't get it," said Cesar before Kay could open her mouth. "He didn't have to tell about that. All he had to do was put the word out about the shoe size. Albers had already started explaining how he was a veteran even though he had turned into Mr. Strong Defense. Poe had probably started kidding him about that."

"So he sent Dr. Poe that pure stuff? To kill him? Just for that?" Stella shook her head in amazement.

"What do you mean, just for that?" asked Cesar.

"Just because he was going to tell everybody about Albers's gym shoes?"

"Not because of the running shoes," said Kay, pursing her mouth just enough to piss off Stella. Cesar didn't like the situation at all. "It was because of the service record."

"*I* know that," said Stella, squaring off to face Kay. "I mean it's unbelievable that someone would take his stupid career so seriously that he would be willing to kill somebody for it. What kind of an *asshole*—"

Cesar was ready to panic, figuring correctly that Stella had decided that Kay Gallery was the kind of asshole who would take her career seriously enough to commit murder over and, looking at Kay, saw that she knew exactly what Stella meant by the crack and was going to pull out her own weapons if something didn't happen real quick.

"And don't forget Mrs. Poe."

Stella and Kay, who had momentarily forgotten Cesar, turned to him. They each had exactly the same expression of irritation and confusion, but he thought it would be dumb to tell them that at that point in time.

"He killed her too."

Neither woman said anything. A voice in the back of

Cesar's mind told him that they had separately decided days ago that Mrs. Poe was a bitch who deserved to die and had dismissed her as an issue. They were irritated to have her dragged back into the scene.

At least they were looking like they wanted to kill him rather than each other, which was better. But then they turned to each other again. Cesar was pretty sure that the soft little hairs on the back of Stella's neck were standing up, so he added, "You know, I spent a lot of time worrying about that picture of the senators. I thought maybe that was some sort of documentation, which could have been a problem, since I was carrying it around." Was that distracting enough? He threw in a charming laugh to distract even more. "Heh-heh." But his tactic failed to divert. The women both looked at him as if he were some jerk who had wandered in off the street, and then they dismissed him, turning back to face each other.

"Do you work?" Kay asked with a cool smile that Cesar had not seen before.

"Do you have a family?" asked Stella.

Cesar slipped out of the room.